MOUTH...
COCO...

"Nancy Coco ...
ting where the ... is a horse-drawn vehi-
cle. She also g... us a delicious mystery complete with doses of
her homemade fudge ... a perfect read to wrap up your summer."
—*Wonder Women Sixty*

"*Oh, Fudge!* is a charm...
Mystery Series. But be w...
of each chapter, so don...
—*S...*

Oh Say Can You Fudge
"Beautiful Mackinac Island provides the setting for a puzzling
series of crimes. Now that Allie McMurphy has taken over her
grandparents' hotel and fudge shop, life on Mackinac is good,
although her little dog, Mal, does tend to nose out trouble. . . .
Allie's third offers plenty of plausible suspects and mouthwatering
fudge recipes."
—*Kirkus Reviews*

"WOW. This is a great book. I loved the series from the beginning
and this book just makes me love it even more. No one can make me
feel like I am in Mackinac Island better than Nancy Coco. She draws
the reader in and makes you feel like you are part of the story. I can-
not wait to read more. FANTASTIC is the only thing I can say further
about this book."
—**Bookschellves.com**

To Fudge or Not to Fudge
"*To Fudge or Not to Fudge* is a superbly crafted, classic, culinary
cozy mystery. If you enjoy them as much as I do, you are in for a
real treat. The setting of Mackinac Island immediately drew me to
the book as it is an amazing location. The only problem I had with
the book was reading about all the mouthwatering fudge made me
hungry."
—**Examiner.com (5 stars)**

"We LOVED it! This mystery is a vacation between the pages of a book. If you've never been to Mackinac Island, you will long to visit, and if you have, the story will help you to recall all of your wonderful memories."
—*Melissa's Mochas, Mysteries and Meows*

"A five-star delicious mystery that has great characters, a good plot, and a surprise ending. If you like a good mystery with more than one suspect and a surprise ending, then rush out to get this book and read it, but be sure you have the time since once you start you won't want to put it down. I give this 5 Stars and a Wow Factor of 5+. The fudge recipes included in the book all sound wonderful. I am thinking that a gift basket filled with the fudge from the recipes in this book, along with a copy of the book, some hot chocolate mix and/or coffee, and a nice mug would be a great Christmas gift."
—**Mystery Reading Nook**

"A charming and funny culinary mystery that parodies reality show competitions and is led by a sweet heroine, eccentric but likable characters, and a skillfully crafted plot that speeds toward an unpredictable conclusion. Allie stands out as a likable and engaging character. Delectable fudge recipes are interspersed throughout the novel."
—*Kings River Life*

All Fudged Up

"A sweet treat with memorable characters, a charming locale, and satisfying mystery."
—**Barbara Allan**, author of the Trash 'n' Treasures Mystery Series

"A fun book with a lively plot, and it's set in one of America's most interesting resorts. All this plus fudge!"
—**JoAnna Carl**, author of the Chocoholic Mystery Series (NAL)

"A sweet confection of a book. Charming setting, clever protagonist, and creamy fudge—a yummy recipe for a great read."
—**Joanna Campbell Slan**, author of the Scrap-N-Craft Mystery Series and The Jane Eyre Chronicles

DEATH
BEE COMES HER

Nancy Coco

KENSINGTON
PUBLISHING CORP.
www.kensingtonbooks.com

KENSINGTON BOOKS are published by

Kensington Publishing Corp.
119 West 40th Street
New York, NY 10018

All Kensington titles, imprints, and distributed lines are available at special quantity discounts for bulk purchases for sales promotion, premiums, fund-raising, educational, or institutional use.

Special book excerpts or customized printings can also be created to fit specific needs. For details, write or phone the office of the Kensington Sales Manager: Attn.: Sales Department. Kensington Publishing Corp., 119 West 40th Street, New York, NY 10018. Phone: 1-800-221-2647.

The Kensington logo is a trademark of Kensington Publishing Corp.

First Printing: January 2020
ISBN-13: 978-1-4967-2702-2
ISBN-10: 1-4967-2702-9

ISBN-13: 978-1-4967-1977-5 (ebook)
ISBN-10: 1-4967-1977-8 (ebook)

10 9 8 7 6 5 4 3 2

Printed in the United States of America

This one is for my grandma Mary. I hope you are dancing a polka with Grandpa again and making your famous homemade bread.

My son, eat honey because it is good, and the honeycomb which is sweet to your taste.
—Proverbs 24:13

Chapter 1

The people who live on the Oregon coast are a bit . . . shall we say quirky? Hippies, grunge fans, and hipsters have melded into a colorful and interesting community. That's the way I like to think of us, anyway. When you think of the West Coast, you might think of sun, surf, and sand, right? That doesn't always apply here. We have fog, cool breezes, and rocky shores. Did you ever see that movie, *Twilight*? It's more like that. In fact, parts of it were filmed nearby.

Now, I've lived here a while and I've never seen a vampire, but I have seen a few sparkly people. One was Emma Jean Baily, who owns a gift shop near the beach. She was out sweeping in front of her shop.

"Glitter is the herpes of the craft world," she'd told me. "Once it's on you, it will never truly go away. I still find it in the most interesting places."

"Hi, Mrs. Baily," I said and smiled at her glittered T-shirt. Her shop was sided with rugged, stained redwood. The porch rose up from the sidewalk and invited people inside.

"Hello, Wren, how are you and Everett doing today?" Emma Jean asked. She was a small woman with a cap of blonde hair and bright blue eyes in a pixie face. She was my mother's age, but looked youthful in jeans and T-shirt.

"We're well," I said. Everett's my cat and constant companion. He purred his reply. Everett is a Havana Brown and his breed is known for their propensity to talk. "We're going for a walk on the beach."

"Good day for it," she said and gestured toward the beach. "I'd stroll with you, but I'm setting up for next week's Halloweentown extravaganza. Lots to do. Is your shop doing anything?"

"I'm making honey taffy. And we're dressing up, of course."

"Of course," she said and leaned against her broom. "This year I'm going as Little Red Riding Hood. What are you going to be?"

"Everett is going as a warlock and I'm going as his familiar." Everett meowed his approval.

Emma Jean laughed.

"I'm just kidding," I laughed. "As much as Everett might like that, I don't know yet what I'm doing exactly . . . maybe a *Wizard of Oz* theme."

"Oh, there's a lot you can do with that," Emma Jean said, her eyes twinkling. "If you need any help, I've got supplies. It would be fun to do Glinda the Good Witch, in glitter."

"I just might take you up on that offer," I said and Everett agreed.

"Well, if you need my help or not, I can't wait to see you both at the costume parade on Halloween."

"Bye." We continued toward the beach, which was only a block or two from my shop. Most people didn't look twice when they saw me walking my cat on a leash. Everett loved going for walks. He was a social cat with slick, chocolate brown, short hair and bright green eyes. My Aunt Eloise was a cat fancier and bred Havana Browns. Everett was the great-grandson of her best show cat, Elton, and just as handsome, if I say so myself.

Aunt Eloise loved Havana Browns because they were charming, outgoing, and playful. Everett fit the bill to a T.

"Hi, Wren," Barbara Miller said as she stepped out of Books and More. "Hello, Everett. Are you two off to the beach?"

"I thought we'd walk the shore for a bit," I said. "I've been making candy all morning and I needed to stretch my legs."

"Are you making honey taffy for the Halloweentown celebration?"

"It is a favorite for Halloweentown," I said. "Funny how people like the taffy for Halloweentown but prefer the dark chocolate for the Big Foot Festival." Halloween-town was a series of Disney movies that were filmed on the coast of Oregon. In honor of the movies, Oceanview celebrated all things magical and scary every year for an entire week in October.

"Everything in your shop is wonderful," she said. "I don't know how people choose. Now that I think of it, I need a couple of new candles. Is someone minding the store?"

"Porsche is there," I said. "She can help you pick out the best beeswax candles for the season."

"Oh, good," Barbara said. "I'm on my way over there now. Tootles." I watched her walk off. Barbara Miller was my grandmother's neighbor. They had grown up together. While my grandma had to use a walker, Barbara still got around quite well in her athletic shoes, jeans, and jacket. Her short hair went from gray in the back to white in the front, but it framed her wide face well.

Everett and I headed down the nearly empty street. Since it was October, most of the large crowds of tourists had left the coast, leaving the die-hards and the locals. It was my favorite time of year. I loved the colors of fall when the ocean was a deep cold blue. The trees had begun to turn red and yellow while the pines were dark green. Orange pumpkins dotted the sidewalks along with autumnal wreathes and Halloween decorations.

The thing about Everett was he was a bit of a talker. He liked to comment on things we saw on our walks. I talked to him often without even realizing that most people didn't understand talking to a cat. "Want to go down to the beach?" I asked him.

"Are you talking to that cat?" Mildred Woolright said as she passed by.

"Oh, hello," I said. "Yes, I guess I was."

She blinked at me. "You're a bit too young to be a crazy cat lady."

"I'm not crazy," I said with a smile. "But I'll admit to being a cat lady."

Mildred rolled her eyes and continued down the street

as I winked at Everett. "Shall we go to the beach?" Cats don't usually care too much for water, but Everett had grown up beside the ocean and as long as we didn't get too close to the water's edge, he didn't mind the sand.

He meowed his agreement and we left the promenade. There were a few slight dunes where the wind had blown the sand between the promenade and the Pacific Ocean. They rolled gently no more than a yard high and were covered with waving beach grass. Everett loved the feel of the grass against his fur.

Bonfires were allowed on the beach and the evidence of them crunched under our feet. Black charcoal spread out in piles large and small. Pieces of charred wood scattered about. The beach was a deep stretch of sand that narrowed during high tide and stretched out during low tide. I was enjoying the sound of the ocean and searching the waves for evidence of whales when I felt Everett pull on his leash. "What?" I asked as I followed him past a clump of dune grass. He led me over to a woman sleeping in the sand. "Hello?" I picked the cat up and looked at the woman. Sometimes people camped on the beach, but rarely in the rounded dunes.

Who was she? Why was she here?

The woman wore nice clothes and didn't look like someone who regularly slept on the beach. "Ma'am?" I squatted down and shook her shoulder, but she was stiff and cold. I put my fingers on the base of her neck. There was no pulse. "Oh, boy." I jumped back and wiped my hand on my long skirt.

I grabbed my phone and dialed 9-1-1.

"Nine-one-one, how can I help you?"

"I think there's a dead woman on the beach." My voice

trembled and came out barely audible. My face felt a little numb and my thoughts tumbled.

"This is the nine-one-one operator. Can you please repeat that?"

"Josie?" I recognized my friend's voice through the jumble of emotions.

"Wren?" she asked. "Are you okay? Did you say there's a dead woman on the beach?"

"When did you start working as a dispatch operator?" I asked because I was in shock and not thinking clearly.

"It's my first day," she said with what sounded like nervous pride. "You're my first call. Where are you? Are you okay?"

"Oh," I said. "I'm okay, yes, I'm fine. I think. There's a woman on the beach and I think she's dead. I guess that would make her a dead body?"

"Where are you exactly?"

"I, um." I glanced around. "I'm about fifty yards from the beach entrance on Main Street."

"Okay, good, an ambulance and police officers are on their way. Are you in danger?"

"No, I seem to be alone on the shore. Should I stay on the line?" I asked.

"Yes," she said. "Please stay on the line. You're sure you're safe?"

"I'm sure," I said.

After a pause that stretched out for what seemed like forever, she said, "the police are on their way."

"Great."

"Please stay on the line so that I know you are safe."

"Okay," I said and waited a couple of long moments in silence. The wind blew against my face and the ocean roared. I felt as stiff as the woman at my feet. "Maybe we should keep talking."

"I can do that. Why don't you tell me what she looks like," Josie asked. "Anyone we know?"

I leaned down closer. "She's dressed like a country club woman. Nice shoes, expensive dress slacks in a swirl pattern, and a tunic-style black top, blonde hair," I said. "She might be in her sixties. Strange, though . . ."

"What?"

"The sun is out, but you know the wind off the ocean . . ."

"Brisk, I bet," she said. "Why?"

"She isn't wearing a jacket."

"Weird," Josie said. "Most ladies that age would be wearing a puffy coat."

"Maybe the killer took it," I said and squatted down to take a closer look.

"Does it look like a mugging? Is she disheveled?"

"No, I don't think so. She still has her wedding ring on and what looks like large single diamond earrings."

"Does she look familiar?"

"There's something familiar, but her face is hidden," I said with some relief.

The woman was on her belly facedown. There didn't appear to be any wounds, but she did have sand stuck in her hair.

"Any idea how she died?"

"I don't see any obvious signs of trauma," I said. "There's some goop in her hair, you know, sand and such."

"And no one else is nearby?"

I glanced around. "There are a couple of kids walking down the shore toward me."

"Keep them away," she said.

"Right." I stood and watched them. "If they get too close, I'll wave them off. I'm just afraid that if I wave now, they will come see what's going on."

"Oh, okay," Josie said. "Can you hear sirens yet?"

I held my breath and listened to my heart beat in my ears. "Not yet," I said.

"Don't worry, they are on the way," she said. "Boy, this job is stressful. I mean, I never imagined anyone dying on my first call . . . you know what, I'll check again."

I looked down at the dead woman at my feet. Everett was lying nearby watching everything from a rise in the dunes. The grass sprung up around him like the vegetation surrounding a lion on the Serengeti. It struck me that I should keep an eye out for tracks or other evidence and make sure no one stepped too close. I glanced around and saw indentations that must have been the woman's original tracks in the sand. Just hers. It didn't look like anyone else had been there.

Her hands were curled into fists. They were drawn against her at the waist. A piece of paper fluttered from the edge of one of her hands, so I took a closer look. She was clutching something. I knew enough to grab a tissue out of the pocket of my skirt and carefully turned her hand to reveal the paper. It whipped about in the breeze. I wanted to take it, but I didn't want to upset a crime scene. Still, it might just blow away in the wind. Thinking quickly, I grabbed my phone and took a few pictures. Then I used the tissue to pry the paper from her fist.

It was a label. A familiar label.

"What's going on, Wren?"

I turned at the sound of a deep, male voice. It was Jim Hampton, a regular on the promenade, a beat cop, and a noticeably handsome man. He reminded me of the actor

Paul Newman. My Aunt Eloise raised me on old movies, and I remember he played a cop in one of them. Jim's blue eyes were guarded and unreadable.

I felt a flash of guilt and I think he picked up on it. "Josie, Jim Hampton's here. I'm going to hang up now."

"Okay," she said. "Call me later?"

"I will."

"Wren?" He raised an eyebrow, looking from me to the body. "What's going on?"

"Everett found her," I said.

Jim was a tall man, maybe six foot, with square shoulders and an athletic frame. He hunkered down and felt for a pulse. "She's dead."

"I know, I called nine-one-one," I said and raised my phone. "Josie said she called the police. I'm glad you're here, but I didn't hear a siren."

Then I heard the siren in the distance coming closer. He looked up at me. "I was walking on the promenade and saw you. You looked . . . upset." He rubbed the back of his neck, his gaze falling to the poor woman.

"I guess I am," I said and hugged my waist. "It's not every day you find a dead body."

"Everett seems to be handling it well," he said glancing toward my cat, who rolled in the sand.

"He's used to dead things," I said, stating the obvious. "He's a cat."

"What's that in your hand?"

"My phone?"

"No, the paper you were looking at."

"Oh, I found it in her hand," I said and held it out. "It's the label off one of my lip balms." He took it from me.

"You mean it belonged to you?"

"No, it's from my store. I make it and sell it. It's

beeswax, coconut oil, and honey. My recipe. I also designed the label. That's why I recognized it."

"Yes, well, it's evidence and you moved it," he said and stood.

"I have a picture of her holding it," I said as if to prove my limited prowess in evidence collecting. "I watch crime shows."

He made a dismissive sound. "I'm not sure that will hold up in court."

The siren went silent as an ambulance stopped at the edge of the promenade. Two EMTs hopped out and went in the back for their gear. Jim stood. "Better call the morgue. This woman is long dead."

"That's what I told Josie," I said and picked up Everett. He took an interest in the vehicle's flashing lights.

"Neither one of you are doctors," the female EMT said. Her shirt tag read RITTER. She was five foot ten with short brown hair and serious brown eyes. Built for power, she hauled a stretcher out. Her partner was a young guy about my height with bleached blond hair and a thin build. He had a surfer's tan and winked at me.

"Gotta let Ritter check her out," surfer EMT said. "We'll call the morgue if she's—"

"Oh, she's dead," Ritter confirmed as she knelt beside the body. "She's stiff. Fender, call Dr. Murphy and let him know that we've got a dead body for him."

"Will do," the younger man said. He grabbed his radio and started talking.

Jim took pictures with his cell phone. Then, he and Ritter turned the body. I saw her face and gasped.

Even without color to her skin, I would know her anywhere. It was Agnes Snow.

"You recognize her?" Ritter studied me.

"It's Agnes," I said. "Agnes Snow." Agnes was my aunt's rival at the local craft fair. They had been feuding over who got the grand champion ribbon for decades. It didn't matter which craft my aunt picked up, Agnes was always there with an award-winning entry.

Aunt Eloise had been acting secretively, hiding her latest craft, certain that Agnes was spying on her. She'd even gone so far as driving all the way to Portland to buy her materials on the off chance that Agnes was somehow keeping track of what my aunt bought at the local craft store.

I should have known Agnes from the way she was dressed. Agnes always wore high-end boutique clothes. She looked like a woman who came down to spend two weekends a year in her million-dollar beach house, but, in fact, Agnes had lived in Oceanview her whole life. She had married into a local family with political clout. Bernie, her husband of nearly forty years, was mayor of Oceanview for over half those years. They never had children. Instead, Agnes had gotten good, very good, at every craft known to man.

"Wait, is she the ex-mayor's wife?" Ritter asked.

"Yes," Jim said. "Bernie Snow's wife and Eloise Johnson's biggest rival." He glanced at me, his blue eyes squinting in the bright autumn light. "Might explain the label you found in her hand."

"Could I see that?" Ritter asked, stepping closer.

"It's from one of my lip balms," I said. "I own Let It Bee. The honey store in town. I make handcrafted lip balms, lotions, candles, and—"

"Candy," Fender said. I turned to him.

"Yes, candy."

"The best candy," he said, grinned a smile worthy of a toothpaste ad, and leaned in. "The honey salted caramel is to die for."

"Let's hope Agnes didn't agree," Jim said.

"I'm sure there's no connection," I said. "Besides, it was a lip balm label, not one from candy."

"You have to admit that it still doesn't look that good for you," Jim said his face suddenly sober.

"Wait, you think I had something to do with Agnes's death? That's nuts. Why would I call nine-one-one if I killed her?"

"You watch crime shows," Jim said. "You know the answer."

"Because I want to involve myself in the investigation?" My voice crept up two octaves. "That's crazy. It doesn't happen in real life. Does it?"

Jim raised an eyebrow. "It happens often enough that they put it in a television show."

"Well." I hugged Everett. "It's silly to think I could hurt anyone."

"Any idea how she died?" Fender asked. He leaned over the dead woman and studied her. "I don't see any obvious trauma."

"Cause of death is for the coroner to determine," Ritter said.

"Stand back," said a woman my age as she walked up with a black bag in her hand. She wore a blue shirt that was marked with CSU. "You all are muddying up my crime scene. Is that a cat?"

"Yes, his name is Everett," I said. "He found the body."

She stepped over to me. "Hello there, handsome," she practically purred and scratched Everett behind the ears. He purred back at her. "Is he wearing a leash?"

"He loves to go for walks and the leash keeps him safe," I said and patted his head.

"Okay," she said and turned on her heel. "All of you, do not move! I need to see where you all have come in and messed up the crime scene." She put down her bag, opened it, then pulled on a pair of gloves. Frowning, she took a large camera out of her kit. "Really, Officer Hampton, you know better."

"We moved the body," he said. "Needed to see if she was hurt."

"I have pictures," I said and held up my phone.

"Someone is smart," she said as snapped away with her camera. "I'm Alison McGovern."

"Wren Johnson," I said.

"Wren, like the bird?"

"Yes," I said. I was used to the question. "My mom loved the name."

"It's cool," Alison said. "Okay, you two can remove the body." I watched in fascination as she continued to bully the EMTs and Jim and work the crime scene. I swear she bullied the grass into giving up its secrets. But she did it in a slow and methodical way.

After a while, Jim stood beside me and watched her work.

"She's good," I said.

"Thorough," he agreed. "I'm surprised that cat is letting you hold him so long."

"Everett? He loves to be held."

"That is not my experience with cats," he said. "My

experience is they lure you in to pet their belly only to scratch and bite and run to hide under the bed for the next day and a half."

I laughed. "Yes, that also sounds like a cat. They're all different, you know. Just like people."

"So where were you for the last twelve hours?"

I turned to him. "Are you still thinking I'm a suspect?"

"Can you answer the question?"

"Can you?" I asked him. "I mean, twelve hours is a lot of time to account for."

"I've been working for the last six," he said.

"That doesn't mean you didn't kill someone," I countered. "Did anyone see you every minute of the last twelve hours?"

He narrowed his eyes. "I'm not a person of interest."

"I'm not either."

"Not yet," he admitted and took out his notepad. "That could change at any minute." He started writing in his pad. "Let's start from the beginning, you found the body?"

"Yes."

"How?"

I went over how I found Agnes step by step right up until the time I pulled the label out of her fist.

"I see," he said as he took notes. "And you know Agnes, how?"

"Like I said—and you know—Agnes and my aunt have this informal competition going."

"Can you explain what you mean by informal competition?"

"The two of them have been competing against each other my entire life," I said. "I think it started when they were in grammar school."

"What kind of competition?"

"Everything," I said, knowing that was the truth. "Most recently it's been about crafts."

"Such as?"

"Quilting, scrapbooking, knitting, crocheting, flower arranging, jelly making . . ."

"Right," he said. "And how do you do any of that competitively?"

"Oh, there are all kinds of contests," I said. "Church contests, county fairs, senior center contests . . ."

"I get it," he said. "I think. So they were rivals."

"Yes, everyone knows that. You even said it yourself."

"Do you think your aunt killed her?"

"What? No, no," I said and hugged Everett just a bit too tight. He squeaked. "She would never. Besides, she was in Portland last night."

"Why was she in Portland?"

"She had a date," I said. "I assume she has an alibi for every minute of her night."

"Did you have a date?" he asked.

"Is that relevant to this case?" I replied, eyebrow raised.

"If it provides you an alibi."

"No, I did not have a date," I said and studied the outgoing tide. "I was home alone making candy and a batch of hand and body scrub."

"Best candy ever," Fender said as he came back from putting the body in the ambulance. He bent down and picked up his bag, then held out his hand. "Rick Fender."

"Hi, Rick, Wren Johnson." I shook his hand.

"Nice to meet you, Wren," he said and grinned. "Can I get a discount on the candy?"

"Come in while I'm there and I'll see what I can do," I said.

"Perfect." He walked back to the ambulance and climbed in the passenger side while Ritter closed the door and walked over to the driver's side. The two EMTs made an odd couple as Ritter was a large woman with square shoulders and Rick was lanky.

"Well, I've got to get back to the store," I said to Jim. "You know where to find me?"

"Wait while I check if they want you to come down to the station," he said.

"Are you kidding me?" I asked, somewhat unnerved by the idea. He held up his palm to quiet me while he turned and spoke to someone on his radio.

I'd been by the police station so I knew where it was, but I'd never been inside. In fact, Jim was the first police officer I'd ever spoken to—it was at a chamber of commerce meeting. I was lucky enough to never have run afoul of the law. Until today.

"You can go for now and take the cat home," he said. "He would be too big a distraction at the station, anyway." He reached over and scratched Everett behind the ears.

Everett meowed as if he agreed.

Relief washed over me. "Then, we're going home."

"I'd advise you not to go anywhere. Right now you're my only lead and it would be better if you didn't do anything suspicious."

"Right." Everett and I left the beach. The wind was colder than I remembered. I felt like the business owners were watching me as I walked by. Suzy from Suzy's Flowers stared. I turned my sweater collar up. Mrs. Beasley, of Beasley's Gifts, watched me from across the street. I waved my hand and she stepped back.

Wallace Hornsby, owner of Hornsby Tailor Shop, peered at me from behind his small round glasses and I sent him an uncomfortable smile. Everett meowed so I hugged him. "It's okay," I said. "They're just curious." I paused and decided I was going to act as natural as possible. I put Everett down, straightened my sweater, and we walked the rest of the way back to my shop. The last thing I wanted to do was act like a murder suspect. No, really, the last thing I ever wanted to do was find a dead body. I guess I needed a new last thing.

A fun antiaging fact: a teaspoon of buckwheat honey in a glass of water taken daily has been scientifically proven to increase healthy antioxidants in the blood.

Chapter 2

"Is it true?" My Aunt Eloise came rushing through the door of my shop. The bells on the door jangled behind her. "Is Agnes dead?"

My aunt was a tall woman with the big bones of our pioneering ancestors. She wore her gray hair in a messy bun on the top of her head. There was always a pen stuck in the bun. Usually it was one of her cat-fancier pens with pictures of Havana Browns. Dressed in no-nonsense jeans and a cat T-shirt and dark, hooded sweatshirt that was unzipped, she always looked as if she didn't suffer fools.

"Yes," I said. "She was lying facedown in the sand dunes close to the promenade." Not that it was much of a dune as the sand was blown by the wind. I guess it was more of a pile. Just a few miles from here the beaches were flat as the ocean tides came in and out, scouring them. They left only the basalt rocks that took millions of years to wear away.

"Who did it? How did it happen?" Aunt Eloise asked, placing her hands on her hips. She looked fierce and not at all happy.

"I don't have any idea," I said. I almost said I didn't have a clue, but that wouldn't be true. There was a clue—one of my lip balm labels. I'd come back to the shop and gone through my records to see if I could tell who might have purchased the balm. It had to be in the last few weeks as the label was relatively new. I was working on a new logo and tried a Halloween twist of a bee with a broom. I thought it was quite clever.

"Well, this can't be right," Aunt Eloise said and paced in front of the counter at the center of the store. When I had set up my store inside what had started out as a two-story cabin in 1909, and had since been everything from a gift shop to a surf shack, I put the counter in the center and to the left as you entered so I could see the entire shop from one perch and be quick to help whenever I thought I saw a customer with questions. "She and Bernie have a big fortieth-anniversary party planned in two weeks. The whole town is going."

"Sounds like they will be going to a funeral instead," Porsche said as she finished restocking a shelf. My sales manager was twenty-five and had two boys. When school started she came in looking for flex hours and I needed some help so it was a win-win. Porsche had gorgeous black hair that was stick straight and beautiful blue eyes, which shined like sapphires. Her mother was Korean and her father a blue-eyed blond American soldier. Porsche was a gorgeous mix of both.

"That's just terrible," Aunt Eloise said. "Poor Bernie. Does he know?"

"I'm sure someone has told him by now," I said. "Forty years, the guy must be a wreck. I'm going to make him a casserole."

"Probably a good idea. I'm not sure he remembers how to cook." Aunt Eloise tapped her index finger on her chin. "You know there was some talk that Agnes was having an affair."

"What?"

"With who?" Porsche asked, leaning on the counter and resting her chin in her hands.

"I don't know," Aunt Eloise said. "But maybe Bernie found out and killed her for it."

"She didn't look like she was hit with anything," I said. "For a crime of passion she looked relatively intact."

"So, no bashing on the head or gunshot wound?" Porsche asked.

"None that I could see," I said.

"Hmmm." Aunt Eloise wrinkled her nose.

"Officer Hampton wondered if you two had fought over something recently," I said to my aunt. "I told him no. There's no way you could have killed Agnes."

"Thanks for defending me," she said and crossed her arms. "I guess this means I can start shopping at the local craft shop again."

"No more reason to go all the way into Portland . . .

unless you have a boyfriend there," Porsche said and waggled her eyebrows.

"My love life is none of your business," Aunt Eloise said.

"Woo-hoo, she is going to meet a boyfriend." Porsche danced around.

"Stop it," Aunt Eloise said and blushed. For all her no-nonsense attitude, she was still embarrassed about her love life.

I had to smile. "When are we going to get to meet this guy?"

"I'm doing things in my own good time, thank you very much. Now, I thought you were going to make a casserole."

"I am," I said. "Porsche, I'll be upstairs if you need me." I walked through my store. It smelled of beeswax, lemon, vanilla, and lavender. I made sure everything was displayed neatly and there was room to move around. As far as I was concerned, there was nothing worse than having to squeeze between and around people to shop.

I'd worked hard to turn the shop into a welcoming haven for bees and bee lovers. Even the music I played was soft and soothing, not the energetic beats of pop music like you got at the T-shirt store down the street. Comforting and inviting were my goals. I wanted to tease all the senses with sweet smells, tastes, fun sights, and soothing sounds. Delight was my goal and I think I reached it.

My apartment was above the shop in the previous owner's apartment. It was convenient and made it easy to be at work. I did a lot of experimenting with my bee products upstairs before they ever hit the shelves downstairs.

I took pride in all of my locally sourced bee products. Bee populations across the United States were still in trouble and by having a bee product shop, I incentivized local beekeepers to raise more bees. Or so I liked to believe. Bees are amazing creatures. Almost as amazing as Everett.

The doorbells to the shop jangled as I took my first step up on the stairs.

"Wren." I turned to find Jim walking toward me.

"Hi," I said, not all that happy to see him.

"Do you have some time to talk?" he asked.

"Sure," I said. "I was just on my way up to put a casserole together for Bernie, Agnes's husband. Can you come up? I have honey and lavender tea."

"Coffee would be better if you have it."

"I can make some," I said. The stairs creaked under our weight. The shop was more than one hundred years old and sat just off of Main Street. I liked the false front and the roomy little two-bedroom apartment above. There was something comforting about knowing that generations of people lived and worked here before me.

The kitchen was tucked up under the eaves. I made coffee in the pot and started a kettle for tea. Jim looked out of place in the quaint living area that was open to the kitchen. He stared out the window. "Nice view."

"You can see the ocean if you are tall enough to look over the Appletons' roof."

"No view of the promenade."

"No," I said. "I'm kind of glad. If I wanted to watch people all day, I would just go downstairs in the shop. I've got a full view of everything going on in the street." I poured his coffee. "Milk or sugar?"

"Black, thanks," he said and took the mug. He sat down on the edge of my love seat. I picked up my tea and sat across from him on the wingback chair. It was covered in blue velvet and I'd gotten it at a yard sale that benefited a local charity.

"Is there any further news on Agnes's death?"

"This is real life, not a crime show," he said softly. "Autopsies and labs take time."

"Then what can I do for you?"

"I'd like to know where you were between midnight and when you found the body," he said. "Do you have an alibi?"

"You really think I did this horrible thing and then called nine-one-one?"

"I told you, I'm simply asking questions at this point. I don't have any hunches or theories."

"I was home alone with Everett," I said. My cat came up and wove his way between my ankles. He liked to move in and out of the slits in my long skirt. "I made a batch of mason jar candles." I pointed to the small wooden table in an alcove next to the kitchen. Jars of pastel-colored wax sat on the tabletop. I'd put them there to cool. Each candle was made of beeswax and a long wick guaranteed to burn clean down to the glass at the bottom. Then, customers could return the jar for twenty percent off their next jar candle. With these candles, I experimented with flowers and flower scents.

"How long does it take you to make a batch that size?"

"An hour or two, depending," I said. "Last night, longer. I was placing flowers in the candles and I wanted them to have a certain look."

"I see." He wrote something in his notepad. "You live here alone?"

"All alone," I said. "I went to bed around one a.m. and got up at seven. Made breakfast and went downstairs to set up the cash register and open up for the morning."

"How was that?"

"Slow," I said. "This time of year most of the crowds appear on the weekends and more toward the afternoon."

"What do you do when no one comes in?"

"I use the time to clean and straighten. My sales manager, Porsche, came in around ten and I took Everett for his walk. I'm sure most of my neighbors saw me go."

"And what about your aunt?"

"I told you, she was in Portland."

"Do you know why?"

"I think you should ask her yourself."

"I will," he said and shifted in his seat. "Do you know who might have had a reason to kill Agnes?"

"Are you sure she was murdered?"

"I'm following the facts. The facts are that you found her body. She had your label in her hand . . . if that is to be believed. So I thought you might know something more about her."

"Wait, am I a suspect?"

"I wouldn't even classify you as a person of interest— yet. But I am trying to understand what happened."

"Me, too," I said. Everett climbed into my lap and purred, letting me know he was also concerned. "I checked my receipts, but I don't make note of the customers unless they pay with a credit card. The label on the balm is new—within the last two weeks or so, but that is over a hundred and fifty purchases. That doesn't count the cash purchases. It was a very popular label."

"I'd like to have the list of credit card payers," he said. "Just in case we need to try to narrow it down."

"Oh, sure." I put Everett down, got up, and woke up my computer. I went to the appropriate file and down-loaded it into a CSV file. "What is your email address? I'll send it to you."

He gave me his official police email. I entered it, at-tached the file, and hit Send. "There you go."

"Thanks," he stood. "Just so you know, I'm talking to all the shop owners on Main. Someone must have seen something."

"I hope you figure it out."

"I will," he said. "You can take that to the bank."

He rose and Everett jumped up on the arm of the love seat to get his attention. Jim scratched the kitty under his chin. "Thanks for being helpful."

"You're welcome," I said. "Please keep me posted."

"You'll know when everyone else does." He ducked his head in a short salute and walked down the stairs.

I heard Porsche mumble something. He replied and then the doorbells jangled. I chewed the inside of my cheek, lost in thought. *Was Agnes truly murdered? Could that killer have been in my shop and bought my lip gloss? Or was Agnes trying to leave a clue to her killer's iden-tity?*

It was evening by the time I finished the casserole. It was my mother's famous beef and honey casserole. Once you braise the beef, you slow cook it in the oven with onion and carrots and beef stock, add honey, then top with mashed potatoes and put it back in the oven until the mashed potatoes brown slightly. I let it cool enough to transport it to Bernie's place.

Agnes and Bernie lived on First Street their entire adult lives. I wondered briefly what it might be like to live in the same home all those years. You see, my dad was in the military, so we moved a lot when I was a kid. Then he died in Afghanistan and mom moved us back to Oregon.

Mom didn't live too many years after. I think she took his death hard. It knocked years off of her. Her heart eventually gave out. Broken heart syndrome is what the doctor called it. I could understand why.

After that, I made a conscious decision to put down roots near my aunt. Aunt Eloise was my only living relative, which meant I was her only remaining family. It felt right to be close by. Besides, I loved my time in Oceanview and wanted to settle into the dynamic beach community. My parents left me enough money to finish college and put a down payment on Let It Bee. That meant the store had to make enough profit in the summer season to maintain my rent during the off-season and help pay Porsche's salary. So far so good. The shop was cool and quirky enough that people loved to stop in and browse. I enjoyed telling them about bee populations.

I had a bee wrangler, Elias Bentwood, who would come in for talks. He started a hive for me in the side of the building. It was encased in glass so that my customers could come and watch the bees work to make honey and comb, and enjoy flying up and out through a hole in my roof. Elias had built this great tool where honey could collect and then pour out of a spigot. Of course there had to be enough honey before that happened. My hive was relatively young and I was not taking honey from it yet.

My shop had dark pine walls and floors. It gave it a bit of a cabin feel. By the beehive were two chairs for anyone who was tired of shopping or wanted to sit and read one of the bee books I had for sale.

I kept the candy in a glass counter beside the cash register. Other shelves were artfully arranged to catch the eye and take a visitor through a journey of discovery. It was amazing how the pattern of the people coming in adjusted naturally to the flow around the store. It was important for me to tell a story.

If people understood more about bees, they tended to be more invested in buying my products. I had a website and had somewhat of an online presence. I was hoping to earn more through word of mouth.

Yesterday, I'd gotten a call from an elementary school group that was interested in coming in and learning about the bees. I figured I'd stock candy and other interesting kid-friendly items—like bee toys and soft plushies. There were plenty of picture books for sale on the subject as well.

The teacher had said something about how studying bees was a great fall science project. I agreed. The cooler air kept the bees calmer. It's, in part, why I didn't have a heater in the bottom floor. The Oregon coast could get quite chilly in the fall and winter, but my customers didn't seem to mind the lack of heat. They were simply interested in the bees.

I covered Bernie's casserole, wrapped it in a thick towel, and carried it from Main to First Street. The Snows' house was a 1930s Foursquare with white shiplap siding and pale blue window shutters. The front door was open and people came and went from inside.

I knocked on the door frame before I entered. It was a habit my mom had taught me. Be polite and don't just barge in, even if the door is open. That bit of advice served me well through many situations.

"Come in, honey, there's no need to be formal. We're all neighbors here," Mrs. Marion Beasley said. The woman was in her late sixties and had worn a beehive hairdo since she was a teenager.

"Thanks, I brought a beef and honey casserole," I said and lifted the dish to prove my point. "It's in plasticware in case he wants to put it in the freezer."

"I'll take that," Joan Shirley said and grabbed the dish out of my hands. The older woman wore a pair of stretchy pants and a long-sleeved blouse. I'd met her before at a chamber of commerce function. Both times I'd met her, she had been a bit overbearing. I tried not to take it personally, since she was much older than I was and well established in the community.

The living room was filled with women young and old. Bernie Snow sat in the corner looking a bit lost. The house was square with the living room taking up most of the front, a dining room to the left, and a kitchen to the right. The hall held a bathroom and then stairs up to what I assumed was the bedrooms. The decor was stuck in the nineties. Agnes had a collection of Hummel figurines in a corner glass cabinet.

I scooted around the women to where Bernie Snow sat alone on a couch. "Hi, Mr. Snow," I said. "Do you mind if I sit?"

"No, go ahead," he said without enthusiasm.

I took a seat beside him. "How are you holding up?"

"I don't know," he said. His expression was dazed with a hint of sadness around his eyes. "I can't believe she isn't coming back." He turned to me. "You found her, right?"

"Yes, sir."

"How was she? Was she . . . I wanted to say *okay*, but that's not the right word here, is it?"

"She looked peaceful," I said. It wasn't a lie. "She was dressed real nice, too. She wouldn't have been embarrassed to be found that way."

He patted my hand. "Thank you for telling me that. It helps."

"Do you know if she had a heart condition or something that would cause her to die suddenly?"

"No," he said. His gaze stared at nothing. "She was healthy as a horse. You can ask her doctor. He'll tell you that she was going to live for another thirty years at least. Long life runs in her family."

"Do you think she was murdered?" I asked softly so that I wouldn't be overheard.

He turned his watery blue gaze on me. "I can only assume so, since she was so healthy. It can't possibly be suicide. She was going shopping to get a dress for our anniversary party. She was so excited about the party and seeing all her friends. I just can't imagine who would do such a thing to her or why."

"Do you know what time she left this morning?"

"We had breakfast at six and I left to play golf. The stores don't really open until ten but she texted me and said she wanted to take a walk along the beach." He wiped his eyes as tears fell. "We were supposed to have lunch at the Okay Café. I was out playing golf when I got the news. Don't you see? I was out playing golf while she was being killed. I should have been with her. I should have protected her."

"There's no way you could have known," I said and gave him a quick hug.

"Did you see anything?" he asked, his voice rough. He seemed to be more and more agitated as if awakening from a bad dream and angry about it. "Did you see anyone?"

"No." I tried to remain calm in the hopes of keeping him calm. "Everett and I were alone on the beach when he spotted her. If it wasn't for my cat, I wouldn't have found her."

He took a deep breath and seemed to settle a bit, except for the incessant tapping of his right foot and the trembling in his hands. "Agnes always did like cats." We sat in silence a moment. I kept him company even though he grew more and more agitated. Finally, he turned to me. "Was she shot or stabbed?"

"I didn't see any wounds," I said.

"Then what could have caused this?" His voice rose at the end to a near shout.

I patted his hand in a poor attempt to comfort him. "I'm no doctor, but it could have been a stroke or an aneurysm."

"Or poison," Joan Shirley said as she stepped toward us. "My guess would be poison. It's the murder weapon of choice for women." The older woman's mouth firmed. Her gray hair was long and braided down her back. I realized she had woven streaks of blue and pink in the braid.

Her words got my attention. "You think she was killed by a woman?"

"Oh come on, honey, everyone knows that aunt of yours and Agnes had a feud going on."

"Not enough to kill her," I said and stood. "Seriously, Mrs. Shirley. Don't you think if my aunt was going to kill

Agnes, she would have done it sooner? I mean, why now?"

"That's the question," Joan said. "Bernie, what was going on that she would have been killed now?"

"I don't know," he said, his face filled with grief and anger. "She was working on an art piece. She wouldn't tell me anything more than that."

"Why would someone kill her over an art piece?" I mused. "I mean, it's not like she sold them or anything."

"Maybe she was having a secret affair," Joan suggested.

"What!" Mr. Snow stood. "Don't you say that. Don't you even think that. My Agnes would never cheat on me. Get out!"

"I'm so sorry," Joan said and blushed. "I overstepped."

"Get out!" Bernie shouted at her. "I want to be alone. Out! Out! Out!"

I had never seen the women in Oceanview move so quickly. Bernie wasn't a tall man but he commanded a room. I guess after being mayor for so long he knew how to take charge. I quashed the urge to flee with the rest of them and lagged behind. "I brought you a casserole," I said. "My Aunt Eloise wanted me to send on her condolences."

"Thanks, but, until I know who did this to my Agnes I'm not going to take any more condolences." He studied the group of shocked and exiting women. "And quit your gossiping. As far as I'm concerned, every single one of you is a suspect."

"Now, wait a minute," I said as gently as I could. "They don't know this was murder and even if it was it could have been random. Agnes might have been in the wrong place at the wrong time and gotten mugged."

"I doubt that," he said and glared at me. "You found her. You said she had no obvious wounds. That doesn't sound like she was mugged to me."

I swallowed hard and decided to retreat. "Right. Please let me know if you need anything."

"I'll thank you and the rest of you to stay away. That's what I need," he said with a full bluster. "You know what? As far as I'm concerned you and your aunt were no friend to my wife and therefore are no friend to me. Now leave!"

I left feeling embarrassed. Social awkwardness was kind of my nemesis. No matter how hard I worked on saying the right thing at the right time, I usually failed. I'd come to comfort a grieving man and left concerned that Mr. Snow thought I or my Aunt Eloise might have had something to do with Agnes's death. Frankly, bees were much easier to understand than complicated human interactions.

Winter Pet Paw Wax

4 ounces beeswax
$\frac{1}{4}$ cup calendula oil
$\frac{1}{4}$ cup coconut oil
$\frac{1}{4}$ cup olive oil

Melt over low heat. Pour into a heat-resistant container wide enough for your pet's paw to fit comfortably. Cools in 20 minutes.

Use by rubbing paws on top of the wax right before you take them out. It is safe for them to lick and keeps the snow, ice, and antifreeze off their skin. It also moisturizes dry pads.

Chapter 3

I arrived back at the shop to find Jim Hampton waiting for me at the door. "Hello," I said. "Do you have more news?"

"I do," he said with a serious look. "I would like you to come with me to the station."

"I'm sorry? Why? I told you everything I know."

"We'll take the squad car." He pointed to a police cruiser that sat at the curb.

I felt panic start to set in. "But, why?"

"We'll discuss that down at the station." He took me by the arm. "I don't want to have to handcuff you in front of your neighbors."

I noticed a small crowd had formed. Panic turned to embarrassment as I noticed tourists and shop owners alike stepping out of the stores along Main Street and craning their necks to see what was going on. I let him lead me around the back of the car to the seat behind the driver. He did the whole thing where they hold down your head as you sit to ensure your safety. I could feel the heat of a blush rush up my cheeks. I refused to bow my head in shame. I had nothing to be ashamed about.

Jim got in and spoke to dispatch, then turned to me. "Buckle up."

I did as he asked and he drove the few blocks to the police station. A local television crew was parked outside along with a reporter and a photographer from the *Ocean-view Gazette*. Unfortunately, I knew both of the *Gazette* employees. Alicia Lankson had been a grade behind me in school. She had been a popular girl, cheerleader, student council president and prom queen. I had been a goody two-shoes, a nerdy girl who ran for treasurer but never got elected. The photographer was Mitchell Grimes. He was in his twenties and sometimes stopped by the shop to buy candles for his mom.

"Officer Hampton," Alicia called out. "Are you arresting Wren Johnson?"

"No one's being arrested," he replied and maneuvered me out of the car and toward the police station door.

"Is she a person of interest?" Alicia called out. "Is that why you picked her up in a squad car?"

Horror went through me at the idea of even being suspected of murder. When he came to my apartment to question me, I took it seriously, but I had never been afraid he would arrest me.

"No comment," he said. "We'll be making a statement later this evening."

Jim ushered me into the station, behind a door, and down the hall to a small room. There was only a table and two chairs in the stark room. "Have a seat," he said.

I swallowed and sat, grateful he hadn't handcuffed me. "What's this about? Do I need a lawyer?"

"You can always call a lawyer," he said and took a seat across from me. "But it's better if you just answer my questions honestly."

I noticed a light blinking on a camera in the corner above his head. "Am I being recorded?"

"It's for your safety."

I put my hands on the table and clasped them tightly together. "What is this all about?"

"Do you make your lip balms by hand?"

"Yes, everything in my shop is handcrafted with care. If I don't make them, then local artists do."

"And is this your label?" He pulled out an evidence bag with the label I had pulled from Agnes's hand.

"Yes, that's what I told you."

"Did you make these on a printer?"

"Why?"

"Could someone else have printed this label?"

"No, you see this little gem here on the underside? I have them on all my labels. It's sort of my own secret thing."

"You are the only one who knows about this gem mark?"

"Well, yes, I think so; I mean, my printer who creates my labels does and probably my aunt and Porsche since they help me place the labels sometimes."

"And is this what the label was on?" He pulled out a second evidence bag. This one had a tube of lip balm.

"I'm not sure, can I look at it closer?"

"Don't touch it," he said and held it closer.

I studied it from different angles and then sat back. "I can't say. This could be anyone's lip balm. I don't have anything to distinguish my lip balm unless you test what's inside. I can tell you exactly the proportion of ingredients inside one of my lip balms. If those aren't there, then it could be any lip balm in the world."

He pulled the bag away and pushed a pen and pad of paper toward me. "Write down the ingredients in your lip balm and the formula."

"Well, now that's proprietary."

"I'm going to be straightforward with you. This lip balm is what killed Agnes," he said. "Write down your ingredients and the proportions or I will be forced to arrest you for the murder of Agnes Snow."

"What? How? I test all my lip balms. There's no way it could kill anyone . . . unless they were highly allergic to bee products. If that's the case, then they wouldn't be shopping in my store."

"The ingredients and the proportions." He pointed at the paper.

"Fine." I wrote down my recipe. "The flavors vary so it might have rose or lavender or clover or citrus. Also my application tubes are BHP free and made out of one hundred percent bioplastics."

"What are those?"

"They are made of vegetable products instead of petroleum products and will biodegrade. It's better for you and better for the environment." I pushed the paper toward him and crossed my arms over my chest. "I'd like to call a lawyer now."

He raised an eyebrow. "I was going to let you go."

"Fine." I stood.

"Good." He stood and I was suddenly aware of how close he stood. Which was strange because I wasn't attracted to him. Right? I felt heat rise in my cheeks.

"Why did you haul me down here in a squad car? I would have told you that at the shop."

"It's procedure and you almost didn't tell me. Bringing you here was to show you I'm serious. I'll get the door."

I hurried through and he walked me out into the lobby.

"Listen, Wren, don't go out of town for a few days. I may have more questions for you."

I swallowed hard. "I'm not going to go anywhere. I own a business here. I'm trying to build a life here."

"I'll be in touch."

I left the police station and stepped out into the cool evening air. The television crew still hung out. I made a sharp left around the building, ducked down through an alley, and around the next block. The thing about Ocean-view is that, like many Oregon coast cities, it was very walkable. I dialed my aunt as I walked.

"Wren," she answered. "Where are you? Are you all right?"

"Officer Hampton took me in for questioning. I'm going to need a lawyer. Is there anyone I can call?"

"Bobby Hanson," she said. "He put together my estate papers. I'll text you his number."

Aunt Eloise loved new tech. She was always up on the latest gadgets, and phones were no different. Aunt Eloise even taught classes at the senior center to help all her friends keep up on new technology.

"Thanks." I heard a car behind me and glanced over my shoulder. It was a blue MINI Cooper. Inside was Alicia, the *Gazette* reporter. She pulled up even with me and rolled down her window.

"Hey, Wren, are you okay? Do you need a ride?"

"I'll call you back, Auntie," I said and hung up my phone. "I'm fine. Just walking home."

Her dark brown eyes were full of sympathy. "Officer Hampton let you go so that's a good sign. Come on, get in."

Just because Alicia was a reporter didn't mean I shouldn't talk to her. I went around and got into her car. She pulled back into the street and navigated the short distance to my shop. It was late and Porsche had closed up for the day.

We parked. "I have some wine," she said. "We can order takeout. It's the least I can do as a friend."

"Thanks," I said. "But I have to make some phone calls." I hated to put her off but I needed some time alone to figure out what happened and how I was going to deal with it. "It's been a very long day."

"Listen, I'm not here to be judge and jury. I'm trying to be your friend. I would really like your story. You know, have you tell your side of things?"

"Talk tomorrow?" I got out of the car.

"Okay," she said. "But I'm here for you, if you need me. This is awful and I don't want you to feel alone."

"Thanks." I opened the shop and punched in the security code. Everett was there to greet me. "Hey, handsome." I scratched his head. "I bet you're hungry. Come on, let's get you some tuna."

My apartment was a sanctuary from a day that was turned upside down. I opened a can of tuna for Everett, plopped it in his bowl, and put it on the floor in the kitchen. When I made the phone call to the lawyer, I got dumped into voice mail so I left a message. Then, I climbed into a hot tub of bubbles to soak my day away.

I didn't sleep much. I'm not sure anyone would have slept after discovering a dead person and then being ques-

tioned as a killer. At 5 a.m. I was up, searching for aller-
gies to my ingredients. Could one of my natural ingredients have killed Agnes?

As far as I could tell the answer was no. I was pretty
sure that if Agnes was allergic to my ingredients, she
wouldn't have been using the lip balm. Then again,
maybe Jim was just fishing for leads. After all, he had
told me that the lab could take weeks or months, and he
picked me up the same day I found Agnes.

I perused the local news. Alicia had written an article
on Agnes's death. It made the front page of the paper. We
didn't get a lot of dead bodies in town. I noticed that she
didn't mention my name at all. I was thankful, although
Oceanview is a small town. Everyone already knew.

Porsche texted me. "Are you up?"

"Yes."

"I'll be right over."

"What about your kids?"

"Jason is handling them."

Porsche lived a few blocks away in a cute beach bungalow. Her husband, Jason, worked for a local company.
I was surprised he was home on a Wednesday.

By the time I was showered and dressed, Porsche was
at my back door with coffees and a bag of donuts. "I
brought you fuel," she said. "I'm guessing you haven't
eaten."

"No," I said as she walked into the kitchen. Everett ran
to greet her, winding through her legs and telling her all
about what happened since the last time he'd seen her.
His meowing could get quite loud.

"Sit, have some coffee and eat something." She pushed
me toward the kitchen table. My apartment kitchen was
basically cupboards against the back wall with a window

over the sink and the door out on the right side. My table was a 1950s chrome set with a Formica top and red vinyl coverings on the chairs.

"Yes, Mom," I teased and took a seat. If I was to be honest, the coffee and donuts helped settle my stomach.

She poured Everett some breakfast and came over, taking a seat at the table. "All right, what's the plan?"

"Plan?"

"Yes." She sipped her coffee. "I know you have a plan. Spill."

"I don't have a plan," I said ruefully. "I'm completely in the weeds."

"Okay, I guess I can understand. Yesterday was a shock and then I heard that Bernie threw you out of his house."

"Yes." I felt the heat of embarrassment rise up in my cheeks again. "He thinks I might have killed Agnes. Then Officer Hampton took me down to the station for questioning."

"Yep," she said and grabbed a cinnamon donut. "I heard all about that. This must be a nightmare. We need a plan. First things first, are you a person of interest?"

"All he told me is that Agnes was killed by a tube of lip balm. And there was one of my labels in her hand so the assumption is that it was my lip balm that killed her." I shuddered as I said it out loud. "Wow, I guess that means I am a person of interest."

"No, I'm not buying it," Porsche said. "You need motive. Where's your motive? I watch television. You need motive, means, and opportunity." She ticked them off on her fingers. "You don't have any of those things . . . well, maybe means."

"It doesn't make any sense. Why would I use my own

lip balm product to murder someone? No one will buy another lip balm from me. Besides, I want to know how he knew it was the lip balm that killed Agnes. He told me the lab wouldn't get to the test results for days."

"Maybe they smelled bitter almonds around her mouth," Porsche said. "Everyone has watched some television show where the victim is killed by poison and the hero smells almonds."

"So, I put almond oil in my balm," I said.

"Bitter almonds smell different than sweet almonds. Someone may have known the difference."

Confused, I asked, "How do you know what bitter almonds smell like?"

"I was a biology major in school, with a botany minor."

I knew that, it was one of the reasons I hired Porsche. She knew as much about bees as I did. "Oh, right, did they teach that?"

"One of the classes I took as an elective was on natural poisons," she said and sipped her coffee. "I've had an interest ever since."

"So, if Agnes was killed by cyanide in the lip balm," I said, "and most people know that cyanide smells like bitter almonds, why would she use it?"

"Maybe she's one of the one in four people who can't detect it?"

"How would the killer know that?" I asked. "None of this is making sense. I thought maybe she was allergic to my bee products, but, if she was, then it would be considered an accidental death, right? I mean, I'm not liable for someone's allergic reaction to my products. Everyone knows it contains bee by-products. It's in the name of my shop."

I had intentionally named my shop "Let It Bee" so that people would remember it and understand immediately what the shop was all about. My interest in bees came about while visiting a friend's farm. They had several beehives on the property to help pollinate their cherry trees. My friend had told me that there were beekeepers who rented beehives out to orchards and blueberry farms to ensure pollination. I found that really interesting. Then, while I was in college, the story was reported that bees were disappearing and dying all over the country, and I became all about the bee.

I had my own hives that I rented out to local farmers. Of course I couldn't keep them in town, but I had great contacts who were happy to rent out space on their land for hives.

"I don't know how the killer would know," Porsche said, and then rested her elbows on my table and put her chin in her hands. "Maybe it was something else."

"I guess beeswax and almond oil would be great ways to apply a lethal dose of any poison, but most poisons are bitter and hard to mask. Besides, who, besides you, knows enough about poison to use it? And who wanted to kill Agnes?"

"I think we need to find out the answers to those questions," Porsche said. "Before you're arrested for murder."

*Havana Brown enthusiasts use the term
"Chocolate Delights" when describing the beautiful chocolate brown cat with bright green eyes. The
breed is known to be affectionate,
intelligent, and sometimes mischievous.*

Chapter 4

"I'm not a trial lawyer, Wren," Bobby Hanson said as he took a seat across from me. Bobby had called me at 9 a.m. and asked me to come in and see him. "Not usually, anyway. I specialize in legal documents."

"You're the only lawyer I know," I said. "And then only through Aunt Eloise."

"Didn't you need a lawyer when you started your business?"

"My realtor took care of the leasing papers and my

friend Emerald took care of the paperwork for permits and licensing. If you aren't a trial lawyer, why have me come down to your office?" I'd walked down to his office this morning to clear my head.

"Because I'm interested in the case," he said. He leaned toward me over his big oak desk. "And my son, Matt, is a trial lawyer. I thought I'd have you come down and meet with him."

There was a knock on the door and the door opened to a handsome man with dark hair and dark eyes. I would guess him to be in his early thirties. He was maybe six feet tall and wore a perfectly fitted, navy blue, pinstriped suit. His black shoes shone and he wore what could only be described as a hipster beard—perfectly groomed and about four inches long. He looked like he just stepped out of a luxury car commercial. That's saying something, as most everyone else in Oceanview wore hooded sweatshirts or flannel. "Sorry for the delay," he said and walked over to where I sat and held out his hand. "I'm Matt Hanson. Has Dad told you I want to take your case?"

I shook his hand without thinking. His handshake was firm and as professional as his Italian-cut suit. "I don't have a lot of money." The words burst out of me. He looked like a high-powered lawyer, and high-powered lawyers usually get paid high-powered salaries. "I'm just a shopkeeper."

He flashed a wide, white-toothed smile. "It's okay, I'm willing to take this pro bono." Sitting on the edge of his father's desk, he faced me. Funny, Oceanview was a relatively small town. Why didn't I remember seeing him around before? He certainly stood out in a crowd.

"Why?" I asked a bit lost.

"We're interested in the case," they both said at the same time.

"I don't understand," I said. "I'm sorry, have we met before?"

"No," Matt said. "I have an office in Portland and Salem. Dad called me in when he heard Agnes was found dead."

"Agnes and Bernie Snow have a high-profile reputation in the area," Bobby said. "We don't think anyone should get railroaded just because the mayor wants answers now."

"That and the mayor and the Snows have been a bit of a thorn in our sides," Matt said and crossed his arms. "Plus, Dad owes your aunt a favor or two."

"So this is political," I deduced.

"Yes," they both said unapologetically.

"Do you know who might have killed Agnes?" I asked.

"No," Bobby said.

"Haven't a clue," Matt said. "Tell us what you know."

I gave them the short story of how I found Agnes, how Bernie Snow kicked me out of his home, and then how Jim pulled me in for questioning. "And now Alicia from the *Gazette* wants me to tell my story," I finished.

"Don't talk to the press," Matt said. "It's never a good idea."

"But if I don't talk to them, they'll make assumptions."

"Assumptions but not accusations," Matt said. He grabbed a chair and pulled it toward me. Then he sat and leaned in. The effect was to create a calm bubble around us. "Listen, do you have any reason to kill Agnes?"

"No."

"What about your Aunt Eloise? Everyone knows they were rivals."

"No," I said. "Aunt Eloise was devastated by Agnes's death. Think about it. Suddenly her rival is gone. Who does she engage with now? Besides, a silly little rivalry doesn't mean you would kill someone. They've been competing for decades. Why kill her now?"

He frowned. "Makes sense."

"Was it okay for me to give Officer Hampton my lip balm formula?"

"Yes," he said. "It shows you are cooperating. But from now on, I'd recommend you don't talk to the police unless I'm with you. If they pick you up again, call me before you say anything. Okay?"

"Okay."

"Good." He leaned back in his chair. "I'll go visit them today and get the story." He smiled again. "My uncle is the district judge."

"Oh." I blinked. "Can he tell you things?"

"No, not officially, but we have ways of guessing," Bobby said.

"Okay, so what do I do now?"

"Now, you go back to your shop and go about your day as if nothing happened," Matt said.

"That's going to be hard to do," I said. "The press is hanging around my shop." It was true. The television news crew had shown up as soon as I stepped outside this morning. I'd told them no comment and I meant it. They were currently camped out on Main Street. "Someone from the news crew is following me. I think they are waiting for me outside." Not to mention Alicia was stopping by tonight with wine and dinner. We were friends. I wanted to hang out and destress.

"Then we have to craft a story that is safe to tell," Matt said.

"There is no need for a story," I said. "I'm innocent."

"Everyone says that," Matt said. "It only makes you look guiltier. Listen, if anyone asks you questions, refer them to me. Here's my card. I'll go check out what the story is on Agnes. You leave your story to me."

Gee, I wish that made me feel more comfortable. I left the law office and walked home. I could have driven, but I needed to think. I did manage to avoid the promenade. There would be a lot of people there and they would all be asking questions.

"You know what the answer is," Aunt Eloise said as she stood by the door to the shop later that afternoon, trying to judge the difference between reporter and shopper.

"Let everyone in and let Porsche run the business until things die down?"

"No," she said and gestured for me to come over. I went to her side and we both looked out at the crowd peering at us. "We need to figure out who's framing you."

"The killer?"

"Exactly," Aunt Eloise said.

"I think the police are going to—"

"Blame it on the easiest person and, my dear, that poor soul unfortunately is you."

I blew out a long breath at the craziness of it all.

"Excuse me," an elderly woman shouted from the lip balm display. She was tiny and wore jeans, a T-shirt that read WORLD'S BEST GRANNY under a black Columbia jacket. Her hair was white and curled perfectly around her round face.

I went over to her. "How can I help you?"

"Is this the lip balm that killed Agnes Snow?" She peered at me from behind round glasses. There was a glint in her eyes.

"What? No," I said horrified. "My lip balm never hurt anyone."

"That's not what I hear," she cackled. "This is great for Halloween. I'll take them all." She shoveled the entire shelf into her Halloween-themed tote bag with one fell swoop of her arm.

"That's over five hundred dollars," I warned her.

"Worth it," she said. "Come on, ring me up. I can't wait to pass these out at work and see who's afraid to put it on."

"I'm sorry, but you can't purchase those," Jim said as he entered the store.

"Why not?" the woman asked. "I have perfectly good credit."

"Because I need to take all of those into evidence," he stated.

"I think you need to have a warrant to seize anything," Aunt Eloise said.

Jim pulled a piece of paper out of his pocket and handed it to me. "Now, I need to take those." He gently but firmly took the tote out of the woman's hand. "In fact, I'm closing the store down. Please everyone, put down whatever you planned to purchase and in an orderly manner leave the store."

"That's ridiculous," I said. "You're going to put me out of business."

"Don't worry, honey," she said as she touched my arm. "Lip balm that's been locked up in evidence is even better. I'm a huge fan of true crime and I have a lot of friends who are as well. Here's my information. The minute he lets those free, you call me and I'll buy the whole lot."

I took the paper and watched in dismay as Jim and Officer Ryan O'Riley shepherded everyone out of the store. Aunt Eloise, Porsche, and I were the only people left. I dialed Matt Hanson's cell phone.

"Hanson," he said as he answered the phone.

"Hi, it's Wren. The police are in my shop. They are making everyone leave the building."

"Did they serve you a warrant?"

"Yes," I said and opened the paper. "I'm not sure that I understand what it says."

"I'll be down. Don't let them search anything until I read the warrant."

"It's too late for that," I said as I watched two more police officers enter the building and begin to systematically take things off the shelves. "They're going to take all my inventory. That's going to put me completely out of business."

"I'll be right there."

I hung up and watched them take items off the shelves. "Excuse me, but that's my property," I said. "You can't seize that."

"Unfortunately, we can," Jim said. "In this case, we

must. We can't take the chance that other products on your shelves are tainted."

I tried to remain calm and make sense of the warrant. "I've called my lawyer. I think you're on a fishing expedition."

"What was the poison that killed Agnes?" Aunt Eloise asked. "Look around, you won't find any poison on the premises."

"I can't share any information," Jim said. "It's best if you ladies go outside and let us do our jobs."

"I need to get Everett," I said and stormed upstairs. My boy was in his favorite box in the bedroom closet. I pulled him out and hugged him close. He meowed his disapproval of being disturbed. But I knew he'd be fine with it. One thing about Everett, he was usually fine with things. "Come on, let's get out of here," I whispered and put his leash on him, then carried him back downstairs and through the shop to the outside. I tried not to cringe at the sound of glass breaking as they jostled things in the shop behind me.

A small crowd had gathered by the time Matt arrived in a blue sports car. He got out and strode into the shop. "May I see the warrant?"

I handed him the paper and snuggled with Everett. My kitty was helping me feel better in the strange circus that had become my life. "It's a bit dramatic in there. Glass is rattling and being dropped. They are just sweeping my inventory into garbage bags. This is going to set me back two months."

"I'll go talk to them." He walked off.

Aunt Eloise put her hand on my shoulder. "This is not the kind of Halloween scare we want around here."

I flinched at the sound of more glass clinking. One of the officers took a bag and put it in his squad car. "I'm going to go to Porsche's house," I announced.

"Good idea," Aunt Eloise said and handed me off to Porsche. "I'll let that cute lawyer of yours know where you're going."

"Come on," Porsche said. "Watching the kids play will take your mind off of this horror." We walked in silence for five blocks. Tears flowed down my cheeks. "Oh, honey, it's okay," she said and hugged me. "We're going to fix this."

"How?"

"We're going to investigate the murder."

"Really? Where would we even begin?"

"Well, we'll do what they do on television. We'll set up a murder board and list suspects."

"How will we know who's a suspect?"

"We'll ask questions and find clues. I'm certain we can get answers that the police can't. We'll get to the bottom of this."

Everett meowed his approval. I wiped away the tears. "Fine, let's do this."

Making a murder board at Porsche's house was easy. She had two boys in elementary school and they had poster board for school projects. We cut a picture of Agnes out of the paper and pinned it to the middle of the board.

"Who is our first suspect?" Porsche asked. Her boys, River and Phoenix, were playing video games in the next room. Everett was sitting on the back of her sofa.

"Well, they always say to look at the husband first," I said. "He would have access to her lip balm."

The sound from the playroom grew loud and something crashed. "Jason, can you go see what the kids are doing?" Porsche asked and rolled her eyes. "Being married for as long as they were is pretty good motive for murder."

Porsche's husband was a shoe designer who worked for Nike. He had a home office but was often traveling to shows around the world. So when Jason was home, they had a deal: He handled the kids. Porsche once told me that as parents you had to double-team your kids or things would get out of hand.

The sounds from the next room quieted down as Jason's voice floated above the fray.

I laughed. "Well, I wouldn't know, but we can't suspect anyone without evidence. We should look into how much insurance Agnes had."

"Got it," Porsche said and made a list. "Oh, and we should ask around. Maybe Bernie has a girlfriend." She wrote "girlfriend" on the board with a question mark.

"Or Agnes had a boyfriend," I said and added "boyfriend" to the list.

"Or Bernie had a boyfriend," Porsche said.

"Or Agnes had a girlfriend," I said and ticked off both columns. I studied my friend. She was dressed in a peasant top with a cold-shoulder sleeve and a pair of jeans. Her long hair was pulled back into a sleek ponytail. I wish I had her upscale style.

In contrast, I wore a maxi dress with a long sweater. My hair was a fuzzy ball of curls that ringed my head like a halo. Sometimes they looked golden. Sometimes there was a hint of red in them.

"So, money, love, revenge—" I started listing things that could be considered motive.

"Your aunt?"

"What? No, no, no," I said. "She would be as likely to have done it as me. Besides, even if she did get mad and do Agnes in, she would have never framed me for the deed."

"True," Porsche said and pursed her lips. "Who do you think wants to frame you?"

"That's a strange question."

"Well, think about it, honey. This is ruining your business and your reputation all in one blow. Is there anyone you know who would want to do that to you?"

"No, I don't have any real enemies . . . I mean, Mrs. Dupont complained about my honey face mask," I said, "but I gave her money back."

"Did she bring back the goods?"

"No," I said.

"She just wanted to see if she could get your product for free." Porsche tapped the marker against her chin. "What about the candle shop? Aren't you in competition with your beeswax candles?"

"Maybe," I agreed. "But that shop is located closer to the beach. I don't think my business is an actual threat. Does Agnes have any family?"

"I think she has a sister in Oregon City. I'm not sure how close they were."

"Well, let's find out who she's related to and add them to the list." I pursed my lips. "Where can we find out more about Agnes?"

"I imagine the craft store," Porsche replied. "She spent more time there than at home from what I hear. Which leads me back to a possible girlfriend for Bernie."

"Maybe she was taking a class and upset the teacher," I suggested.

Porsche wrote "craft store" and "teacher" on the board. We heard a crash in the next room. "Hold my pen," she said and stormed off to yell at whatever child was upsetting the place.

I held the pen in my hand and studied the board. There was a lot we didn't know.

How were we going to figure this out? How was my business going to survive if I didn't?

*Honey's antibiotic properties can help heal
wounds and sooth burns.*

Chapter 5

"They took over half my inventory." I stood in the center of my shop and stared at the disarray the police had left behind.

"I had them note everything they took," Matt said. "We're going to submit it to your insurance company."

"I don't think they'll pay for a search and seizure."

"Then we'll sue whoever is framing you."

I smiled wryly. "We have to figure that out first. It seems the police are looking squarely at me." Everett meowed from my arms and studied the mess with distain. My cat liked things in their place neat and tidy. He didn't necessarily like what it took to get them that way, but he appreciated the end result.

"I've got a call in to the judge," Matt said. "They executed the warrant and that means they think they have good cause."

"They were fishing for something," I surmised. "But there is no way they found it."

"Maybe this is like that old Tylenol case where someone tampered with the product," Aunt Eloise suggested.

"My advice to you is to take the rest of the evening off," Matt said. "You can spend all day tomorrow cleaning up and then determine what it would take to reopen. They've released the store so it will take a second search warrant for them to come back. I'll make that as hard as possible. They're going to have to put the murder weapon in your hand."

I started to tremble at the idea. "Perish the thought."

Matt gave me a short hug. "Don't worry. I've got your back."

"Come on, Wren," Aunt Eloise said. "I'll go upstairs and make you some dinner. You shouldn't be alone tonight."

We let Matt out and locked up the shop. So many people walked by and stared. It was unusual to have foot traffic in the evenings for the off-season, and I knew they had to be gossiping about me. I waved at them and smiled, holding my chin high. Most looked away, ashamed.

Upstairs I saw that they had also thoroughly searched my apartment. I wondered if I had left anything embarrassing lying around. I didn't think so.

"Well, this is certainly a fine kettle of fish," Aunt Eloise said. Today her long gray hair was plated down her back. She had on her "Portland Rose Kitty" T-shirt, jeans, and a long black sweater. "The least they could have done is cleaned up after themselves."

"It's okay," I said and put Everett down. "I'd rather do that myself."

"Why don't we put your bedroom together first? That way, after dinner you can take a nice hot bath and get some rest. Everything else will keep."

"What about you? Do you have plans for the evening?"

"No, no. I was going to try my new candle-painting craft. That can certainly wait now that Agnes is gone and you need help." She ushered me into my bedroom. There was something comforting about her familiar orange blossom perfume.

"What about your kitties?" I asked. She always had at least three Havana Browns. She'd given up showing and breeding cats after Everett's mother died. Instead she started a Havana Brown rescue group. She had Everett's sisters Ember and Evangeline spayed. They'd recently fostered a rescue named Sir Hamilton Princeworthy, but preferred to be called Lug.

"The girls are doing quite well with Lug. I think we might have a home for him soon," she said. "I'm talking to a great gal in Eugene who is looking for a cat."

I stopped just inside my bedroom and tried to hide my horror.

They had stripped my bed and searched under the mattress. Stuff was everywhere. I felt sick to my stomach to think that anyone, let alone the very people who are supposed to protect and serve, could just go through my things. It devastated me. My dismay must have shown.

"Go get some clean sheets," Aunt Eloise said, her tone all business.

I was numb as I went out into the hall and took clean

linens from the closet. The hallway was strewn with things from the rest of the house. My pictures hung crookedly. Tears filled my eyes as I hugged the sheets. Everett wandered down the hall sniffing at random objects.

"All right," Aunt Eloise said. "It's going to be okay. Come on, help me make the bed." She had somehow muscled the mattress back on top of the box springs, cleaned up the floor, and deposited clothes in the hamper in the corner of the room.

"They destroyed my home. I won't know what they took until I go through everything."

"Matt will get you an inventory," she said as she made the bed. "Come on, give me a hand. Action will help. We'll have this room back to normal in no time. Don't worry, I'll help you wash your clothes."

"Thank you," I said as I tucked in the top sheet. "I don't know what they touched and didn't touch. I'll feel better after everything is cleaned."

"You should charge them for your dry-cleaning bill," she said.

"I think I've got bigger issues than a laundry bill. Porsche thinks we should figure out who's framing me."

"Now that's an excellent idea," she said.

"We set up a murder board in her living room. You know, like all the police detective shows? I realized that I don't have the first idea how to begin an investigation."

"Who was your first suspect?"

"We wrote down Mr. Snow because husbands are the best suspects in the murder of a woman. But then I asked why he would murder her the week before their fortieth anniversary bash."

"It does seem strange," Aunt Eloise said. "Unless

Agnes was having an affair. Then it might have been a crime of passion."

"I've been thinking about that and I don't think so. A crime of passion would have been more . . . blunt. Wouldn't it? I mean, it would have taken a murderous rage. Yet, she looked so peaceful there in the sand."

"Poison is usually a woman's weapon," Aunt Eloise said.

"So what woman wanted Agnes dead and me out of business?"

"That is the question of the day. Come on, let's go make some dinner."

I picked up Everett's favorite cardboard box and placed it back on the closet shelf. The room was nearly back to normal. Except for the large pile of clothes in the laundry basket, you could barely tell anyone had been in it. The rest of the apartment had a long way to go.

I worked in silence while straightening my home and returning everything to its normal position. I noticed the police had taken my accounting books and my laptop. "What am I supposed to do now?" I muttered.

"What's missing?" Aunt Eloise asked when she noticed I'd paused just inside the combination living room and kitchen.

"They took my account books and my laptop."

"You have your stuff backed up in the cloud, right?" she asked as she pulled a skillet out of the cupboard. I realized that she had already straightened the kitchen.

"Wow, you act fast."

"Thanks," she said. "I prefer a tidy kitchen to make dinner in. Now, what stopped you in your tracks?"

Everett wound around me, as I hadn't budged from the

spot where I entered the living room. I knew he was worried. "I need my laptop."

"If you have things backed up, you can get a cheap replacement to use until yours comes back," she suggested.

I reached down and picked Everett up to reassure him and somehow touching him reassured me. "Yeah, I think I have it backed up."

"Don't worry, we'll go down tomorrow morning to the discount store and get you a used laptop. You can download your accounts from the cloud and use it until you get yours back. Easy peasy."

"You don't think they locked my accounts, do you?"

"Did Matt tell you the warrant covered your accounts?" she asked.

"No."

"I think it's safe to say that the warrant didn't cover your accounts. Matt would have told you. Really, they have no reason to freeze them." She came over and hugged me. "This has rattled you. Let's have some dinner and discuss the next steps. There's always next steps."

"Right," I said and hugged her back. "I can salvage what's left of my inventory and download the backup of my files. It's going to be all right."

"You betcha," she said. "Now, skillet mac and cheese is on the menu. Go clean up and set the table. Dinner will be done before you know it."

Aunt Eloise was right, dinner made things better. "You know you can always come stay with me until things settle down," she said. "I still have your room set up." After mom died, I lived with Aunt Eloise. It was a comforting thought to go back, but I needed to move forward not backward.

"Thanks, but Everett and I can get through this. Right, Everett?" He meowed his agreement and jumped up in my lap.

"The room is always there if you need it." She pulled a pad of paper and a pen out of her cat tote and placed them on the table. "Okay, we'll do dishes in a moment," she said and pushed her plate aside. "First, let's look at the next steps. You've identified possible killers. Do you have any motives?"

"No motives," I said. "And I don't understand what motive the police think I have."

"All right, we need to find out all of Agnes's dirty little secrets." Aunt Eloise rubbed her hands together. Her eyes glinted.

"You're having too much fun with this."

"Maybe," she said casually. "I will talk to my friends at the senior center tomorrow. Someone knows something. This is a small town and the seniors all have their ears to the ground."

"Okay," I said. "What can I do?"

"Snoop around the craft store. Agnes practically lived there and no way could I even go into it without her knowing. Someone there knows something and they will more likely talk to you than me."

"Okay," I said. "I feel better now with a task."

"Several tasks," she said. "Now, I have to go."

"And leave me with the dishes?" I widened my eyes.

She laughed. "Yes." She got up, leaned over, and kissed me on the forehead. "Now, you do the dishes and take a nice hot bath. You're going to be fine. You're a very strong woman."

"I take after my auntie."

* * *

The next morning, I was up before the sun. Everett was mad that I kicked him out of bed so early to make it. He went off and sulked in his box. After doing two loads of laundry and completely organizing my apartment, I felt energized. By the time 10 a.m. came around, I had already straightened half my store. Porsche arrived and slipped in through the back. Out front was a TV news crew as well as local reporters.

"Hey girl," Porsche said. "The kids are in school and all is right with the world. Wow, you really did a lot this morning."

"I did," I said. "I feel good and I'm not going to let anything get me down. You and Aunt Eloise are right. Let's figure out who is framing me and why."

"Great," she said and went to the back door. "Because I had to take the murder board out of the house. The kids kept asking questions." She brought the poster board into the shop. "Now I don't think we should keep it in the shop, but upstairs might do."

"Let's put it in my den." I had a second very tiny bedroom. I had thought of making it a master closet, but then decided instead to make it my den. That didn't mean I did much in there. I was a laptop girl, which meant, as everyone who searched my place yesterday found out, I did most of my work from my living room couch. I took the poster from her and went upstairs.

Everett came out to see me when I entered the apartment. The second bedroom was off the living room and about eight feet by eight feet in size. I think at the turn of the twentieth century it was good enough for someone to sleep in, but for today's homes, it would barely fit a twin bed. Inside I had a soft, cream shag rug and a futon in my favorite color, purple.

I cleared the tiny writing desk that fit under the eaves and put the board up on it. Porsche had filled in the place-holders of boyfriend and girlfriend with black silhouette cutouts. Bernie's photo was one from an old campaign poster where he was smiling and waving with a baby in his arm, which made me think. If anyone knew what was going on, it would be Bernie's secretary and campaign manager, Judy Sellers. Judy didn't run in my limited social circles. I figured I needed to meet more people and made a mental note to figure out how to get introduced to Judy. If anyone knew Bernie's secrets, it would be her.

I grabbed my crossbody bag and slung it over my shoulder, careful to put my wallet and my phone safely inside. Then, I grabbed a pair of sunglasses and went downstairs.

"You should go out the back," Porsche advised. "There's a real crowd out front."

"Do you think the back is safe?" I peered out the peep-hole. My back alley also held a crowd. I chewed the inside of my cheek and pondered what to do. Everett rubbed up against my leg and meowed. "Good idea," I said and took his leash off the wall. "You go distract them." I handed Everett over to Porsche.

The moment the front door opened on Everett and Porsche, the crowd swelled. Photo flashes went off. People were shouting questions. Porsche waited long enough for the people in the back to run around to the front before she took off her hood and let them all know it was her and not me who was facing the crowd with Everett beside her.

I slipped out the back as soon as it was clear and made

it to the craft store undetected. It felt like a victory and my heartbeat sped up as I slipped inside. Walking through the store, I made a careful note of the three ladies inside. The cashier was Hanna Graebill. She had graduated high school last year and was taking a year off to figure out what she wanted to do with her life. I doubted Agnes would have much to do with a nineteen-year-old. In the back stocking shelves was Marcy Reynolds. Marcy was my mom's age and had spent her life working part-time at the craft store. Her husband was a local fisherman and they didn't need her to work a full-time job. The third was store manager Brenda Emperies. Brenda was my age and had graduated college with a business degree before going into retail management. She'd taken the job as craft store manager and never looked back.

My guess was that Marcy would be most likely to give me the information I needed. So, I sidled up to the yarn section where she was stocking shelves and grabbed a pattern for a pair of socks. Then, I found some oversized knitting needles and went to the yarn, looking for a great color.

"Do you need any help?" Marcy asked.

"Oh, no," I said. "I'm going to make a pair of socks. I was just looking at yarn." I flashed her my pattern book.

She glanced at the needles. "Oh, no, honey, those needles are way too big to use to knit socks. Have you ever knitted before?"

"No," I said. "But my aunt said I need to get a hobby and these socks look pretty easy to make."

"Let's take you back to the knitting needles and find you the right gauge. Actually you might want these." The needles she picked up were small and made a loop.

"Oh, gosh, I guess that makes sense if you're going to

knit something round like socks. I guess I thought you would stitch up the back." I took the needles.

"Let's get you the right yarn for your project."

"The store is pretty empty today," I commented as she went through the wall of yarn and showed me a variety of colors in a lightweight texture.

"Oh, everyone is out at the community center. There's an event for Bernie Snow."

"Huh," I said. "I thought he didn't want any fuss."

She studied me for a moment. "You're Wren Johnson, aren't you? You're the one who found Agnes dead."

"Yes," I said. "It was quite traumatic."

"Aren't you a person of interest in the case? I mean, that's what they are saying on the news."

"I'm afraid that's only speculation. I haven't done anything but discover her body. Still the whole thing is quite something, isn't it? It's why I came here today. I needed a project to calm my nerves."

"Well, knitting will do that." She turned back to the yarn. "Hard to start with a pair of socks. You should really start with something simple like a hat and scarf set."

"I thought the socks were cute."

"Suit yourself," she said, "but don't say I didn't warn you."

"I need something a bit challenging to take my mind off of finding Agnes and the rest of the mess. I understand that she came here often. Did you know her well?"

"Yeah, she came in here all the time, and I loved to talk to her. She always had an opinion. You know, she was getting ready to teach a class for us. I think it was on candle painting. Yes, that's right, candle painting."

"Funny, that's the craft my aunt just started working on."

"It's like Agnes had a craft radar. She always knew

what the next hot craft was going to be. In fact, she started scrapbooking before it became a fad. Don't get me started on her needlepoint."

"I wonder what got her interested in crafts. Was she sick as a child or something?"

"Agnes, sick? Goodness, no, that woman was healthy as a horse her entire life. That's why her death is so suspicious," she said and pulled a skein of yarn off the shelf. "How's this?"

"It's perfect," I said and took it from her. She had picked out a bright orange and black mixture. "These might make great witchy socks for Halloween."

"That's only a few days away," Marcy said. "You'd better get to knitting."

"I'm sure I'll have a lot of time on my hands." I studied her. "You think Agnes was murdered. Who do you think would want to kill Agnes? Did she have any enemies?"

"That nice police officer asked me the same thing. I'll tell you what I told him. Agnes could get a person's nose out of joint pretty quickly. But then she had a way of always drawing someone back in. It was a gift. So while a lot of people might not like her, she never got anyone mad enough to want to see her dead." She studied me. "Did she?"

"What about Bernie?" I persisted. "Do you think someone would have wanted her dead to get back at him? He was the mayor for years and years."

She laughed. "If anyone wanted to get back at him, they would have done it before he retired."

"Hmm, that's true." Then I leaned in close. "I heard Agnes might have been having an affair. Do you think that's true?"

"What? An affair? Agnes?" She laughed so hard tears came to her eyes. "I'd eat the entire yarn section if she was having an affair. That woman was too busy crafting to be getting into that kind of trouble, if you know what I mean."

"I do," I said. "Thanks for the information and the yarn."

"You're welcome. Bring those socks in when you're done. I'd love to see what they look like."

"I will," I said bravely. Then I made my way to the front. Hanna was reading a gossip magazine. I set my stuff down on the counter. She looked up at me. "Oh, my gosh, are you Wren Johnson?"

"Yes," I said. "Hi."

"Aren't you a person of interest in Agnes Snow's death?"

"Me? No," I said. "Definitely not me, I can't imagine having a reason to kill Agnes."

"Oh, I can," Hanna said as she rang me up. "That old biddy was into some nasty stuff."

"Really." My eyes grew wide open. "Like what?"

Hanna stopped swiping my stuff over the reader and leaned toward me. "You didn't hear this from me, but I heard Agnes getting into a fight with Rhonda Doll."

"Really? Over what?"

"Rhonda wanted Agnes's place as president of the garden club. She told Agnes that she'd been president far too long and it was time for a fresh face and fresh ideas." She leaned on the counter. "Then two weeks later, they were both in here when they started shouting at each other. Rhonda saw Agnes through the window and stormed in to confront her. Turns out Rhonda had initiated a coup of the garden club. She thought she had enough members to overturn Agnes's position, but Agnes wasn't going down without a fight. That woman knew everybody's secrets."

"I take it Rhonda wasn't successful."

"No," Hanna said and straightened. "Agnes managed to convince the club to keep her as president. That's when Rhonda came in here gunning for her. She was so mad she was shouting about how Agnes was a master manipulator and control freak. She told Agnes to watch her back, she was coming for her."

"Wow." I glanced over my shoulder. "Did Marcy witness this, too?"

"Naw, she was on break at the time." Hanna finished up checking me out and I paid with a credit card. "If I were the cops, I'd check out what the heck was going on in the garden club."

"Thanks," I said as I grabbed my stuff.

"Anytime," Hanna said and returned to her magazine. "You'd be surprised what you see from behind the cashier counter."

Honey Taffy Candy

½ tablespoon butter
½ cup heavy whipping cream
1½ cups honey
⅛ teaspoon baking soda

    Take a large heavy pot (you will need room for this to bubble up) and add the whipping cream and honey. Heat over high heat, stirring constantly until the mixture comes to a boil. Then, cook uncovered without stirring until the mixture reaches 280°F on a candy thermometer. (This can take 15–20 minutes so be patient but don't leave it unsupervised.) While this is cooking take an 8-by-8-inch baking pan and butter it. Place it in the refrigerator to cool. Once your candy mixture reaches 280°F, remove from heat and mix in the baking soda. Pour into your greased pan being careful not to scrape the sides of the pot. Let cool until it is easy to handle. Then, butter your hands and pick up the candy. Pull and stretch the taffy until it becomes lighter and firm ridges form. Braid taffy or roll. Then, slice into one-inch pieces. It's fun to wrap individually with waxed paper. Store in the refrigerator. Enjoy!

Chapter 6

I left the craft store and texted Aunt Eloise about the garden club. She texted back that she had made progress at the senior center and we should meet up at her home—out of the press's sight. Aunt Eloise lived in a lovely bungalow just four blocks from the beach. It was built in the 1930s and had white clapboard siding and blue shutters. She kept flower boxes under the sills, and they were currently filled with orange, red, and yellow mums.

I went to the back door and knocked.

"It's open." I heard my aunt say from inside so I went in and closed the door behind me. A quick look down the street told me that no one had followed me. The back door led to a small enclosed porch where my aunt kept her collection of cat vases and jars on shelves. I took off my shoes and entered the kitchen. It was warm and smelled like family. To my right was a double window and a small dinette table with three chairs under it. To my left was a gorgeous kitchen with cabinets that went from floor to ceiling. It was not a large space but the cabinets made up for it.

"Oh good, Wren, you're here," she said as she came out from the bedroom to the left of the kitchen. Emma, a gorgeous brown cat with mint green eyes, followed her out. She greeted me with a meow and I bent to give her a few long strokes. "I'll make us a cup of tea."

Evangeline chased Lug into the kitchen. Lug jumped up on the table and watched me carefully. But Evangeline had no reservations. She came up and put her paw on my arm to say I should pet her as well. "Hello, ladies," I said and gave them love. "How are my favorite girls?"

"They're doing well," Aunt Eloise said. "Making Lug feel right at home." I stood and studied Lug.

"Would you like to say hello?" I asked him. When I was a small child, Aunt Eloise had taught me to let cats approach me, rather than run to them and start petting. It could be intimidating for the poor dears—especially the ones rescued from bad homes or bad situations. "What's his story?" I asked as I sidled up to the table and waited for him to ask for pets.

"He's about five years old and his owner died suddenly of a heart attack. Her son couldn't keep him because his daughters are allergic. So he found the rescue group and I have him until we find him a good home." She handed me a cup of tea. "Come on, let's sit in the living room and let him warm up to you."

The kitchen was decorated in red and white with

strawberry wallpaper and accents. The dining room contained an old dining table and buffet that belonged to my grandparents. Here, Aunt Eloise kept her cat cookie jar collection. My favorite was the cookie jar with two cats driving a convertible. The dining room opened up to the living room with two chairs, a couch, a television that I had never seen on, and a card table with the current craft in progress in the corner.

"What's in your bag?" Aunt Eloise asked.

"Oh, yarn and things to make socks," I said and sat down on the couch. "It's been a while since I knitted, but I thought making socks might be cool."

"Ambitious," she said and sat down. The crocheted throw on the back of her chair had a cat motif.

"I really went to check out the craft store. I heard some interesting information," I said and sipped my tea. "What did you find out?"

"I learned that Agnes was blackmailing Bill McCarty," Aunt Eloise said.

"Over what?" I asked. Bill was the tourism board manager at the local chamber of commerce. Like so many other residents, he'd grown up in Oceanview and, after a brief stint away in college, returned to create a career in the small town. He'd been at the chamber of commerce as long as I could remember.

Bill was a memorable guy with his long gray beard and bald head. I didn't know how old he was, but I figured at least my mother's age.

"No one knows for sure," Aunt Eloise said. "But it had to be something big because every Friday for the last three months, Bill would go into the bank and withdraw two hundred dollars in cash."

"Who told you this?"

"Eleanor Stone," she said. "She's a teller at Cascade Federal Bank."

"How did she know that he was paying Agnes?"

"Because Agnes would come into the bank within minutes of his withdrawal and deposit the same amount into her account. So, Eleanor got suspicious. One day, she took a quick break and followed Bill after he left with his cash and she saw that Bill went to the back alley and Agnes met him there. He handed her the cash and she took it without a word. Eleanor hurried back to the bank and then soon enough Agnes was in the bank making her weekly deposit. Eleanor joked with her one time about blackmailing someone."

"And?"

"Agnes didn't even flinch."

"I wonder what Agnes had on Bill?"

"Eleanor has no clue, but it is certainly another avenue to explore," Aunt Eloise said. "How did it go at the craft store? Did you get anything other than knitting supplies?"

Lug leapt up on the edge of the couch and pretended not to notice me. Meanwhile Evangeline curled up on my lap. Emma had the prime spot on Aunt Eloise's lap.

"I ran into Marcy. She told me I should start with a hat and scarf," I said. "But I was pretty insistent on getting stuff to make socks."

"You spoke to Marcy?" Aunt Eloise put her teacup down on the end table and leaned toward me, her right hand petting Emma. "Did she have any idea who might have killed Agnes?"

"Marcy was suspicious of me. She heard I was a person of interest."

"What did you do?"

"I played it off as just fake news," I said. "Then, I asked if she knew anyone who might want to hurt Agnes, but she swore she didn't know anyone who would want to do such a thing."

"So the craft store was a dead end?"

"Not really. The cashier, Hanna, told me that Agnes and Rhonda were in a fight in the store the other day. Rhonda was trying to oust Agnes from her position in the garden club."

"Oh, I remember that," Aunt Eloise said. "Rhonda had worked hard to gain enough signatures to force a new vote for president, but in the end the club voted Agnes back in."

"Hanna told me that Rhonda followed Agnes into the store and screamed and yelled at her. Words like 'control freak' and 'manipulator' were used."

"Oh, interesting," Aunt Eloise said. "We need to add Rhonda to the murder board. It sounds like both she and Bill had motive—certainly more motive than you."

"There might be even more people with motive," I said. "Hanna said that Agnes had something on most of the garden club members. Apparently, that's how she maintained her power."

"Small towns," Aunt Eloise said. "You learn everybody's secrets if you pay attention."

"I don't have any secrets," I said.

"Yes you do," Aunt Eloise countered. "We all have secrets."

"What are yours?"

"Wouldn't you like to know," she teased. "I doubt anything I'm holding next to my heart is worthy of blackmail."

"Do you think that Agnes was blackmailing more than one person?"

"Maybe," she said and looked at me. "Do you think Bernie knew?"

"Well, if he didn't, he will soon. Won't the bank report all of her accounts?"

"Oh, I hadn't thought of that," my aunt said. "I guess, yes, they will all come out in probate."

"Any one of her blackmail victims might have killed her," I said. "We need to figure out the entire list of suspects."

"Bernie might know more than we think," Aunt Eloise suggested.

"You think he might be in on it?" I remembered how Bernie looked the night when I brought the casserole over. There was so much grief on his face.

"He hasn't made any noise about her accounts," she pointed out. "He might not know yet, but I suspect if we know someone has told him. Wouldn't you be trying to find out why your spouse had secret accounts?"

"Do you think the cops might say something to him?"

"If we can find out about Bill, they will find out about Bill," Aunt Eloise surmised. "The real question is which of her blackmail victims is also angry enough with you to frame you?"

"I don't know Bill or Rhonda," I said. "I don't run in their circles."

"It doesn't mean they wouldn't try to frame you,"

Aunt Eloise said. "People get strange ideas and trust me if you're poisoning someone, you're not thinking straight. Let's approach this from a different angle. Who wants you out of business or in jail or both?"

My eyes widened at the thought. "No one," I said. "I don't have anyone who hates me that much."

"Anyone who might want your business?"

"Gosh, I don't think so. I mean, I've been so busy the last year getting the store up and running, I haven't had time to make enemies let alone friends."

"What about old boyfriends?"

"I haven't had a boyfriend since Rick," I said. "You know that." Rick was my college boyfriend who left me for adventures in Europe. I didn't regret it. We were close, but I wasn't ready to give up my idea of owning a honey shop.

She made a face. "Why would anyone be doing this to you?"

"Maybe it's not about me," I mused. "Like you said, people get strange ideas. Maybe the killer simply needed a way to get Agnes to ingest the poison, and once the police started looking at me, they had a scapegoat."

"If you think about it, it was ingenious. I mean, people keep putting on lip balm as it wears off and most women store a tube in their purses or their cars. We don't think about others having access to it."

"Agnes was holding the label from one of my tubes when she died," I said. "But what if the label was not the original?"

"So you think the killer tore your label off of her tube, glued it on the poison tube, and put it back in her purse?"

"I didn't find a purse," I said. "Maybe it was in her jacket pocket."

"So, who was close enough to her to slip a poisoned lip balm into her jacket pocket?"

"Not someone she was blackmailing," I said thoughtfully. "Think about it. You don't hug your blackmailer."

"That leads us back to Bernie."

"Except poison is most likely the weapon of a female killer."

"One of Agnes's friends?"

"Maybe someone from the garden club."

"This is all too difficult," Aunt Eloise said. "How do the police do it? On television it looks so easy."

I glanced at the clock. It was well past Everett's dinner. "I have to go," I said and stood. Evangeline deftly leapt off my lap. Lug put a paw on my arm as if to say I should pet him before I go. I ran my hand along his silky fur.

"Update the murder board," Aunt Eloise advised. "We have to keep track of everything we learned."

"I will." I picked up my bag of knitting supplies, gave the cats one last pet, and left.

As I arrived back at the store I saw that the crowd had disappeared. It seemed that the interest in my being a suspect in Agnes's murder had died down. Thank goodness people had short attention spans. Now, maybe I could get back to selling bee products.

I went in through the front door and the bells jangled behind me. Everything was in its place again. The shop smelled of the honey almond candles we specialized in as Porsche had some burning behind the counter where I stashed my bag of yarn and needles.

Helen Dower was browsing the body creams. Thankfully I could count on my regulars, and Helen was one of them. She was a fortysomething, high school teacher with blonde hair and big blue eyes. When I opened my store, she told me she would make a point of stopping by as she had a special place in her heart for the bees. "I made a new lavender honey face cream," I said and pulled one off the shelf beside her. "I know you love my face creams. This one is great for bedtime. It's soothing and it helps firm your skin while you sleep. Not that you need that, but it's good to get in the habit."

"Oh, thanks, Wren," Helen said and took the jar from me. "This sounds perfect. What's in it?"

"Honey and lavender along with coconut and avocado oil."

"Did you know women used to use arsenic on their skin to make it whiter and more translucent?"

"What?"

"I teach history and love all those kinds of details," she said.

"You can rest assured, there's no arsenic in my products."

"Well, now that's not what the press is saying," she said and peered up at me through her round tortoiseshell glasses.

"I wouldn't know the first thing about even obtaining arsenic," I said and put my hands on my hips. "I use only natural ingredients."

"A lot of poisons are natural, honey," she said. "Arsenic is a mineral that occurs in the earth."

"So, what? There are just arsenic mines somewhere?"

She laughed and held out her hands. "How would I know?"

"Well," I took the jar from her, unscrewed the top and stuck my finger into the perfect swirl. "This cream is perfectly safe." I rubbed some on my cheek. "See?"

"I'll take it," she said and snatched it back from my hands. Helen was all of five foot one inches tall. She wore jeans and a T-shirt that had a teddy bear motif. "I didn't mean to insult you. You know I love your stuff. I actually came in looking for pumpkin spice. You, know, keeping up with the season."

I calmed down. She was actually going to buy and that's exactly what I needed right now. Customers.

After helping Helen with her purchases, I turned to Porsche, who was going over the inventory. "How bad is it?" I asked.

"They took a good one-third of the inventory," she said. "That includes all of the lip balm." She pointed to the empty basket where I had displayed it. "And most of the skin care."

"I've got enough ingredients to replenish some of the favorites," I said. "The rest will have to wait until I get more supplies. How bad is it going to affect the bottom line this month?"

She did some quick calculating in her head. "Probably as much as you're going to pay me."

"Oh, so twelve dollars and fifty cents?" I teased.

She laughed. "You never know. We might have a run

on our store. I mean, people like gruesome during Halloween. And murder is pretty gruesome."

"I didn't have anything to do with Agnes's death," I said.

Porsche raised her hands. "I didn't say you did, and I didn't realize you were so touchy about the subject."

"It's been a strange twenty-four hours," I said. "Anyone would be touchy."

"I suppose you're right. How'd it go at the craft store?"

I went behind the counter and opened the bag of yarn to show her my haul. "Apparently I'm going to make socks," I said. "Unless you want to try."

"No way, I've got enough going on. Did you find out anything about Agnes?"

"Yes. Do you know Hanna Graebill?"

"Sure, she babysits for me sometimes."

"She cashiers at the craft store and she told me that Agnes and Rhonda Doll got into a fight in the store recently."

"Oh, that's good, a clue. What was it about?"

"Rhonda wanted to oust Agnes from her position as president of the garden club. But Hanna said that Agnes had dirt on members of the club and pulled strings to keep her position."

"That must have really ticked Rhonda off," Porsche surmised. "Rhonda can be a force to be reckoned with. My mom found that out a few years ago when she started a book club. Rhonda came in and took it over. Before my mother even realized what was happening, the book club was meeting at Rhonda's house every month and Rhonda was not only picking the book but leading the discussion."

I winced. "She sounds like a handful."

"To say the least. You think that your aunt and Agnes were a problem?" Porsche's mouth firmed. "Rhonda makes trouble wherever she goes."

The door to the shop opened and Jim walked in, taking off his hat. My heart sank. "What can I do for you?"

"Have you come to take more from her?" Porsche closed in ranks beside me.

"I'm sorry about that," he said and came over to the counter. "We had to ensure that none of your products were tainted."

"And did you do that?"

"The lab hasn't had time to process what we took," he said. "Listen, I heard you were asking people questions, and I wanted to let you know that we take our investigation seriously. We don't need any help from amateurs."

I raised my chin and stood my ground. "You're crazy if you think I'm going to just sit around and wring my hands while you try to prove I murdered Agnes Snow. Because I'm innocent."

"Everyone is innocent until proven guilty, right?" Porsche said and put her arm around me.

"I haven't arrested you yet, have I?" He looked perplexed. "I'm trying to do my job and keep everyone safe. I'm asking you to please let me do that."

"Fine," I said.

"Good," he said his expression cautious. "Thank you."

"I'll walk you out," I said and purposefully moved him toward the door. "Listen, we think that Agnes was blackmailing Bill McCarty. Did you know about that?"

"Why do you think that?"

"The bank teller began to notice a pattern of Bill withdrawing cash and Agnes depositing cash."

"Who's the bank teller?" he asked.

"I'm sure you can figure that out yourself," I hedged. "Also, you should check out Rhonda Doll. She wasn't a fan of Agnes."

"We know," he said and stopped at the door. "Seriously, Wren, let me do my job. You have to trust me."

"Why?" I crossed my arms. "All you've done is rummage through my home, take my things, and destroy my business."

We stood eye to eye. "This is serious, Wren. I'm not trying to ruin anyone. I'm only doing my job."

A spark of something went between us for a moment and I felt the store closing in around us. I could see why women thought Paul Newman was a heartthrob. Right now my heart found itself enthralled with Jim Hampton's blue eyes. "My dreams and my life are at stake here," I stressed but it came out as a whisper.

"I'm going to find the killer and see Agnes gets justice." He turned and walked out of the shop, stopping only long enough to put his hat on before stepping out into the street.

"What was that all about?" Porsche asked.

"Small town," I said and blew out a long breath. Everett wound around my ankles so I picked him up. "He wants me to stop my investigation before it's even started."

"You aren't going to do that, are you?"

"No," I said and stared at the door. "Do you think Jim Hampton is good-looking?"

"Maybe in that dangerous, I'm-in-charge-guy kind of way. Why?"

I tried to play innocent. "No reason."

"Ohhh, someone has a crush," she teased. "You should follow that."

"Please, he thinks I'm a killer."

"Guys like bad girls, too, you know. His suspecting you of murder might be even better." She winked at me.

"I've got enough drama in my life right now. I don't need to add to it by getting involved with a man who wants to put me in jail."

"Yes, but wouldn't it be fun?"

Studies have shown that honey can improve both short- and long-term memory.

Chapter 7

I was up again early Friday morning. Perhaps I was becoming a morning person, although more likely I was becoming an insomniac. Sleep seemed to elude me that week. I used the time to create Halloween-themed lip balms and hand lotions. The holiday was a few days away. If I made extra pumpkin spice and candy corn scents, I could continue to sell them through Thanksgiving.

By the time Porsche showed up to open the shop, I had two batches of lip balm and a dozen candles done and cooling on my production table. "Hey," Porsche called to me as I headed downstairs. "You might want to come see this."

"See what?" I asked as I hit the ground floor.

"This was pinned to your back door." She handed me a piece of paper.

It was a picture of a dead cat hanging from a noose. "Oh, that's awful!" I put the picture down. "Who would do such a thing?"

"It looks like a threat. Maybe you should call the cops."

"Why would anyone want to threaten me?"

"Perhaps your investigation uncovered something that someone doesn't want uncovered," she suggested.

"What? Like Bill McCarty being one of Agnes's blackmail victims?"

"Maybe," Porsche said and leaned in. "Maybe someone really has it in for you."

"Right, like I did anything to tick anyone off," I protested. "That's the problem with Agnes's murder. Why am I being framed for it?"

"You're right, there really are two motives here. One, the killer needs a motive to plan out and murder Agnes." She ticked off on her fingers. "And two, they need a motive to frame you for the deed."

"I've been racking my brain trying to figure out who would want me to go out of business. I don't have any direct competitors and I don't have any enemies. Frankly, I've been too busy trying to get my shop off the ground to tick anyone off."

"That you know of," she said.

"Well, if there's anything I know about people, it's that they let you know when they don't like you."

"Mostly true." She tapped her finger on her chin. "What if they didn't mean to frame you?"

"Well, that doesn't make sense. They used my lip balm."

"All we really know is that you found your lip balm label in Agnes's hand."

"And the police suspect Agnes was poisoned by lip balm," I added.

"But did they find the lip balm container?"

"I think so. Jim showed me one anyway."

"And was it yours?"

"It was hard to tell. I told him it could have been any-one's. He said they were going to test for the ingredients and had me write down what was in my lip balm."

"We're just going round and round here," she said and twirled her finger to emphasize the circle. "What I guess I'm trying to say is that framing you might have hap-pened accidently."

"Oh," I said and tilted my head. "Huh."

"We need to find out if Agnes was in the habit of peel-ing labels off of things. If so, then we should consider that the killer only meant to get rid of Agnes, and every-thing that followed was by pure accident."

"And now that we're investigating—"

"They're nervous and sending you threats." She pointed toward the paper. "You should call the cops."

I scrunched up my face in frustration and then resigna-tion. "You're right." I dialed the police station to report the threat. They promised to send an officer by when they could. We put the paper on the counter behind the cash register and opened for business. It was the Friday before the Halloweentown celebration and Oceanview was al-ready starting to buzz. "Are you ready for a week of Hal-loweentown?" I asked Porsche.

"We need to dress up every day for a week, right?"

"Yes, starting Sunday," I said. "But if you can't, I

understand. The big day is a week from tomorrow, and I'd save my best costume for that day."

"Oh, I have enough costumes," she said with a laugh. "I love dressing up for Halloween and have been looking forward to this all year. Sunday I'll be working as Morticia Addams from the old *Addams Family* television show."

"Oh, boy."

"What are you wearing?"

"I was going with a *Wizard of Oz* theme starting with Dorothy. I thought Everett wouldn't mind hanging out in a basket all day."

"Oh, a cat as Toto, that is surprising. And on the big day?"

"I'll be the Wicked Witch—"

"Of the West!" we finished together.

The bells over the door rang and a pair of women came in to browse. I went over to show them how to sample the hand creams.

The rest of the morning went by in a blur as Friday traffic picked up. People often took the entire day or half the day off and came out to the coast from Portland and surrounding cities. Word had spread about my being subject to a search warrant, and people were curious to see the shop and me.

"I guess no publicity is bad publicity," I said after lunch.

"The pumpkin spice is super popular in candles and creams," Porsche said. "You should give them funky names like Death by Candlelight and Dark Surprise."

"That's a great idea," I said. "For next year, though. For this month, I've got the labels finished."

"You know packaging is the ticket to good sales these days. Women will pay extra for fun or funky packaging."

"Now that is something we can both agree on," I said. "I thought the whole mason jar, country chic thing would do better."

"Oh, it's not doing badly, but you might skew a younger generation with something more poppy."

"How did you get so smart?"

"I'm taking a nighttime course on marketing," Porsche said. "I've been paying attention to the way other brands market. Looks like your bees are a huge hit." She pointed to three women who were avidly watching the hive.

"Cue me," I said and made my way over. "Isn't the beehive interesting?"

"Do they stay in there all the time?" one woman with a long blonde ponytail asked.

"No, there are cutouts near the eaves that allow them to fly in and out."

"What do they pollenate to make honey this close to the ocean?" a woman with a short black bob asked.

"Bees average a two-mile radius when they're hunting for food," I said. "But some have been known to go two or three times that. The best part about Oregon is that we have a lot of wild berries and particularly the blackberries that grow everywhere. The bees love them. Then there are all the flower gardens people in town have."

"Do you get all your honey from this hive?"

"Oh, no," I said. "I locally source all my ingredients, but some of the honey and honeycomb and beeswax comes from as far away as the Tualatin Valley and the orchards around Mount Hood."

"So some of your ingredients could have come from my backyard bees," the blonde woman said with glee.

"I guess you could think of it like that," I agreed. "Although most bees that beekeepers keep are loaned out to various farmers to help pollinate crops. So it's more likely it came from one of the orchards or farms near you."

"Wait, aren't you the woman they think killed the old lady on Tuesday?" the third woman, who had long brown hair, asked.

"Oh, no," I said with a short smile. "I didn't kill anyone. If I did, they certainly wouldn't let me work in my shop. Would they?"

"That sounds right," the blonde said. "You must just look like her."

I kept my game face on at her strange comment. "Bee pollen is really good for your skin and your health," I said. "Porsche over there can explain." I motioned to Porsche. She got the tin and came over, and escorted the ladies to the edibles.

"I didn't know honey candy was good for you," the blonde said with a laugh. "I'll take a pound."

"Wren."

I turned to see Jim coming toward me. "Are you stalking me?" I teased.

"You called about a threat?"

"Oh, right, yes, I did." I felt the heat of embarrassment reach my cheeks. "I completely forgot about it—it's been an insanely busy morning. It's over here." I took him behind the cash register. He put on a glove and then picked up the letter and placed it in an evidence bag.

"This looks a bit gruesome, but there isn't an obvious

threat. It might have been a Halloween prank by kids." He looked at me and I felt a pull toward his blue gaze.

"Maybe," I agreed. "But I thought it was better to be safe than sorry and let you know right away. It's all in the spirit of letting you investigate."

"I appreciate that," he said. "Where was this found?"

"Porsche found it tacked to the back door when she came in. She parks in the back lot." I took him down the hall to the back door and we stepped out into the cool ocean breeze of the alley.

We closed the door and he studied it. "Was it tacked with a thumbtack?"

"I think so," I said.

"Where's the tack?"

"Oh, Porsche must have it." I opened the back door and we went inside.

"Do you keep it locked?" he asked and studied the door.

"Yes, except during business hours."

"Maybe you should keep it locked all the time."

"I'll have to check the fire code on that." I took him back into the shop. The three ladies were leaving with bags filled with honey products. "Nice sale."

"They were great, having a girls' weekend and wanted stuff for self-care." Porsche looked Jim up and down. "I see you're back. Can't keep away from our girl?"

My eyes went wide. "Porsche."

"I'm here about the threat," he said without flinching. "You said it was tacked to the back door. Do you have the tack?"

"Actually, I said it was pinned," she said and reached into a drawer and removed a hat pin. "This is what held it to the door."

He took the pin in his gloved hand. "Interesting."

"That's what I thought," Porsche said. "Who even has hat pins anymore? I mean, maybe my great-grandma has one or two in her dresser from when she wore hats in the fifties."

"You're right," I said. "Our moms didn't use hat pins—even in the eighties."

"Maybe it's someone who collects hat pins," he suggested.

"That looks like it has a pearl on the end. If you collect hat pins, that might be one of your best. Why would you use it for a note to the door when tape would do?" I asked.

"They want us to know who they are," Porsche said.

"I agree it could be a clue," I said.

"Stop," Jim said and held up his hand. "We don't know what it means. I will catalog it and add it to the investigation, but for all we know this is simply a prank."

"What about the hat pin?" Porsche asked.

"It could have been what was handy. Kids wouldn't know if it had meaning or not."

"Right," I said and sent Porsche a look that I hoped told her to leave the topic alone.

"I'll write up a report," he said. "But we have no proof this is connected to the murder." He wrote something on a notepad near the cashier station. "This is your case number. Let me know if you get any more threats."

"We will," I said and held Porsche back as we watched him walk out of the shop.

"That was so condescending," she said. Her face looked like steam was coming out of her ears. "He just dismissed everything."

"I think he's trying to keep us calm," I said. "Think

about it. What would you be more comfortable with? Him saying this is a note from the killer and the hat pin is a clue or it's just a prank?"

"Prank," Porsche said.

"Yes," I said. "But we know better than the standard line."

She looked relieved. "Oh, good, we're going to look into who owned the hat pin?"

"Yes." I patted her on the back. "Aunt Eloise can most likely point us in the right direction." I picked up the phone and called my aunt. She promised to come right over.

"But Officer Hampton took the pin," Porsche said.

"I have a photo," I said. "I snapped it when you took it out. It's a little out of focus, but it should do, plus I took a photo of the note in case we needed to refer to it." I showed her the picture on my phone.

"You are brilliant."

"I came as soon as I could," Aunt Eloise said as she stormed through the door. "What's going on?"

I glanced over at the two browsers and noticed that they watched us with interest. "Let's go upstairs," I said and put my arm through my aunt's. She got my drift and went upstairs to my apartment quietly.

"What's going on?" she asked as soon as we closed the door. Porsche stayed behind to help the customers.

"Porsche found this pinned to my back door this morning," I said and showed her the picture of the note.

Aunt Eloise winced. "That's horrible. Is Everett okay? Who would do such a thing?"

"Yes, I think he's okay. We called the police. Officer Hampton came over and took our statements and the note. He said he would start a case file and gave me the number of the file to refer to, but he said he didn't think it was related to Agnes's murder."

"Okay?" She looked at me quizzically.

"Porsche and I think it is. We think it's a clue to the killer."

"Why?"

"Look at this hat pin they used to attach it to the door. Why would the person leaving the threat use a hat pin and not a piece of tape or a thumbtack?"

She took my phone from me and zoomed in on the photo. "That's a good question. That hat pin is at least sixty years old. It could be even older *and* that looks like a real pearl."

"Do you think someone is trying to tell us something?"

"I'm not sure," she said and handed me the phone. "But I can find out who owned a hat pin with a pearl end."

"You don't think it was a random flea market find?"

She crossed her arms over her chest. "Please, who buys hat pins anymore?"

"So it's older—vintage—not something from the eighties?"

"Eighteen eighties maybe," she said. "Listen, Agnes's wake is tomorrow. You should close the shop early and we'll all go. Maybe we can find someone who will recognize the pin."

"I don't know. It seems like my going would be in poor taste. Besides, how would we show it to people without drawing suspicion? We were explicitly told to stop investigating the murder."

"We won't be investigating the murder," she said airily. "We'll be investigating the hat pin."

"That's all well and good, but I'm going to stay away from the wake."

My aunt pursed her lips and tapped her cheek. "I know, you can volunteer at the senior coffee tomorrow afternoon. It's before the wake and people might be more willing to talk."

"But I have to work."

"Take a late lunch. I'm sure Porsche will cover for you. Oh, and make some cookies to smooth the way into people's hearts."

As if a cookie would reveal a killer.

Dab honey on a cold sore to reduce itchiness and heal it quickly.

Chapter 8

"Are you sure this is a good idea?" I asked my aunt the next afternoon as we walked to the church. The town was laid out in a grid pattern that wound between the foot of the mountains and the branches of the river and creek that spilled from them. The founders of the town numbered the east-west facing streets except for Main Street, of course. They named the north-south facing streets after trees.

Lumber is historically big business in Oregon and that means everyone has a special place in their heart for trees. Most of the houses in town were built between 1900 and 1930. The sidewalks were old and often lifted by tree roots. Trees grew tall and wide, shading homes. The streets alternated between paved and brick, creating a sense of history.

"They're always looking for volunteers to work the dessert tables at the senior coffees," she assured me. "You're volunteering. Volunteering is always a good idea. Now, you have that plate of honey almond cookies, right?"

I held up the plate. "Right here."

"Cookies and volunteering, you are such a good person," she said and directed me into the church. The building was a hundred years old and I knew the basement where they held the coffee would smell distinctly of age. It was the afternoon, and a light rain had started falling. I loved autumn in Oregon. The bright light of summer turned to the cool gray of a rainy Oregon winter. It was afternoon so it was light outside, but the gray mist probably wouldn't end for months.

I wore a bright green raincoat I'd gotten from a second-hand shop when I was a teen. It was a departure from the usual black or gray that most locals wore during the rainy season. I hadn't figured out why they didn't wear color. Maybe it was to blend in with the weather.

We shook out our umbrellas and entered the church basement. Barbara Miller from the Books and More shop was cutting into a large sheet cake and dishing out pieces onto plates, while Judy Sellers was making punch with frozen strawberries, ice cream, and lemon-lime soda.

"Good afternoon, ladies. We're here to help," Aunt Eloise said as we went over to the tables in the back of the room.

"I brought cookies," I said and lifted the plate. I felt uncomfortable and tried to hide it by being a tad too cheery.

"Well, Wren Johnson," Judy Sellers said and came over to shake my hand. "So nice to finally meet you. How are you?"

Holding the plate in one hand I shook her hand. "It's nice to meet you, too," I said. "Things have been a little crazy since . . . well, I assume everyone knows."

"Oh, yes, the elephant in the room, should we say?" Judy winced. "What a terrible thing to come across. Poor Agnes, I hear you found her facedown in the sand. She would have had a fit being found like that. I'm sure there was sand in her hair."

"I don't think she was aware," I said and put my cookie platter down next to the plates of cake. "Aunt Eloise said you ladies needed volunteers for the church coffee this afternoon so I thought I'd help."

"Good thing," Barbara said. Today she wore a black hoodie and black slacks with sturdy sensible shoes. "All the other ladies are prepping for Agnes's wake. We thought we might cancel the coffee, but a lot of the seniors said they wanted to come before the wake and have a short meeting."

"What are these coffees about?" I asked and hung up my raincoat.

"We talk about fund-raisers for the church and get together for social time," Barbara replied. "Although I don't think anyone will be feeling too social. But we have cake and punch just in case. Agnes would want it that way."

"Maybe we could take the leftovers to the wake," I suggested. "Where is it being held?"

"At the Blue Siren Bar and Grill," Judy interjected.

"But I think it's best if you don't go, dear. I understand your presence upset Bernie the other day."

"I didn't do anything," I said pointing out the obvious.

"Yes, Eloise told us the whole thing," Judy said. She was a tiny but fierce lady with white hair that hung in a perfect bob around her shoulders. I understand at one time it was red, but like some redheads she went all white at a young age. Her blue eyes were a very striking pale shade, and she played them up by wearing turquoise-colored blouses. "But you can't tell that man anything once he's made up his mind."

"And she would know," Barbara said. "She was his personal secretary before he retired."

"I spent more time with that man than I did my own husband."

"Oh, right, what was that like?" I asked.

"Sixty-hour workweeks over twenty years make for a lot of hours. My husband Fred and I have only been married ten years."

Aunt Eloise had been right about my volunteering at the church. Here was my chance to find out what Judy knew. "So you would know how close he was to Agnes."

"Oh, he only had eyes for her, no matter what some ladies will tell you," Judy said.

"What ladies?" I asked, sure I looked as aghast as I felt. Bernie was far from handsome.

"Why most of the women in town over fifty," Barbara said. "Except for me, of course. Ever since my Albert died, I've been devoted to my bookstore."

"I'm sorry, what do they find in Bernie?" I asked.

"Well, honey, you might think he's old, but some

women are pretty lonely and Bernie was in a powerful position," Judy said.

"You'd be surprised how power plays into attraction," Barbara said. "Do you mind manning the punch bowl?"

"Not at all," I said. "Wherever I can be useful."

People filed into the room and I went to my station. As the room filled up, I counted twenty-five people. I was surprised there were so many people here on a Saturday afternoon. Although most people were somber, they managed to eat cake and drink punch before the meeting.

Aunt Eloise took my plate of cookies around and made sure they were taken and tasted. She gossiped with some of the ladies while I tried to identify everyone in the room. I wasn't as familiar with Oceanview society as my aunt was. I'd only lived here for three years before college and then came back after my mother died to start the store.

"What brings a young lady like you to the senior coffee?"

I turned to see Richard Horowitz standing at the punch bowl with an empty cup in his hand. I took his cup and filled it up. Richard came into the shop often to see the bees. He told me once he was seventy-two years old, but he looked sixty-five if I were to guess. He was my height and round with a bald head. Today he wore jeans and a plaid shirt. "I heard you needed volunteers. Since Agnes's death, I feel terrible about not being more involved in the community, so I thought I'd step in."

"That's mighty nice of you," Richard said. "I would have thought you'd be investigating old Agnes's murder."

"Why would you say that?" I handed him his cup of punch.

"Because you're a person of interest, and I think you're innocent," he stated. "If it were me, I'd be investigating."

"Why? Do you know someone who would want to murder Agnes and frame me?"

"Well, now that's a very good question," he said and sipped his punch, his dark eyes twinkling.

"Are you telling me you know who?" I raised my eyebrows.

"I have my suspicions."

"Who do you think it was?"

He leaned in and I could smell wood smoke. Some of the older people still used wood-burning stoves to heat their homes. "My guess is it's Linda Sloan. She has that candle shop on the other end of Main Street."

"Linda? Why?"

"Agnes and she got into a fight last week," he said. "At the senior center, and I wasn't the only witness. It was quite heated because Agnes tried to get Linda to sell Agnes's painted candles. Linda was reluctant, but Agnes threated to kick her off the garden club board if she didn't do what Agnes wanted. Linda has been the treasurer of the club for years. I don't know what Agnes thought she had on Linda, but Linda was mad. The next day I noticed she had put Agnes's candles in her front window."

I winced. "I can see why she would have wanted to kill Agnes, but why frame me?"

"Your bee store is a direct candle competitor," he pointed out. "Linda and Eloise have had a number of tiffs over the years. If you went to jail, Linda would be getting three birds for the price of one."

"She sounds like she has motive," I agreed.

"I think she has means, too."

"What do you mean?" I asked.

"She has been known to buy poisons for the garden club. They take care of the flowers and such around town. Not to mention having prize gardens in their own homes."

"Maybe I should pay Linda a visit."

"You can't," he said. "She's working on Agnes's wake. I'm going to be interested in seeing how guilty she looks at the ceremony. I'm not the most astute guy, but I can tell when someone's lying. I just might ask Linda myself how she feels about Agnes's murder. It could get a rise out of her."

"Mr. Horowitz," I said. "Maybe you shouldn't confront her. If Linda is a killer, you don't want her coming after you."

He winked at me. "I'm a bachelor. I'm used to women like Linda coming after me."

I stayed to help clean up after the coffee, and Aunt Eloise and I closed up the church basement. "Did you find out anything?" I asked her.

"Judith Cantrell loves to talk about her parrot, Pete," Aunt Eloise said. "And Lori Anderson thinks that Amber Firth, the caterer of the Snows' anniversary party, has got to be pulling her hair out. Lori is sure she has all the food prep done for the now-canceled party."

"But Bernie will let her keep the deposit, right?"

"Sure, but what do you do with all that food?"

"She could bring it over for the wake," I said. "You

saw how they devoured the cake and cookies. I'm sure the crowd at Agnes's wake would enjoy the caterer's food."

"Barbara already thought of that," Aunt Eloise said. "But Amber's crowd is at the Mulligan's family reunion today. They didn't have anyone to spare to finish cooking and then serving the food."

"Sounds like some charity is going to enjoy great catered food," I said. "There are a lot of homeless shelters in the area."

"That's what I suggested," Aunt Eloise said. "Did you find out anything?"

"Mr. Horowitz has a theory of who killed Agnes."

"Oh, and who does he think did it?" Aunt Eloise asked me as we walked back to the shop.

I explained his theory about Linda.

"That's all well and good," Aunt Eloise said. "But Linda and Agnes were like sisters, they fought and made up immediately. It happens."

"But, I'm sure my losing so much of my inventory isn't going to hurt her candle shop, either," I said. "Not with Halloweentown week starting tomorrow. I've got some candles made, but I'm behind and waiting for supplies to be shipped in. In the meantime, Linda has some gorgeous black and orange candles for sale. Even if I sold out, I wouldn't be a threat to her now."

"Hmmm, it may not hurt to pay Linda a visit," Aunt Eloise said. "Tomorrow morning, you and I should pop over to her place before the shops open. Maybe we can see if Mr. Horowitz's theory holds any water."

"Sounds good to me," I said. "But we have to do it

early. I need to be in costume by ten when the store opens."

"Is there a lot of makeup involved?"

"I'm going to be Dorothy from the *Wizard of Oz*," I said. "So, no, not too much makeup. It's good to go tomorrow, because after that my costumes get more and more elaborate. I wouldn't have time to do them up right if I spent the morning at Linda's place. Are you going to be in costume?"

"I'm going to be a zombie cat lady," Aunt Eloise said with a smile. "I've got face makeup and then I'm going to give Lug and the girls an outing. Emma will be on her leash and Evangeline will be in my cat pack on the back and Lug in my front-facing cat pack."

"Back pack and front pack? Won't Emma be jealous?"

"No, she prefers to be on a leash instead of carried."

"Oh, you could join me in my *Wizard of Oz* costume as the bicycling witch and put them all in a basket in front of your bicycle."

"They love each other, but three in one basket might overstress them," Aunt Eloise said. "It's a thought, though."

"Oh, man, I didn't have time to ask anyone about the hat pin," I said and felt disappointed in myself. "Do you think that Linda put it on my back door?"

"It's hard to tell, but she could have. Linda has an extensive costume jewelry collection. I wouldn't put it past her to have hat pins in the collection."

"If they are her collection, then why sacrifice one in my back door?"

"Maybe some part of her wanted you to know the threat came from her," Aunt Eloise said.

"Why would she think I'd connect the hat pin to her?"

"You had to be investigating," my aunt said. "That would be my guess."

"We need to go see Linda."

"I agree," she said.

"Listen, I've got to get back to work. There's nothing more we can do today because I have to make more inventory. Thanks for taking me to the coffee, though. I think it added to our investigation."

"What about Officer Hampton?" she asked and gave me the side eye.

"I think he's doing a fine job of ensuring I'm indicted."

Aunt Eloise looked thoughtful. "I think he likes you."

"Seriously?" I studied her eyes to see if she was teasing.

"Really," she said sincerely. "You should see the way he looks at you when you're not looking. Why do you think he's always around?"

"I thought he was making sure I didn't leave town or, worse, hurt someone else."

"Hmm," she said. Her mouth formed a crooked line. "You really haven't dated in a while, have you?"

"I've been focused on getting the store up and running and I'm making my inventory myself. It's a lot of work."

"All work and no play makes for a hard life."

"Making hand lotions, lip balms, body lotions, candles, and candy are playing for me," I argued.

"It's Saturday night and you are young. I think you should think about going out to dinner with the man."

"What?" I must have looked shocked. "Again, he's trying to put me in jail. What is up with you and Porsche? She said the same thing."

Aunt Eloise gave me a side eye. "Keep your friends close and your enemies closer."

We parted ways and I went into the store. It was four o'clock, time for Porsche to go home and take care of her family. Everett and I would close up at seven and then take our nightly walk. It dawned on me that I was as much a creature of habit as my cat. That meant that a bad guy could easily know my whereabouts on any day. Combine that with the fact that my products were easily bought with cash, and I was an excellent target. No wonder the killer had chosen to frame me.

Honey's antioxidant properties are being studied as a possible cancer treatment.

Chapter 9

My mother used to say that when you go visiting someone you should take a hostess gift. For me it was honey almond cookies. I had a plate ready and went knocking on Linda's door. It was 10 a.m. on Sunday and I knew she would be home from church. I hadn't waited for Aunt Eloise because I had a new idea of how to get Linda to open up. I hoped it would work.

"Coming," came the call from inside. Linda opened the door and seemed momentarily surprised. An average-sized woman, Linda was my aunt's age and had been running the candle shop her entire life. Today she wore a pink tunic with black leggings and black socks. Her blonde hair was cut in a fresh bob. She had the look of a woman of standing and wealth. "Wren Johnson, what are you doing here?"

"I wanted to visit and I brought you some cookies." I tried to look innocent and held my plate out to her.

She took it without thinking. For an awkward moment she debated letting me in or not. Finally, she blurted, "I have no idea why you would come visit me."

I had my story ready. "I need your help."

"Whatever for?"

"May I come in?" I asked.

She bit her bottom lip then relented. "Yes, come on in." She held the door for me with her back. Her hands were full of cookies. "Take a seat in the living room and I'll make us some coffee. You do drink coffee, right?"

"I do," I said as she disappeared down the center hall to what I assumed was the kitchen. The house was warm and designer decorated. To my left was a living room and beyond was a formal dining area. To the right was a closed door, most likely leading to a bedroom. Behind that were the kitchen and, I assumed, the stairs to the second floor.

I remembered she was in stockinged feet. "Would you like me to remove my shoes?" I called after her. Some people don't like shoes on their carpets. Her place was spotless, so I guessed the same was true for her.

"Please."

I slipped off my knockoff Keds, set them in the hallway near the door, then stepped into the living room. Five pillar candles burned in the fireplace instead of logs and the room smelled of pumpkin spice and maple. The decor was clean and beachy with white walls and pale blue furniture. I took a seat on the couch.

The picture over the fireplace was a wide-angle shot of the shops along Main Street with Sloan's Candle Store in the center.

The home had candles on nearly every flat surface.

They seemed to watch me disapprovingly. I leaned back on the couch as Linda entered with a tray of coffee and my plate of cookies. She set them down on the coffee table and took a seat in a blue-and-white floral-printed chair. "I have cream and sugar if you want some." She gestured toward the tray.

I picked up my cup. "No thank you, I like my coffee black." As I put my cup to my lips it occurred to me that Agnes was murdered by poison. It might not be a good idea to eat or drink anything in Linda's home. I pretended to sip and put my cup down.

"So, what do you need from me?" she asked. "Isn't there someone else you can bug?"

I ignored her dig. "No, actually, you are the best person for this. You see, the police took almost a third of my inventory when they searched my shop and home. I know you have beeswax candles in your shop."

"I do and they are locally made."

Her pause was brimming with the insinuation that her candles were better than mine. I let it go. "Wonderful," I said and brightened my expression. "You see, with Halloweentown this week, I know we'll have a nice tourist rush."

"Yes," she agreed. "I was preparing today's costume when you knocked on my door. My shop opens at eleven." She looked at her watch as if to rush me.

"So does mine," I said. "I'll make this brief. I was wondering if I could sell some of your candles in my shop. My inventory is low and I don't want bare shelves. We are on opposite ends of Main Street. If I could put your candles on my shelves, I could put up a sign and drive more people to your shop. It is a winning situation all the way around. You get more shelf space and good advertising and I get to keep my shop open with shelves that look full."

She sipped her coffee and studied me.

"I suppose I could share a few of my candles. But you must let me brand the shelf you use."

"Wonderful," I said and sent her a reassuring smile. "Perfect. Thank you."

"Is that all you wanted?"

"I understand you and Agnes were close. I'm sorry for your loss."

"We weren't that close," she said and drank her coffee. "In fact, Agnes was quite upset with me before she died."

"Oh, really? I thought you featured her things in your shop. I assumed you were best friends."

"Far from it," she said. "Frankly I'm glad the old biddy is gone. Don't tell the cops that, though. She was so controlling that she would come into my store and tell me how to showcase her things as if she was the star of my show, for goodness' sakes."

"If you didn't like that why didn't you tell her?"

"She threatened to have Bernie put an ugly piece of sculpture in front of my store. When he was mayor he could have done just that. Why do you think that awful metal creature was placed in front of Hank Worthington's men's clothing shop? Hank and Bernie didn't get along."

"How was Bernie able to keep his job as mayor if he intimidated people?"

"He had some high-paying supporters who made sure that his competition looked bad. In return he gave his supporters clout in the town and along the coast. That's how the Seaside Hotel got zoned and built. That terrible monstrosity doesn't even go with the charm of the town. But no matter, it's a done deal now."

"I had no idea," I said.

"You wouldn't. You've only been a business owner for what, a year? I was wagering you wouldn't make it this long."

"I did, though. I'll celebrate my second anniversary in May of next year."

"If you last that long," she said.

I blinked. "What do you mean?"

"I mean, you're already in trouble if you have to come here and ask me for help."

"Oh, right."

"Don't take it personally," she said, reaching over to pat my hand. "Main Street businesses are cutthroat. It's prime property during tourist season. I'm surprised you got your place at all. I suppose because it is just off Main, you got a good price."

"Aunt Eloise helped me secure the lease."

"Your aunt is a strong woman."

"She is," I agreed and stood. "I need to get back and get dressed for the shop opening. You can send your candles over anytime. I live above the shop so I'll be there. Porsche and I will ensure they are branded to your standards. Thanks for helping."

"It will be an interesting co-marketing experience." She stood as well and walked me to the door. "Are you going to stop selling candles?"

"Oh, no," I said and slipped on my shoes. "Mine aren't as good as yours, of course," I flattered her. "But I make them because beeswax is so pretty in candles. Don't you think?"

"It is," she said and opened the door. "It has a nice melting point."

I stepped outside "Bye, Linda."

"See you soon," she said as she watched me walk away. I wasn't sure how productive the visit was, but it was interesting. If Linda was the killer, then I was inviting her into my home, which was probably not a smart idea. Still, if she poisoned any more of my things, she would implicate herself, since we were co-marketing. It could work out in my favor.

Halloweentown was a tradition on the Oregon coast. It was fun to have showings of the films around Halloween. People loved to dress up and bring their kids around to trick or treat. I had made salted honey caramels for treats.

My blue-checkered dress and white apron with red-sequined pumps gave away my costume pretty quickly. Especially since I carried Everett in a basket. To punk it up a bit, I created zombie makeup for my face.

"You look smashing, darling," said Porsche. She was dressed in a long black Morticia costume from the old *Addams Family* television show.

"You aren't so bad yourself," I said and gave her a wolf whistle.

"You know us girls," she said. "We love to show off our figures at Halloween."

The shop was all decked out in orange and black with tiny skulls and witches' cauldrons. The front window was ringed in glowing bats, and we had a steaming Crock-Pot of mulled cider at the door. Instead of bells, the door cackled every time someone walked in.

Costumed people roamed the streets as we unlocked

the shop and put up our open sign. Porsche stood at the door and gave away candy as the little kids came in and shouted, "Trick or treat!"

"Oh, trick, please," Porsche said.

A little boy in a puppy costume studied her. "You're supposed to give me candy when I say that."

"You mean I can't choose trick?" she asked.

"No tricks," he said. "Only candy."

"Well, if you insist." She put a piece of candy in his orange plastic pumpkin. "But next time think up a fun trick for me. Okay?"

"Okay," he said.

At first most of the visitors were kids and their parents looking for candy. But after a while, the crowd began to shop. I didn't mind the kids and their parents not shopping as it was still good publicity. People got to come in and see what we sold in the shop. I knew from experience that they would come back around later to purchase something they saw.

The beehive was also a nice draw. Kids found the bees scary and fascinating at the same time.

It was after 4 p.m. when the door cackled and a tall man with broad shoulders walked in. I recognized him immediately. "Conrad? Conrad Hassel?" Conrad was a guy I'd gone to college with. I'd had a huge crush on him, but he was dating another girl so I never let him know.

"Well, if it isn't my old friend, Wren." He gave me a bear hug. The man was a serious heartthrob of muscle and blond hair with a movie-star grin. "How are you?"

"Good. I didn't know you were in Oregon—"

"Moved to Portland last spring to work as COO of a software service company. Man, you look good."

"Oh, thanks." I felt the heat of a blush and then realized I was wearing zombie makeup. "How can you tell in my costume?"

"If you look that good in zombie makeup, then you must be really hot in regular makeup."

I blinked at him. Was that a pickup line or did he really mean it? "Thanks, what brings you to Oceanview?"

"I've got a buddy who wants to start a whale-watching business. He knows about whales and boats and I know about business. So I came over to check it out. Funny how everyone here is in costume. Halloween isn't until Saturday."

"It's the Halloweentown celebration," I said. "It's an entire week of Halloween and you are out of costume."

"Well, then I'll need to get one." He looked around. "This place is great."

"Thanks."

He studied the beehive. "Is this your store?"

"Yes, it is," I said. "I've been open about eighteen months."

"You were always good with business concepts." He turned and studied me. "Need an investor?"

"No, thanks," I said and smiled. "I want to prove I can do this on my own."

"Then let me take you out to dinner."

"I—"

"She'll go," Porsche said. "I've got the store covered."

"Porsche!"

"Go," she encouraged. Then she stage-whispered, "It isn't every day a handsome man shows up and asks you to dinner."

"Stop," I said and my cheeks felt hotter. "Are you sure?" I asked Conrad.

"I couldn't be more sure," he said.

"Now?"

"Yes, now! I don't mind taking a zombie out to dinner. I know this nice pub that has been smoking brisket all day and they make a mean sandwich."

"Okay," I said. "I'll get my purse."

"I thought that was your purse," Conrad said and looked down at the basket.

"No, this is my cat." I opened the top of the basket and Everett opened a sleepy eye and looked at me grumpily.

"Nice."

"Porsche, will you watch Everett?"

"Sure," she said, her gaze focused on what was going on.

I put the basket down on the counter and ran upstairs, got my purse and stopped to check my reflection in the mirror. I guess the black and white and slightly green tone of the makeup wasn't an altogether bad look.

Hurrying down the stairs, I reached the bottom to see Conrad standing there and my mouth became dry. He looked gorgeous—like the actor who played Thor.

"Let's go," he said and cocked his arm. I put my arm through it and waved goodbye to Porsche. Everett watched from the counter as if something was happening that he'd never seen before. Probably because he'd never seen it before.

Out on the street I felt as if everyone was watching us. It was a strange feeling. I tried to ignore it. But Oceanview was a small town and small-town people noticed everything and liked to comment. I guess I'd hear about it tomorrow.

He opened the door to the Four Horsemen Pub. Inside it smelled like smoked meat and IPAs.

"Welcome," the host said. "Table for two?"

"Yes," we both said at the same time and then laughed.

"I've got a quiet seat back here." He took us to the back of the building. Tall booths closed in the customers as if each table was in its own secret room. The host put the menus on each side of the table and I took the side that looked toward the back. I know some guys liked to have their backs to the wall so they could see the entrance. I wondered if Conrad was one of those guys.

"If it's okay with you, I'll order us both the smoked brisket," Conrad said.

"I'm in," I agreed. His eyes were so blue and his hair blond with a touch of red. "So you're thinking about investing in a whale-watching business?"

"I know there are several already," he said. "So another in the mix will be hard to be successful. That's why I'm here, I'm trying to figure out an angle that will bring people to us."

"Have you come up with any?"

"Well, maybe a secret cove or private picnic island adventure."

"I'm not sure there is any place on the coast that's secret."

"We'll see," he said. "Maybe I shouldn't go into the business. Tell me, if you weren't running your honey business, what business would you be in?"

"Probably a pet store or a florist shop." I thought for a moment. "Actually, definitely a pet store."

"There isn't one in Oceanview?"

"No, we have to go to Astoria or Beaverton, which is closer to you."

"Well, then pet shop it is," he said. The waiter brought us our drinks and brisket.

The rest of the time went by quickly as we caught up on all that had happened since college. I had taken a year to learn about bees and the bee craft. Then another year to apprentice beekeeping. Then another to earn enough money to stock my shop. Then finally time to create my inventory.

Meanwhile Conrad had gone straight to San Jose and gotten involved in a start-up that went viral. Now he was an angel investor. I teased him that he should be one of the guys on *Shark Tank*. "Don't I wish," he said.

We walked back to the shop. Darkness had fallen and the streets were quiet. A few high school kids in costumes were running around—up to no good, I'm sure.

"So," Conrad said as we hit the door of the shop. "Can I call you?"

"Yes," I said and gave him my number. We hugged and I watched him walk away. The date had been so much fun. I felt light and happy. It was nice to be out with a man who made my heart go zing just by looking at him. Maybe things were looking up for me.

Strawberry Honey Lip Balm

½ cup coconut oil
¼ cup beeswax
1½ tablespoons honey
1 teaspoon strawberry extract

Heat coconut oil, beeswax, and honey over low heat until melted. Remove from heat and add extract. Stir until blended. Pour into twelve half-ounce tins and let sit to cool. (Note: Any extract will work, so if you like vanilla and honey that would work as well.)

Chapter 10

The next day I was dressed as the Tin Man. Of course, I had to put my zombie spin on the costume. Silver face makeup and dark circles around my eyes created the Undead Tin Man look. Porsche arrived at the shop dressed like Wednesday Addams, complete with long dark braids. Five minutes before we opened, Linda knocked at the door dressed as Queen Elizabeth. She carried a carton of candles.

"Well, this is a surprise," Porsche said.

"No, we were expecting her," I said and opened the door. "Linda, thanks for coming by and adding to my inventory. I realized last night that we didn't discuss commission."

"I'll give you ten percent and if I see an uptick in sales due to the candles being here, then we can negotiate a higher percentage."

"Great," I said.

Porsche rolled her eyes behind Linda.

"Where do you want them?" Linda asked.

"I've got a lighted shelf right here." I took her to the right-hand corner of the shop. The glass shelves on the wall had lighting underneath to make anything on them stand out.

"I can set them up," I said and tried to take the carton.

"Oh, no," Linda said and wrenched it away from me. "My goods, my setup."

I raised my hand in the air like a stickup victim. "Works for me. I'll just go over to the counter and finish opening. Let me know if you need me for anything."

"I'll be fine. I was selling candles when you were still in diapers," Linda grumbled.

Porsche pretended to dust the shelves on the other side of the room with a feather duster. She gave me a look.

"I'll tell you later," I mouthed and went over to Everett, who sat on the counter. I stroked his thick fur.

We watched as Linda carefully arranged the shelf with her candles and sign.

"All right, girls," she said as she walked over with her empty box. "I think you're going to see my candles go faster than your things, but if you want to co-market, so be it."

"Thank you so much," I said.

Linda left and Porsche turned to me. "What the heck?"

"We think that Linda might have killed Agnes and is framing me because we compete in candles."

"So you invited her in?"

"Yes," I said. "If she poisons anything else of mine, well, we can say her things might be just as contaminated."

"Oh, brilliant."

"Besides," I went on, "I needed extra inventory. The shipment of new supplies doesn't come in until tomorrow."

"Have you heard anything more from your lawyer on getting your stuff back?"

"I haven't," I said. "I'm kind of afraid to find out what happens next."

"You should probably keep an eye on that."

"Aunt Eloise also thinks Officer Hampton is sweet on me and might be trying to keep me out of trouble."

"I told you," she said. "Besides, he should be looking after you. You're innocent."

"Of course I am," I said. "But I'm sure he's getting pressured to arrest someone in the case. I haven't seen our reporter friend around in a few days."

"Maybe she's on to someone else," Porsche said. "You should call her."

"I will," I said. "But it's time to open the doors. I can see the kids walking down the sidewalk."

We opened the doors and handed out candy to the kids in costumes who were trick or treating. By noon the crowd had slowed, so I went up to my office and called Alicia.

"This is Alicia," she said.

"Hey, it's Wren. How is the investigation into Agnes's murder going?" I asked.

"It's sort of stalled out," she said. "I haven't heard a peep in days. The medical examiner is busy with the autopsy and not all of the labs have come back. At least that's what the cops are saying. Why? Do you know something?"

"We should meet for tea this afternoon."

"Sounds good. How about the Tree House Tea House at three?"

"I'll be there," I said and hung up. Talking to Alicia was tricky. I didn't want to give up too much of what I knew. Just enough that she could run down that path with her connections.

I went downstairs to find somewhat of a crowd in the store. I loved a good rush—especially on a Monday. It meant we were going to make a profit for the day.

"Aren't these candles from the candle shop?" a woman asked.

"Yes," I said. "We're co-marketing. I also have some beautiful all-natural beeswax ones here. They melt very nicely." I showed her the candles I'd made the other night.

"I need about two hundred of these in this blue," she said and held up a color swatch. "Next week, can you do that? You see I'm getting married and I've decided to have candles for all the guests. I know it's last minute but is it possible?"

"I certainly could do that," I said and took the color swatch. "Do you want tapered or in mason jars?"

"I like the mason jars," she said. "We're having an out-door country wedding. We were going to have it at one p.m. so there would be plenty of light, but then my aunt can't come into town until late, so candlelight it is."

"Perfect," I said and told her the price, giving her a nice quantity discount.

"Oh, you're a lifesaver," she said and gave me a quick hug. "The candle shop said they couldn't do that many so quickly."

"Huh," I said, puzzled. "Well, don't worry, I'm your girl! Hi, I'm Wren."

"Nice to meet you, Wren. I'm Amy . . . Amy Packard, soon to be Amy Timagowa." She flashed a hefty diamond ring at me.

"When do you need to pick up your candles?" I asked.

"Would it be a bother to bring them to the wedding venue?" she asked and crinkled her face.

"There will be a delivery charge. Where is the venue?"

"It's at the White Horse Winery."

"That's about thirty miles from here," I said. "Sure, I can do it. Hang on while I write you up a work order and quote for the work."

I went over to the counter and pulled up a form I used for just such transactions. I filled it out as she stood by the counter. "Here you go," I said. "I'll need a third down to begin."

"Sure, anything," she said. "You are a lifesaver," she repeated.

The door cackled and I looked up to see Jim coming toward me with a very serious face. "If you'll excuse me," I said to Amy. "Porsche will finish ringing you up."

I met Jim halfway. "You need to come with me," he said quietly.

"Okay, where are we going?"

"Down to the station." He wrapped his hand around my arm.

I glanced over at Porsche. "I'll be right back," I said. She let me exit the building with little fuss.

"What is going on?" I asked. "You can let go of me, I'm coming willingly."

"I should have put cuffs on you, but I thought I'd save you from that," he said gruffly. "I'm going to keep my hand on you." He opened the back door of his squad car and tucked me in. I felt the door close and lock, and dread filled me. Something must have happened.

He got into the driver's seat.

"Has there been a break in the case?" I asked and leaned forward as he pulled out into traffic.

"A witness has come forward."

"Oh, that's good news," I said. "Isn't it?"

"Yes and no," he said.

"Why are you taking me in if you have a witness?"

"I want you in the lineup."

"In the what?"

He pulled into the police station and let me out of the car. "I want you in the lineup for the witness."

My heartbeat picked up. "Wait, aren't witnesses unreliable? What if they wrongly identify me? Should I call my lawyer?"

"You can call your lawyer," he said as he pulled me toward the station. "After the lineup."

I tried not to make too big a fuss as he dragged me into the station, through the lobby to the rooms in the back. I didn't say anything further. Matt had told me not to say anything without him present, and I was going to follow that rule. Jim sat me in a chair just inside the squad room. Three other women my age sat in chairs with our backs against the same wall.

"Stay here until we call you in."

"Yes, sir," I said and sent him a mock salute.

He gave me the side eye and disappeared into the depths of the squad room. I pulled out my phone and texted Aunt Eloise what was going on. I promised not to say anything and asked her to call my lawyer and get him down to the station as soon as possible. If I was going to be arrested, I wanted Matt here.

"Try not to think bad thoughts," Aunt Eloise texted me. "It might just be to rule you out."

"I'd like to know who the witness is," I texted. I craned my neck and looked around the squad room. "I don't see anyone I recognize."

"I'll find out where Linda is," she texted back. "So help me if it is her—"

"Don't say anything more," I texted. "Call Matt."

"All right, ladies, come with me, please," a female cop said. I noted that she was brunette, around my age, and her name tag said Shelley. I wondered if it was her first name or her last name. "Please wash off your makeup. Cold cream and washcloths have been provided for you."

There were four of us in various costumes, all in strong face makeup. My zombie Tin Man face paint was silver and red. I hated to take it off before the end of the day. It had taken me a full hour to do properly, but there was nothing to do but what I was asked.

Once we were all clean faced, she had us sit back down in the chairs for what seemed an eternity. Finally, she came back. "Please follow me." We walked down a hall and around a corner. She opened a door into a narrow room, and we lined up against the wall and faced a mirror. I'd seen this on television. But I'd never wanted to be part of the lineup in real life.

She closed the door and I craned my neck to look down the line. We all sort of looked similar. Our heights varied a bit and our hair color went from dark brown to my soft auburn. A disembodied voice came over a speaker. "Please look straight ahead. When I call the number in front of you, please step forward."

I dutifully looked ahead. My number was four. The officer asked us one by one to step forward. Turn to the left.

Turn to the right. Step back. My heart rate picked up when my number was called. I took one large step forward, turned left and then right and stepped back. The ensuing silence felt like forever.

"Number two, please step forward." I resisted the urge to look at number two as she stepped forward, then turned side to side again.

"Number four, please step forward."

Great, I was one of two suspects getting a closer look. I did exactly as I was told. We stood in our line for another eternity before the door opened and the policewoman stood there with Jim. "Wren Johnson, please come with me," he said.

I followed him with only a slight look back. All the other "possible suspects" got to turn the opposite direction and follow the female officer down the hall.

"What's going on?" I asked.

"I'm taking you to an interview room," he said. His tone was authoritative and clipped.

"I didn't do anything."

He didn't answer me. He stopped in front of a door and opened it. "Please go in and take a seat."

"I need to see my lawyer."

He studied me with a steel gaze. "You have your phone. You can make a phone call." Then he stood in the doorway and crossed his arms over his chest.

I turned my back on him and called Matt's law office.

"Hanson and Company, this is Sherry. How can I help you?"

"Hi, Sherry, it's Wren Johnson. I'm being held at the police station. Please have Matt come straight away. He told me to call if I needed something and before I talked to the police."

"Oh, okay," Sherry said. "Your aunt already called and Matt is on his way."

"Thanks." I hung up. Jim walked up to me and held out his hand.

"I need your phone and anything else that is in your pockets."

"Are you kidding me?"

"No, I'm serious."

"Fine," I said and was not ashamed to say I might have pouted a bit. "Here." I put my phone in his hand and pulled fifty cents, an unused tissue, and a lip balm out of my pocket. "That's all I have."

He studied what I put in his hand. "Take a seat. We'll be in shortly."

"Are you going to tell me what's going on?"

"Shortly." He turned and walked out of the room. I heard a click as the door locked behind him.

I put my elbows on the table, resting my chin in my hands. If Linda was trying to frame me, I was going to have to figure out what to do about it. Clearly having her candles in my shop was not enough to keep me out of jail.

Chapter 11

"I'm glad you called me," Matt said as he entered the room with a briefcase in his hand. "Do you know what they are holding you for?"

"No clue," I said. "Officer Hampton brought me in for a lineup. I thought it was to take me out of suspicion, but afterward they kept me and let everyone else go."

"Okay, have you said anything to them?"

"I asked to call you."

"Good," he said. "I'll go find out what the heck is going on."

He was gone for what felt like forever. I'd already waited long enough so I stood and paced the length of the small room. Finally, the door opened and Jim came in with Matt.

"So? What's going on?" I asked.

"Please have a seat," Jim said.

I sat down and Matt sat next to me.

"As I told you earlier," Jim began, "we had a witness come forward."

"Did they see who killed Agnes?"

"The witness picked you out of a lineup," Jim said.

"What?" I turned to Matt. "That's impossible. I didn't do anything."

Matt patted my hand. "Let's just take a breath." He turned to Jim. "What are they claiming they saw my client do?"

"They say they saw your client talking to Agnes about a half an hour before she was found dead. They also said they saw you hand Agnes the lip balm."

"They are lying," I said. "Didn't you say Agnes had been dead a while? How could I have met with her only a half an hour before? Besides, I didn't even know the time of death—"

"Stop talking." Matt put his hand on my arm and stared at Jim. "Who is the witness?"

"It's Mildred Woolright," Jim said. "The thing is, the judge said we are to let you go. There isn't enough evidence to arrest you . . . yet."

"There never will be," I said and stood.

Matt stood with me. "We're done here." He took my arm and pulled me out of the room, through the bullpen to the reception desk, where they returned my phone and other belongings. We left the building and I took a deep breath of free air. His BMW SUV was parked across from the entrance and thankfully the news crews were no longer there. That thought made me realize that I had missed Alicia and the tea house. How was I going to explain that to a reporter?

"I'll take you home," Matt said and unlocked his passenger door, so I climbed in. As he closed the door and went around the car, I glanced at my hands and realized I was shaking.

"Are you okay?" he asked as he turned on the ignition.

"Let's leave, please."

"Fine," he said. We headed down the street to the alley behind my store. He parked in the back parking space next to Porsche's Dodge van and looked at me as he turned off the car. "What happened? Did you see Agnes the morning she died?"

"No," I said. "I only saw her when Everett found the body. I don't know who Mildred thought she saw, but it wasn't me."

"I believe you," he said. "Right now all they have is the word of one woman. It has taken her a while to come forward so her testimony will be suspect. I'll need to discredit her. Do you know why she would identify you?"

"No. Maybe her eyes are bad or she thought she saw me but it was just another girl with auburn hair."

"That's why they did the lineup," he said. "To see if she can pick the killer out. Unfortunately, she picked you out right away."

"It's ridiculous. I was in my apartment that entire night making new product and then sleeping. How do you prove where you were if you were alone?"

"It's a question we face a lot in the court system. Luckily you are innocent until proven guilty. It's why I need any information you can give me about your relationship with Mrs. Woolright. I can use it to help the jury understand why she would lie."

"I don't have a relationship with Mildred."

"Have you done something to make her angry?" he asked.

"No," I said and made a face. "I barely know her. I

think the last time I saw her was the morning I found
Agnes. She caught me talking to Everett and called me a
crazy cat lady. I think I told her I wasn't crazy but I was a
cat lady."

"And?"

"She walked away."

"Where did you see her?"

"On the promenade, right before we found Agnes."

"Well, that is interesting," he said.

"Do you think she's involved in Agnes's death? Did
she have an eye for Bernie? I understand he has a way
with the ladies her age."

"As far as I know, Bernie only had eyes for Agnes,"
Matt said. "Dad's been paying attention to anything coming out of the Snow household."

"Did you go to her wake?" I asked.

"Yes," he said. "I'm glad you stayed away."

"The seniors advised me not to go," I said. "Besides,
Bernie kicked me out of his house when I brought a casserole. I wasn't about to be publicly humiliated again."

"It was a smart choice. It's best to lay low as much as
possible right now."

"Low is the only way I can lie right now," I mused.
"They made me take off my makeup. With Halloweentown this entire week, I'm going to have to go straight
upstairs and reapply the Tin Man face."

"It'll be worth it," he said.

"What do you mean?"

"I mean, by voluntarily going down to the station and
washing off your makeup, you have shown them that you
are willing to cooperate. It's a good thing."

I blew out a breath and opened the car door. "Thanks
for coming down and taking care of things."

"My pleasure. Do you want me to walk you inside?"

"No, I'm sure I'll be fine," I said and got out of his car. I leaned into the open window. "I sure hope you get to the bottom of this soon. I won't have much reputation left."

"We're doing our best," he said. "I promise."

Inside, the shop was crowded with people in costume. I helped Porsche out at the counter for an hour and a half as we worked through the crowd. By the time things died down, it was an hour from closing. Not enough time to make replacing my full face makeup worthwhile.

Josie arrived dressed in a classic witch costume complete with black dress, striped stockings, pointed shoes, black hat, and green makeup. "Wren! How are you doing?" Josie was five foot five and enviously thin with a narrow face and large eyes. Her red hair was covered by a green wig and witch hat, but her freckles shone through the makeup. She rushed over and gave me a big hug. "You've been on my mind ever since that first call."

I hugged her back. "Things are a bit crazy."

"I know," she said. "I heard about today. I've been telling everyone at the station they are barking up the wrong tree, but I'm a newbie and so they aren't listening."

"Hello," Porsche said and came out from around the counter.

"Porsche, this is Josie," I introduced them. "Josie and I were both on the debate team my senior year of high school."

"Nice to meet you," Porsche said.

"It's been a while since Wren and I have touched base," Josie said and sent me a look. "I do follow you on Instagram, but we were supposed to have lunch last year—"

"Oh my gosh, has it been that long?" I felt the heat of embarrassment rush up my cheeks. "I'm so sorry."

"I understand," she said and her eyes showed that she did truly understand and was only teasing. "I could have reached out myself, but I was busy training as a nine-one-one dispatcher."

"You're an emergency dispatcher?" Porsche asked.

"Yes, my first day I got Wren's call about Agnes. It was like taking a test," Josie said.

"You did very well," I said and gave her arm a squeeze.

"I heard they made you do a lineup and Mildred claims she saw you that day talking to Agnes and giving her lip balm?" Josie said. "Scary."

"I know it's crazy," I said. "I don't know why Mildred is saying this."

"That's not good," Porsche said. "We need to figure out what is going on with these old women, and we need to figure it out soon."

Just then Aunt Eloise barreled into the shop and the door cackled with a sharp sense of doom. Her crazy cat lady costume was in full force. She held Emma in her arm while wearing Evangeline in a backpack and Lug in a front-facing carrier. Her face was painted in white and gray zombie makeup.

"I know who killed Agnes," she announced.

That stopped all three of us. "Who? How? Why?" we asked.

"It wasn't Mildred," Aunt Eloise declared, "although that woman had plenty of reasons to want Agnes dead."

"Then who?" Porsche asked.

"It was Theodore Woolright," Eloise stated.

"What?" Josie asked.

"Why?" I asked.

"It would certainly explain why Mildred claims to have witnessed you giving Agnes the lip balm," Porsche said.

"Who are you?" Aunt Eloise asked Josie pointedly. She glanced at me. "Should we take this upstairs?"

"Aunt Eloise, this is Josie. We knew each other from school. She's the new nine-one-one dispatcher."

"Nice to meet you," Eloise said and took me by the arm. "I don't think we should be talking around her. She works with the cops." She glanced over her shoulder at Josie. "No offense."

"None taken," Josie said. "I fully understand. You don't want to put me in a difficult situation. So, I'll just go for now." She gave me another hug. "Nice to meet everyone."

"That was rude," I said as we watched her leave. The store was completely empty now except for Porsche and Eloise and me.

"We shouldn't be talking about our investigation around her. It puts her in a bad position of having to report it or keeping secrets from her bosses," Aunt Eloise insisted.

"She seemed to understand," Porsche pointed out.

"Fine," I said. "Tell us why you think Theodore Woolright murdered Agnes and is framing me."

"Well, Theodore went to Bernie today demanding that he get his money back," Aunt Eloise said.

"Okay, first of all, how do you know that? And second, what money did he want back?" I asked.

"He demanded that Bernie pay him the money that he'd paid to Agnes," Aunt Eloise said. "I know because I was talking to Eleanor Stone—remember she works at the bank. She said that Theodore and Bernie went to the bank today. Bernie wanted to see Agnes's accounts. It seems she didn't tell him about her blackmail schemes. She'd been hoarding the money. Bernie nearly passed out when he saw the amount she had in the bank."

"So, Bernie didn't kill her for money," I surmised.

"No, and he gave Theodore his money back right down to the penny," Aunt Eloise said. "So whatever Agnes was blackmailing Theodore over, Bernie didn't want to continue the ruse."

"It was pretty gutsy of Mr. Woolright to go to Bernie and acknowledge that Agnes took money from him, don't you think?" I asked. "I mean, if your blackmailer died wouldn't you be relieved and let it alone? Especially if he killed her for it."

"I hadn't thought of that," Aunt Eloise said and tapped her finger on her chin. "What if he killed her and then realized that killing her isn't enough to keep his secret? I mean, Bernie had to find out about the secret bank account, right? Maybe he thinks by demanding his money back, he'll seem innocent of the murder."

"Why would that make him seem innocent?" Porsche said. "I'm confused."

"I bet he asked for his money back to throw everyone off the scent that he killed Agnes. Think about it. While he was making a scene about getting his money back, his wife was at the police station identifying Wren as the killer."

"In a twisted way that makes sense," I said.

"You have to be twisted to murder someone," Porsche pointed out.

"I'll call Matt."

"Before you do that . . ." My aunt touched my wrist.

"We really need to have some solid proof that backs my theory."

"Okay, how are we going to get it?" I asked.

"We need a plan," Porsche said.

"Maybe I can invite the Woolrights over to my house for game night. Then, while I'm keeping them busy, you two gals can go in and leave a recording device. Then we can listen in to their daily conversations. After all, if they are working together on this crime, then they're bound to talk about it. We can collect the information later and give it to the police."

"Or even call the police and let them find the recording in the house," Porsche said.

"Oh, my goodness," I said and rolled my eyes. "This is not a cop show. One, we don't have a listening device, and two, we don't have a recording device that will run around the clock and long enough to maybe catch them talking about their plan. And three, the only way to legally record a conversation is if one of us is there. I'm pretty sure one person has to know they are being recorded."

Porsche and Aunt Eloise looked defeated.

"It was a nice thought, though," I said, trying to cheer them up.

"What do you suggest we do?" Aunt Eloise asked and hugged Porsche. Suddenly I was the one in the hot seat again.

"Let's see if I have any record that proves Mr. Woolright bought a lip balm from me," I said. "Aunt Eloise, come with me. I keep the sales receipts from the last month in my office."

We went upstairs, leaving Porsche downstairs to take care of any last-minute shoppers. My new computer held

all of my downloaded transactions. The problem was I
didn't keep customer names of people who paid with
cash—unless they signed up for my newsletter. Right
now twenty percent of my customers paid in cash and of
that, only twenty percent signed up for a news-letter. That
meant that the purchaser of the lip balm could still be
missing from my lists and information.

We scoured the names. My hunch was right. Whoever
bought the lip balm must have done it fully aware that
they were going to use it to kill someone. They had to
have paid in cash and not signed up. Of all the lip balms I
sold in the last two weeks, there were five that didn't
have a name attached. Those that used their name didn't
include Mr. or Mrs. Woolright or Mildred.

"This was a dead end," I said and sat back from my
computer. Aunt Eloise stood over my shoulder.

"Well, this proves whoever killed Agnes planned to
frame you," she said.

"Does it?" I asked. I did a filter of my database for
Agnes. "Look, Agnes bought a lip balm from me every
three months. It was a regular pattern."

"Did she buy one of the new labeled ones?" Aunt
Eloise asked.

I sorted the dates. "Here." I pointed to the screen. "I
did have the new labels in stock the last time she bought
it. Now, she might not have bought a new label one. I didn't
make a note of the label, only the date."

"So we're back to where we started with no proof of
anything," Aunt Eloise said.

"We did run through some theories," I said and gave
her a hug. "It's okay. We'll figure it out."

Everett meowed from my desktop. He put a paw on
Aunt Eloise as he tried to comfort her. "I don't want you

to go to jail over this," Aunt Eloise said. "If they try to indict you, I'm going to say I did it."

"Aunt Eloise, no!"

"What are they going to do? Put this old woman in jail?"

"Yes," I said, "and I don't think you'll like the orange jumpsuits."

"I'll be fine; I can handle myself."

"Let's not even think about this now." I went over to the murder board. "We really don't have any good suspects. I mean, the spouse is usually the main suspect, but Bernie did seem truly devastated by Agnes's death."

"Plus, I haven't been able to dig up any girlfriends or any other motive for him to want Agnes dead."

"Linda is still a good suspect," I mused. "I've got her candles in the shop. So far I've sold one. I'm not sure the co-marketing is making any difference. What I don't understand is how Linda fits into the picture."

"Agnes was blackmailing Theodore, right?"

"I think so," I said. "According to your insider at the bank anyway. We should ask Mr. Woolright about that."

"Why would he tell you?" Aunt Eloise mused.

"That's a good point," I said and drummed my fingers. "What if I get my reporter friend to ask him? Maybe he'll tell her more."

"Or maybe he won't because he doesn't want to run Agnes through the muck now that she's dead."

"Why wouldn't he if she was blackmailing him and he already made a big show of confronting Bernie to get his money back?"

"Because he doesn't want everyone to know what Agnes was blackmailing him for," she said.

"Okay, so how can we find out?"

"We need to find Agnes's book of business," Aunt Eloise said.

"Her what?"

"When someone is blackmailing as many people as we suspect Agnes was, then they have to keep the information somewhere. I bet she kept it in a diary or journal."

"Like a ledger?"

"Exactly, "Aunt Eloise said. "Or even just a list of clients. Anyway, she had to keep track somehow."

"Wouldn't she keep that in her office or desk?" I asked. "It's not like you keep something like that out in the open."

"I say we sneak into the Snows' house and find Agnes's client list. Then, we can see who she was blackmailing and make sure everyone is on our suspect list."

"It's not a bad idea," I said. "Except we don't know how to break and enter into someone's home. We will most likely get caught. Then, we really will be guilty."

"Don't be so defeatist," Aunt Eloise said. "I have a plan."

Great, I thought. I just hoped her plan wasn't going to get us put in jail or worse . . . killed.

Chapter 12

The next morning, I was up at 5 a.m. I dressed in jeans and a T-shirt and went downstairs and let Aunt Eloise in. She was dressed all in black.

"Maybe I should have gotten ski masks for our faces," she said. "It would help hide your very pale face."

"And yours," I teased her. We both had the light complexions of our Scottish forebears. "Let's have some coffee. I can't break and enter without caffeine in my system."

"I told you it wasn't breaking and entering. It will be 'searching for Everett.'" She used air quotes.

"Right, then how would we explain the ski masks? I mean, who wears ski masks in the morning when they are looking for a lost cat?"

"That takes the wind out my sails," she said with a pout. "But you're right, if we are to do everything planned, then we need to make it look as if we were only going for a walk and then Everett ran off and well, the Snows' door was open, so we slipped inside to get him."

I poured us both coffee and added cream to mine. My mugs were white with Oregon coast views on them. I never got tired of Oregon's beautiful shoreline. I pushed the creamer and sugar dishes toward my aunt.

"Thanks," she said and dumped two teaspoons full of sugar into her mug and stirred.

"Are you sure Mr. Snow will leave the house open?"

"The word is that he goes to the YMCA every morning at six thirty to swim laps and work out. That means we'll have an hour to get in and get out. Everett is our ruse to get in."

"Meow," we heard from the bedroom door.

We laughed. My cat looked as sleepy as I felt. "Yes, Everett," I said. "We are talking about you." I picked him up. "Do you really think this is going to work?"

"It has to work," my aunt said. "We can't have you going to jail."

"But this will be the most illegal thing I've ever done. We could go to jail for *this*."

"We won't go to jail and we aren't taking anything. We're going to explore and if we find a ledger or client list then we'll take photos of it."

"Let's go then," I said. "Before I lose my nerve."

We checked the time. It was nearly six. I lived far enough away from the Snows' house that we would get there after Mr. Snow left. I put Everett on his leash and we walked out into the cool dark air. Everett loved to walk on his leash. He talked to us about everything we saw or passed along the way.

"He knows we're going in a different way," I said.

"Of course, cats are not stupid. Have you ever taken him by the Snows' house?"

"Maybe once when I first got him," I said. "But you get into a routine, you know? I learned he loved the beach and that's where we would go every day."

"That's even better, really. It would make more sense for him to get into the Snow house if he doesn't usually go that way. It would seem more plausible that he would get lost."

We made our way quietly for the next block or two. We got to the Snows' house. It was a regal 1920s craftsman-style home with rock trim and a side portico. The driveway was lined by hedges so we hurried toward the house. That way it would look like we were chasing after Everett if anyone saw us. My aunt went right up the side steps and opened the door with a doggy door in the bottom, inviting Everett inside.

I dropped his leash and my kitty ran right in.

"What if Bernie is inside?" I whispered.

"Well, we're only going in to get Everett." She opened the door wider. "Everett. Here kitty, kitty."

I looked around but didn't see anyone who might see us go into the house and went in myself. We entered the kitchen. I remembered the house from the night I brought over the casserole. It was quiet and I figured either Mr. Snow was in bed or he was gone. I prayed he was gone. "Everett," I called.

"Here, kitty," Aunt Eloise said as she went straight through the kitchen to a back room. I followed. "This is Agnes's craft room." She flipped on a light and rummaged through drawers. Every kind of craft supply imaginable seemed to be located in the room. Agnes's awards covered every wall. She had framed her grand prize ribbons and had two shelves full of trophies.

I went over to the shelf. One trophy read BEST KNITTER, another WORLD CHAMPION EMBROIDERY. "She really did win a lot of prizes."

"Stop looking at those silly things and help me go through drawers. If you were a client list or ledger, where would you be?" She opened and closed drawers rapidly. She had to, as the room was filled with drawers of bits and pieces of fabric and fluff and paint and twine.

"If I had a blackmail book I would keep it somewhere safe, like in a safe."

"I don't think there's a safe in the house." My aunt kept opening drawers.

"What about a false bottom drawer?"

"Oh, man, you mean I need to go back through the drawers and knock on them for a false bottom?" She looked at the half wall of drawers that she had just gone through.

"Maybe," I said and moved two of the awards on the shelf that were used as bookends. "Or maybe you hide it in plain sight." I pulled a notebook out from two that were marked journal. This notebook was bound, but black and unassuming. I opened it and there inside was a list of names and amounts of money along with dates. "I found it."

"Wonderful! Quick, open it and I'll take pictures."

I laid the notebook on the counter and tipped a goose-necked lamp so that the light shone directly on the book.

Aunt Eloise pulled out her phone and snapped page after page as I flipped through them.

"Okay, put it back," she said. "I'll find Everett and we'll get out of here."

"Great!" I put the notebook back on the shelf as my aunt made her way out of the room calling Everett's name. I waited and heard her going through the house. I hoped Everett hadn't gone and hidden under a bed somewhere. Cats were notorious for sneaking into obscure places and not coming out for days.

Suddenly my aunt screamed.

Racing toward the sound, I went upstairs. Aunt Eloise stood in front of a door. The light was on but she blocked my view. She screamed again. I pushed her aside and saw Bernie Snow facedown on the hardwood floor. Everett stood on top of him. Blood was everywhere. I grabbed my kitty and shakily called 9-1-1.

"Nine-one-one, what is your emergency?"

"Josie?"

"Yes, is this Wren?"

"Yes."

"Okay, you sound upset. Take a deep breath and then tell me what's going on."

I took a deep breath. "I'm at the Snow house. We need an ambulance as soon as possible. Mr. Snow is hurt."

"Help is on the way," she said. "How bad is he hurt?"

"He's lying in a pool of blood."

"Oh dear, okay, is he breathing?"

I looked at Bernie. "I can't tell." Aunt Eloise held her stomach. She looked stricken and staggered against the wall in the hallway. "I think he might be dead."

"We need to go through this one step at a time," she

said. "I need you to put two fingers on his neck near his collarbone and feel for a pulse."

"I don't want to touch him," I said and tried not to sound whiney. "The police already think I killed his wife."

"I understand," she said with more confidence than the last time I had called her. "But you need to check for a pulse."

"Okay," I said and blew out a breath. I hitched Everett up on my hip and knelt down. "He's lying facedown."

"You can still check for a pulse."

"Right." I put my phone on speaker and maneuvered it so that it and Everett were in the same hand and then I reached down to put my fingers to Mr. Snow's neck. He was ice cold. I jerked my hand back, scrambled back and fumbled my phone. "He's really cold. I think he's dead."

"Okay," she said and I heard her swallow. "Are you safe?"

I looked around, suddenly aware that my aunt and I were at a crime scene. "Maybe? I don't know."

"Then stay on the line," the operator said. "I've called an ambulance and the police. It will be a few minutes before they can get to you. Did you take CPR?"

"No," I said. "It was on my list of things to do but I never got around to it."

"No problem, I'll walk you through it. Did you feel a pulse when you touched him?"

"No, all I felt was cold."

"You have to see if he has a pulse," Josie said.

"His neck is cold."

"It might be shock," she said. "You don't want him to die while you watch, do you?"

"What? No! Of course not, but I think he's already dead."

"Listen, Wren, you're not a trained doctor," she said calmly. "I need you to at least try to save him. Feel for a pulse."

I gave Everett to my aunt, knelt back down by the body, careful not to step in the blood, and pushed my fingers into the space just above his collarbone. "I don't feel anything. There's no pulse."

"Okay," she said. "It doesn't necessarily mean he's dead. Put your ear on his chest and see if you can hear a heartbeat."

"I can't, he's chest down," I said.

"Okay," she continued. "Does he appear to have a neck injury?"

"Not that I can tell."

"Try to turn him over."

"Do you think that's good advice?" I asked her.

"Is there anyone with you?"

"Yes," I said. "My aunt is here."

"Then one of you carefully hold his head while the other turns him. If you're going to be doing CPR you'll need him on his back."

I motioned my aunt over. She seemed frozen to the spot. "Aunt Eloise," I said. "Please, we have to help him."

"Can't we just wait for the EMTs?"

"Every moment counts," Josie said.

"She said every moment counts," I repeated.

"Fine," Aunt Eloise said. "I'll hold his head." She put Everett on the top of the dresser and carefully walked to Bernie's head. "This is terrible. I don't think I can do it."

"We have to try," I said. "Hold him steady and I'll roll him over. One, two, three . . ."

We shoved and pushed and struggled until he turned. He was very heavy and very limp, flipping like a dead fish. "I think we're too late," I said.

"Open his airway," Josie said.

"You don't understand," I said into the phone. "He's dead."

"Tip his head back, open his mouth, and swipe a finger in his mouth to see if his airway is clear," she continued.

I looked up at my aunt, whose mouth was a tight line. She wasn't going to help. I blew out a deep breath and did exactly what Josie said. It was rather disgusting. "I didn't feel anything."

"Okay, now is he breathing?"

"It doesn't sound like it. Seriously, he's really cold and white and his eyes are open and he's staring blankly at the ceiling." All I could think about was that CSI McGovern was going to be very upset with us for messing up another crime scene.

"Check for breathing and start heart compressions," Josie said, as if reading from a list of instructions.

Luckily, I heard sirens. The door downstairs bust open and a man's voice shouted: "Where are you?"

"We're upstairs," I yelled back.

Jim came through the door to find me and my aunt hunkered down beside a dead man. "Step away from him."

We both scrambled upright and stepped back with our hands raised. "The dispatcher told us to turn him over and check for a pulse."

He knelt down and put his finger to the same spot as I

had. "He doesn't have a pulse and he's cold. I think this man is dead and has been for some time. You moved the body?"

"She told us to," I said and pointed to my phone.

"Let me talk to her," he said and took my phone from me. "This is Hampton." He walked off to the other room. I looked at Aunt Eloise.

"I told her I didn't want to touch him."

"Let's get out of here," Aunt Eloise said. She picked up Everett and we both hustled downstairs into the kitchen.

"Don't go anywhere, you two," Hampton hollered at us.

"We'll just step outside," I said. "We don't want to further contaminate the crime scene."

"Fine, but don't go far. I have questions."

We stepped outside as the EMTs came through the doorway with a stretcher and their kits in hand. I went over to stand under the ancient basketball hoop that hung on the garage. Aunt Eloise had told me that years ago Bernie had hung the hoop to encourage neighborhood kids to play at their house. I found it sad that most people overlooked the hoop with the missing net. Taking Everett from my aunt, I hugged him until he squeaked.

"I've never seen a dead man before," Aunt Eloise said. "Well, not one that wasn't already in a casket with waxy makeup on."

"We had to touch him," I shivered. "I put my finger in his mouth."

"If he had had a blockage you would have saved his life by finding it," she pointed out.

"But I didn't."

"No, you didn't." She put her hand on my arm to comfort me. "But you tried and that says a lot about you."

"Do you think I need to call my lawyer?"

"Yes," Aunt Eloise said gravely, placing a reassuring hand on my shoulder.

"We should have never tried looking for her client list."

"We have it now," she said. "Those pictures in your phone will help us figure out who is doing this."

"I hope so," I said. "I just want my life to go back to normal."

"Here, give me Everett." She held out her hands. More sirens moved toward us. "Call your lawyer."

I dialed Matt's number with shaking hands. By now the sun had come up.

"It's pretty early to call, Wren," Matt said as he picked up. "Are you in trouble?"

"I think maybe," I said.

"Where are you?"

"I'm at the Snows' home," I said. "I'm with my aunt and my cat. We found Bernie Snow on the floor of his bedroom and I'm pretty sure he's dead."

"Have you called the police?"

"Yes," I said. "Can't you hear the sirens?" Another cop car pulled up and cut the siren as it stopped in front of us. "I think you should be here in case they think I did it. I had to touch him. The dispatcher asked us to turn him over and look for a pulse. Jim arrived before we could start CPR. He told us to stay away from the body."

"I'll be there in fifteen minutes," he said. "Don't say anything to anyone until I get there."

"Okay," I said and hung up the phone.

"Don't talk?" Aunt Eloise suggested.

"Not until he gets here."

A female officer came out and said, "Officer Hampton said to come out and get your statement." She pulled out a recording device. "I'm Officer Morris. You are . . ." She looked at her notebook. "Eloise Johnson?"

"That's me," my aunt said.

"And Wren Johnson?" she asked and eyed me.

"Yes," I said. "I just called my lawyer. I'm not going to speak to anyone until he's here."

"Fine," she said and turned to my aunt. "I'll get your story first. Ms. Johnson, please step over to the squad car. I need you out of hearing distance, but not far. Don't make me put you in the squad car."

"Got it," I said and walked ten steps away. I turned and leaned on the car and watched the goings-on. Someone had put up police tape at the end of the driveway. The neighbors had gathered to see what was going on. I could feel them staring at me. I'm sure they were curious why we were even in the Snows' house.

My phone lit up with texts from Porsche and Alicia asking me what was going on. Word traveled fast in a small town. Alicia arrived and stood right outside the police line and waved at me. I waved back. She texted. "What happened?"

I texted back. "Can't talk until my lawyer gets here."

"What about the other day when you stood me up?"

"We'll talk later," I texted back.

"But you will tell me what's going on, right? Is it Bernie Snow?"

"I can't say." I put my phone away. Anything I texted would be written in stone and probably used as evidence. I watched as Officer Morris finished taking my aunt's statement. At least I knew what the story was. We had gone for a walk and Everett had slipped into the Snow home. The cat was with my aunt right now. She had taken off his leash. At least that part of the story seemed to be working. I glanced around again. Our plan to slip in and out unnoticed was certainly out the window.

Honey is a natural humectant and emollient. You can use it to condition your hair. It seals moisture and reduces breakage. Wash your hair, then apply a quarter-size amount of honey to your ends. Let sit for thirty minutes and then rinse with warm water.

Chapter 13

"Tell me you didn't say anything to anyone," Matt said as he walked up. He was dressed in a button-down shirt, dress slacks, and a relaxed sports coat. He looked like he just walked off a television set.

"I waited."

"Let me go in and see what's going on." He went to the house but got stopped at the door. I watched as he argued, but they weren't letting him in. Instead, Officer Morris stepped back out and walked straight to me.

"I see you have your lawyer," she said. "So I'm going to get your story now."

"Okay," I said and motioned for Matt to come over. "Ask away."

"Why were you in Mr. Snow's house?"

"My Aunt Eloise and I went for a walk with Everett."

"Who's Everett?"

"My cat." I pointed to Everett, snuggled in the arms of my aunt. "But then my aunt told you this, didn't she?"

"I'm simply asking questions," Officer Morris said.

She went on to ask me more and I told her how we found Everett and then Mr. Snow.

"You called nine-one-one?"

I looked at Matt and he nodded to let me know to answer.

"Yes," I said. "I'm sure the recording will show that I found him facedown and was told to roll him over. Which we did as carefully as possible. I cleared his airway and was about to start CPR when Officer Hampton came in and told us to step away. That Mr. Snow was dead." I felt a tremor in my voice.

"I think my client has answered enough questions for now," Matt said.

Officer Morris pulled out a card. "If you think of anything else, please call me."

"Are we free to go?"

"You and your aunt are free to go," she said.

"Thanks." I walked over to Aunt Eloise and took Everett from her. I slipped his leash on him. "Let's go home. Matt, thanks for coming. You probably didn't need to be here, but you did say for me to call you before I talked to anyone."

"I'm glad you called me," Matt said low with his back

to the crowd. "With you as a person of interest in Mrs. Snow's death, we need to keep you as helpful but as safe as possible. I'll walk with you. There are a lot of people here and you need to not speak to anyone."

"She can certainly talk to me," Alicia said as he lifted the police tape for us to duck under.

"I've advised my client not to speak to anyone," he said. "Especially the press."

"Well, she's my friend," Alicia said.

"And you are the press," he pointed out. "I will write up an official statement that you can use if you need to, otherwise you'll have to get your story from the police like everyone else."

Aunt Eloise put her arm through mine and we walked behind Matt the entire way back to the shop. The downtown was bustling as it was now nearly 10 a.m. and the stores were opening. People eyed us through their store windows. Word must have spread about Bernie's death.

We went into my shop through the back. I gave Matt a hug and he walked back to the Snows' house to get his car. Aunt Eloise let Everett free once we were safely inside.

Porsche waited for us at the counter. "What happened? Is it true you found Bernie Snow dead in a pool of his own blood?"

"Yes, it's true," I said.

"Oh, dear," Porsche said.

"I can't say anything. Matt won't let me, but Aunt Eloise will tell you what happened."

I left my aunt to fill Porsche in and went upstairs, where I stripped and went straight to the shower. I didn't want to feel as if I had any evidence on me. I had after all knelt down and turned Berne's body over. I tried to replay the scene in my mind. Did I see a bullet hole? No. Any obvious trauma? Not really. All I really remembered were his wide unseeing eyes.

I got dressed and went downstairs to face the day. Today's costume was the Cowardly Lion. I was glad I didn't have much face makeup to put on, as I didn't feel like being a zombie after finding Bernie Snow. The rest of my outfit was a straight-up lion suit with a hoodie mane.

Porsche was dressed as Tiffany from *Bride of Chucky*. She had opened the shop while I showered and dressed, and the place was packed with shoppers.

"How are things going?" I asked.

"Your aunt said to tell you she was going home to shower and get some rest. I guess finding a dead man has left her in a bit of shock."

"I understand that," I said. "The hot shower helped me, and work will help, too."

"People have been asking for you," Porsche said.

"I can't talk to anyone about this morning," I said and stretched my neck to peer around the room. "Did Alicia come in?"

"She texted and I said you weren't working today."

"Thanks," I said. "Is anyone buying?"

"Yes, quite a bit," she said. "Even Linda's candles are going."

"Well, that's something," I said and stepped out from behind the counter. "Maybe with my costume, people won't bug me about this morning."

"Yeah, well, good luck with that," she said.

"Oh, Wren, good to see you. Porsche, here, told us you weren't working today."

"June," I addressed the mother of two who came in

often and sent Porsche a look. "I wasn't feeling very well, but I'm going to try to make a go of it. What brings you in today?"

"I was looking for a new hand cream," June Walters said and put three tubes on the counter. She was a lovely Asian woman with perfect skin and shiny black hair that fell to her shoulders. "I love your rose-scented ones."

"I thought maybe the pumpkin spice was what you came for," I said and rang up the three tubes. "These have been available for months."

She didn't look at me. "I prefer the rose and just ran out is all."

"Well, I'm glad I had some for you." I watched as she swiped her credit card and I bagged up her lotions. "Thanks for coming in."

The store slowly emptied when people realized I wasn't going to be talking about finding Bernie Snow this morning. Luckily most people felt guilty enough to buy at least one item, and nearly all the candy sold.

While Porsche went to lunch, I restocked shelves. The doorbells cackled as it opened and I looked over my shoulder to see Conrad coming toward me. "Wren, I heard what happened this morning. Are you all right?"

"Yes, I'm fine," I said.

He put his hands on my forearms and drew me toward him. "Thank goodness. I can't imagine what it must have been like to come upon someone like that. What were you doing in his house? Were you alone?"

"I can't discuss the details," I hedged as I leaned into the cologne-scented warmth of his chest. I closed my eyes for a second and enjoyed his embrace. Then, I realized I was dressed like the Cowardly Lion with my own frizzy mane underneath. Not the most romantic of looks.

"Not even with me?" he asked with concern in his gaze. "You really should talk to someone about it. It's not good to bottle that all up inside."

"I'm sure I'll be fine."

"Let me take you to dinner," he said. "You close at seven, right? I'll pick you up at eight. You can wear the costume if you like. I think it's cute."

"I think that says more about you than me," I teased him.

"Have dinner with me."

"Don't you have a business deal to work on? Something about a whaling boat operation?"

"I won't be working on that at dinner," he said. "I'll pick you up at eight. We can go out to the Northwest Inn. They have a Tuesday special on roast beef."

"Sounds yummy," I said.

He gave me another hug and kissed my cheek. "I'll see you then. Try not to get involved with anymore dead men."

"Bye, Conrad," I said.

Porsche came back in as he was leaving and grinned at me. "What'd I miss?"

"I'm going out to dinner," I said. "And not because someone wants to hear my story." I couldn't help the grin that ran across my face.

"Good," she said. "It's about time you got a little action."

"What's it like out on the street?" I asked. "I know you didn't just go home for lunch."

"People are all abuzz. There's speculation that you killed Bernie, but the betting pool says it was your Aunt Eloise that did them both in."

"Why would Aunt Eloise kill Bernie Snow?"

"They think she was caught in a love triangle and got rid of Agnes. And when Bernie found out, he dumped her—so she killed him."

"That's ridiculous," I said and put my hands on my hips.

"I know that and you know that," she said. "At least very few people think you killed Bernie."

"I have no motive."

"Unless you killed him for rejecting your casserole," she pointed out and went to the counter.

"That's ridiculous," I repeated. "I'm going to go call my aunt and check on her." I grabbed my phone and went upstairs. Everett followed me up. I dialed my aunt.

She answered the phone with, "Wren, how are you?"

"I'm fine. The store had a nice run this morning until everyone decided I wasn't going to be telling the story after all. It's been quiet so far this afternoon. How are you? Porsche says you are the talk of the neighborhood. Something about you having an affair with Bernie Snow and offing Agnes to be with your true love who then—"

"Rejected me so I offed him," she said with a chuckle. "Right. Bernie was no fan of mine and I was no fan of his. He once tried to say my prize kitties had to be bred outside of the city limits. 'No livestock within city limits,' he'd grumbled. That is until I mentioned that Agnes was breeding parakeets. That shut him up."

"She bred parakeets? For how long?"

"Only two years before the birds drove Bernie nuts and he shut her down. They can be quite noisy in a flock."

I laughed then got serious. "We need to meet and go over the photos of Agnes's ledger."

"Not for a day or so," she said. "We need to lay low for a bit."

"Right," I said. "But what if the killer is found on those pages?"

"What pages?" asked a mellow baritone voice behind me.

I whipped around to see Jim standing in my doorway. "I thought I closed my door."

"It was open," he said and stepped in. "Are you talking to your aunt?"

"Yes."

"I'd prefer you hung up."

"Why? Am I being arrested?"

"Who is that?" Aunt Eloise asked.

"It's Officer Hampton," I said. "He wants me to hang up."

"Tell him your lawyer told you not to talk to anyone without him present."

"Right." I looked at Jim. His eyes were so darn blue. "My lawyer said I can't talk to anyone without him present."

"Then hang up with your aunt and call your lawyer."

I swallowed hard as my stomach leapt into my throat. "Are you arresting me?"

"Don't let him intimidate you, dear!"

"Hang up the phone," he said as calm as could be.

"I'm coming right over," my aunt said.

"Talk to you soon," I answered and hung up the phone. "There, I did what you asked." I crossed my arms and hugged myself. "What can I do for you?"

"I want to talk about what you were doing in Bernie Snow's house when you found him."

"I wasn't killing him, if that's what you are implying."

He raised an eyebrow. "I don't imply or infer things. My job is to stick with the facts."

"Okay, what do you want to know that my aunt and I didn't already tell you this morning?"

"Why were you walking in the Snows' neighborhood? I learned from the neighbors that you aren't usually in that area. It's a small town. Someone would have noticed if you walked there every morning."

"I switched my route so I wouldn't have to walk by the beach where I found Agnes's body." That was the story Aunt Eloise had given me.

"So you walked by Agnes's home instead? How is that any better?"

"I had not seen Agnes dead there for one," I said. "But anyway, Aunt Eloise and I were talking and I had no idea where I was until Everett ran off." As if on cue my kitty jumped up on the back of a nearby chair and meowed for attention. I picked him up.

"Why was Everett off his leash?" Jim took a step to the side and filled the door frame.

"He wasn't off his leash," I said. "That's the crazy part. I was talking to Aunt Eloise and Everett must not have been getting enough attention. He yanked on his leash and pulled it out of my hand. Before I could grab it, he took off—right into the Snow's house."

"He opened the back door?"

"He went through the doggie door," I said. "We knocked and no one answered, but then we saw the door was left open."

"Didn't you find that suspicious?"

"No, Aunt Eloise told me that Bernie has a habit of leaving his door unlocked. I was too worried about Everett to think about the door being open. The idea was to find Everett and get out."

"But not before you took pictures of Agnes's accounting book," he said.

I waited a heartbeat.

"That's what you were talking about when I came in, right?"

I still didn't answer.

"We have your fingerprints on the ledger," he stated. "We printed the entire house. There were three sets of prints. One belonged to Agnes, one to you, and one I assume will turn out to be your aunt's. We won't know until we get a copy of her prints in the system."

I felt the blood rush out of my face. "You're going to fingerprint my aunt?"

"Sit down," he ordered and I collapsed into the chair beside me. "Put your head between your knees." He encouraged me with a gentle hand to the back of my neck.

I studied the floor under my chair. "I don't think I'm going to faint."

"Good," he said and got up. "Don't move." I heard him walk away. Then a clank of glassware and the faucet turned on. He walked back across the room. "Here, take a sip of this."

I sat up and saw stars in my view. I willed them away and took a sip of the water. "You can't arrest Aunt Eloise. It would kill her."

"My guess is that your aunt is made of sterner stuff than that," he said.

"I am," Aunt Eloise said from the still open door. "What did he do to you?" she asked as she rushed across the room. "You look deathly white."

"I didn't do anything," he said and stepped back to let her get a good look at me.

"He got me water," I said, "that's all."

"We found Wren's fingerprints on Agnes's ledger," he said. "Along with a second pair that isn't catalogued. I believe they belong to you. We'd like to have you come down to the station and give us your prints for comparison."

She looked from him to me. "Do I need a lawyer?"

"Mine will take care of you," I said and stood. I nearly lost my balance as the world went black. Darn it for freaking out.

"There you go." My aunt and Jim grabbed my elbows and pushed me back down into the chair. "Sit still."

"I won't let them charge you with murder."

"Well, dear, that's funny," she said and straightened. "I thought they were looking at you for the murder."

"I'm not convinced either one of you did it," he said. "I simply need the prints to prove a point."

"That's what you said about the lineup, and that nearly put me in jail."

"I'm sorry for that," he said. "Whoever killed the Snows is slippery."

"What if they work for the police?" I asked. "That would make it easy to frame me and my aunt."

"Why would a police officer frame you?"

"I don't know," I said. "Why would anyone frame me?"

"Wren," came a call up the stairs. I recognized Linda's voice.

"Up here," I called and stood. This time I kept my balance as Linda scurried through the doorway. "Linda, what can I do for you?"

"I wanted to say that your co-marketing idea is working. I had ten new customers who bought candles and said they saw them first at Let It Bee and then came to see what else I had."

"Wonderful!" I said.

"I brought you another box of candles," she said and looked around curiously. "I think you have plenty of space on your empty shelves."

"Great. Thanks. I can set them up for you."

"I already did it," she said. "I saw Eloise come running through the store and wanted to make sure you were all right." She gave Jim the side eye. "Is everything all right?"

"It's fine," he answered for me. "I had a couple of questions about Bernie Snow." He put his hands on his hips and his posture dared us to say anything further.

"Yes, well, I guess I'll be going then," Linda said. She gave me a quick hug. "Goodbye, dear."

"I'm not going anywhere," Aunt Eloise said.

Jim sighed and crossed his arms. "Fine." He walked over and closed the door. "I know you two are lying."

Honey makes a great facial scrub to reveal radiant skin. The enzymes in honey make for a gentle exfoliator. Mix a teaspoon of raw honey with a teaspoon of olive oil and gently rub in circles on your skin. Rinse with warm water and enjoy smoother, plumper skin.

Chapter 14

"I need my lawyer," I said, raising my chin and crossing my arms.

"Call him," Jim said. "But I know you two planned that expedition into the Snow house." He looked directly at Aunt Eloise with his steely blue stare. "Betty Forrester told me you asked about Bernie's trip to the health club every morning. She told me that she let it be known that Bernie was gone at six thirty every morning and he didn't lock his house."

"That doesn't mean we were lying," I said.

"Funny how coincidental it was that Betty told you about it and then you were walking down the Snows' street the very next day at precisely the time Bernie usually checks in at the fitness center."

"Purely coincidental," Aunt Eloise said, her hands behind her back. I had a feeling she was crossing her fingers. It was what she did whenever she was lying.

"And strange how your cat, who is very good on a leash, suddenly bolted into the Snows' house so that you had to go in and search for him."

"We didn't kill Bernie," I said.

"I know," he said. "The ME's preliminary report said the time of death was around four a.m. You were seen coming down the street at six thirty-five."

"Who was in the Snow house at four a.m.?" I asked.

"Bernie had to have been up," Aunt Eloise said. "He was dressed for the gym in sweats and a T-shirt."

"Bernie was meeting a friend for coffee after his workout. Betty was expecting him at five thirty at the health club—it opens at five a.m.—but Bernie didn't show so she thought he must have overslept."

"Betty seems to know a lot about Bernie," I mused.

"She should," he said. "She was his sister."

I turned to my aunt. "You asked his sister about his daily trip to the gym? What were you thinking?"

"I know Betty from school. She was interested in our investigation."

"She probably told Bernie," I pointed out.

"She would not tell Bernie," Aunt Eloise said. "She had heard that Agnes was into something and knew that Bernie was in denial. She wanted us to help figure out what actually happened . . . to help her brother."

"Betty had motive to kill her brother," Jim said. "She might have set you up."

"What? Betty? Why?" Aunt Eloise asked.

"Bernie and Betty's mom died two months ago. Their parents left nearly two million dollars to Bernie and only one hundred thousand to Betty. She has been working with a lawyer to fight that in court."

"But with Bernie's connections, she had no shot at winning," I surmised.

"Exactly," Jim said. "Bernie and Agnes had no children. That means the money goes to Betty."

My aunt and I looked at each other—stunned. "How do we prove Betty did it?" I asked.

"That's what I need your help with," Jim said. "Eloise, I want you to set up a meeting with Betty."

"And me?"

"Wren, I'm going to ask you to record what is said. You can wear a wire or you can use your phone."

"I'll use my phone," I said.

"What do we need to talk about?" Aunt Eloise asked. "We can't just come out and ask her if she killed her brother and set us up."

"No," he agreed. "I need you to try and find out how she felt about Agnes. See if you can get her to talk about the lawsuit and her parents' money."

"What will that prove?" I asked.

He turned his blue gaze on me. "It will help us build a case for motive."

"Will it give her a chance to frame me further?" I asked.

"Don't worry, dear," Aunt Eloise said and patted my hand. "I won't let that happen. I will go to jail before you do."

"No one's going to jail," Jim said. "Try to set up some time with Betty tomorrow. Wren, you have my phone number. Text me when you have it set up and then record the encounter. I will come by tomorrow night and gather the evidence." He turned. "Thank you, ladies."

We both watched him leave. I waited for two breaths and went to the door to ensure he was gone. Then I turned and leaned against the door. "Do you think he's setting us up?"

"What? Why would he do that?" Aunt Eloise asked.

"I don't know," I said. "But it seems odd that he wants us to gather evidence for him. He's been pushing me to stop investigating since I found Agnes. Now he wants my help? I don't buy it."

Aunt Eloise pursed her lips and tapped her chin. "True."

"I say we trust no one. For all we know, Linda is the one framing me. Just because she brought me more candles doesn't mean she didn't kill Agnes."

"Oh, my dear, this is so exhausting. I think you're getting paranoid."

I hugged my waist. "I feel paranoid," I agreed. "I'm going to ask Matt if he thinks I should be involved in this Betty thing."

"Now that is the best idea ever," she said. "Come on now. It might be early, but it's been a long day. Let's have a glass of wine and make a nice dinner."

Everett meowed at the word "dinner."

"See?" Aunt Eloise said. "Everett agrees."

"I'm afraid I have to take a rain check," I said and felt a blush rush over my cheeks. "I have a date."

"Hear that, Everett? Our little girl is getting a life." Aunt Eloise seemed positively gleeful.

"Meow," Everett said, seeming to agree.

She held out her hand and he gave her a high five. I rolled my eyes.

The next morning, I got up early. A shipment of supplies had come in yesterday and I needed to create more inventory. Everett climbed up on the back of my flowered wingback chair and watched me with one eye closed. Today I was making lip balms and lotions. I liked putting my lotions in tins and glass pots with threaded lids that twisted on. It added to the charm of the brand. I grabbed a stack of preprinted labels and put them on the table next to jars that were prepped for use.

Next I created the lotions by mixing ingredients in a large pot and heating them so that they blended together. Finally, I added fragrance and a drop of coloring to create a beautiful sensory experience. It was important that the look, feel, and smell all brought the senses to life.

There was a knock on my inside door. I glanced at the time. The store opened in fifteen minutes and I wasn't in costume yet.

"Wren, how are you doing?" It was Porsche.

I opened my door. Porsche was dressed as Raggedy Ann in zombie makeup. "I'm fine. Time got away from me."

"Clearly." She walked in and headed to my coffeepot. "You know I need coffee in the morning. With all the deaths, I got worried when I came in and the pot downstairs was cold."

"This one is fresh," I said as I pulled off my apron. "I've got to get dressed. Love your costume, by the way."

She poured herself a large mug, took a sip, and closed her eyes in delight. "My sons weren't a fan of this one."

"I think it's very clever and will give little kids night-mares."

"Yes, well, after Tiffany from *Bride of Chucky* was such a hit, I thought I might continue in the twisted doll theme. Which *Wizard of Oz* character are you today?"

"I planned on being the Wicked Witch of the East."

"Oh, I was hoping for a zombie Glinda the Good Witch."

"That's tomorrow," I said and hurried to my bedroom to slip on the costume.

"You've been doing a lot of work on inventory," she said from the living room. "We really need it. I'm sur-prised how much we are selling this week."

"Foot traffic is up," I said as I left my bedroom in full costume and headed to the bathroom to apply the zombie face makeup. "I think people are curious about the mur-ders."

"How was your date last night?"

"Good," I said.

She walked to the bathroom doorway holding her cup of coffee. "Spill the details—all the details."

"What's to talk about? Conrad picked me up, we went to dinner and caught up on our lives, then we had a drink and he left me at the front door."

"Sounds boring," she said and pouted. "Did he even try to kiss you?"

"I don't kiss and tell."

"So he did kiss you? Is he a good kisser? Did he come up for a nightcap?"

I ignored her and continued to put on my makeup.

"Fine, I'll change the subject. What did Officer Hamp-ton want yesterday afternoon?" She leaned against the bathroom door frame and clung to her coffee mug.

"He thinks that Bernie's sister Betty killed the Snows. He wants us to help him prove it."

"Wow, that's interesting. Are you going to do it?"

"I contacted Matt last night. He said he doesn't have a problem with it. As far as he can tell, it shouldn't hurt my case in any way and will actually show my good faith in trying to be cooperative."

"What do you need me to do?"

"I'm going to have to meet with Aunt Eloise and Betty at three this afternoon. Can you watch the store while I'm gone?"

"Sure, but I've got to leave at four today. The boys have soccer and Jason is out of town on a business trip."

"Of course," I said. "Thanks for putting in the extra hours. Did you see that Linda brought more candles?"

"Yeah." She grinned and sipped her coffee. "I think she sees you less as competition now and more as an ally."

"Which is a good thing," I said. "I need all the friends I can get."

"What about Conrad? Do you have another date?"

"He'll be back this weekend," I said and finished up my makeup. A glance at the time told me we were going to be late opening. "Come on. People will be wondering why we aren't open."

"And I'm wondering why you aren't talking about your love life," she said as she followed me downstairs.

"Maybe because I don't like to kiss and tell," I repeated.

I was right, people were pacing in front of the door. Some had little kids in tow. With school in session, most of the kids who came into town were toddlers and preschoolers. After 3 p.m. there would be schoolchildren. I grabbed the bowl of candy and unlocked the door while Porsche set up the cash register.

"Trick or treat," a tiny girl in a Disney princess costume said.

I held the bowl down to her level. "Pick one."

She looked at me solemnly. "Can I take one for my brother? He's in school."

"Yes," I said.

She grabbed two pieces of honey taffy. "You aren't a bad witch after all."

The day flew by. I went upstairs at lunch and brought the new pots of lotion down and restocked the shelves. Aunt Eloise texted me.

"Are you ready to meet with Betty?"

"Yes," I texted back. "Matt didn't have a problem with us doing this."

"Good, let's see if we can't put a bad guy in jail."

"You sound pretty cop-like," I texted. "I can almost hear 'Bad boys, bad boys' in the background."

She texted back an emoji that was crying as it laughed. "Now I'm going to have that song stuck in my head."

"Do you really think Betty set us up?"

"I don't know what to think." She texted back. "Meet us at the Coffee Bar at 3 p.m."

I sent her a thumbs-up emoji and finished straightening shelves. My five hours' worth of work this morning had only begun to replace the missing inventory. If I wasn't careful, I could lose Porsche. She wasn't working for me for no reason. I could take the pay cut. After all, Let It

Bee gave me free living space. I could always eat at Aunt Eloise's place. But austere measures only worked for a short time.

Making a list of ingredients needed to build more inventory, I worked the room. I felt a tug at my skirt and turned to see a little boy with big brown eyes dressed as a cowboy. "Excuse me," he said in the cutest voice.

"What can I do for you?" I glanced around to see if he had a parent with him. There weren't many people in the shop besides Porsche and me, but that didn't mean much. "Are you lost?"

"I like your bees. I have bees in my backyard. I . . . I went barefoot, one time, and stepped on one. It hurt. Mama told me that a bee dies after it stings you. Did I kill that bee by stepping on it?"

"Yes, honey," I said and got down on his level. "I'm afraid that honeybees are the only bees that die when they sting you. You see, the stinger is useful for protection against other insects. But people's skin is too tough for the stinger and the bee gets stuck. Once the bee is stuck, getting unstuck will kill it."

"That's quite a gruesome tale," a male voice said.

I glanced up to see Conrad standing over the boy with his hand on his shoulder. "He asked me if it was true."

The boy turned to Conrad. "I accidently killed the bee." He looked close to tears. "Grammy says I have to wear shoes so it doesn't happen 'gain."

"That's a very good idea," I said and stood

"Cowboy boots will work too, right?" he asked.

"Yes," Conrad and I answered at the same time.

"Is this your boy?" I asked.

"Yes, this is William. William this is my friend, Wren."

"No," William said solemnly with a shake of his head. "That is the Wicked Witch."

"Well, yes, I am wearing a Wicked Witch costume," I said. "But underneath, I'm a normal person named Wren."

"Why?"

"Because I'm dressed up for Halloween. Just like you are dressed as a cowboy."

"I am a cowboy," he said.

"I see," I said. "I'm sorry but I didn't know."

"I'm going to go watch the bees." He sprinted off to the bee wall.

"I didn't know you had a son," I said.

"Yeah," Conrad said. "I thought I'd bring him by today to meet you. How are you?"

"I thought you were out of town until the weekend?"

"William's grandmother had an emergency and needed me to come get him."

"Where's William's mom?" I crossed my arms over my chest and tried not to let my disappointment show. Was Conrad married?

"She died when William was two. A drunk driver took her from us."

"I'm sorry," I said, overcome with the urge to hug him. "That's terrible."

"We're getting better every day," he said. "Sandy, my wife, well, her mom lives in Oceanview. It's also why I want to move here. William needs a woman in his life."

"It must be tough being a single parent."

"It has its good days and its bad days." He smiled at me. "I like your costume."

"I'm sorry, I thought he was wearing a costume."

"Oh, he is," Conrad said. "It's just that he's an all-in

kind of guy. If he's dressed as a cowboy, then he's a cow-boy."

I smiled. "I have a bee book you can have for him. He really seems interested."

"Thanks," he said. "Is it a picture book?"

"Yes, and age appropriate. I get a lot of preschoolers interested in the beehive. I like that." I went over to the book rack and pulled out a bee book that was at the bottom of the rack. "He'll like this."

"Great." Conrad pulled out his wallet.

"No, this one is on me," I said. "It's the least I can do."

"Thanks, Wren." He smiled. "Are we still on for din-ner on Saturday?"

"Yes, I'd like that."

"Me, too." He peered around the store, spotting his son trying to reach a candle. "Well, I'd better get William. It's snack time."

"I wouldn't want to get in the way of a growing boy's snack time."

He laughed and gathered up his boy. "Say goodbye, William."

"Goodbye, William," the boy repeated and waved to me.

"Goodbye," I said and waved back.

"So, Conrad has a son?" Porsche asked.

"Yeah," I said.

"And the mom?"

"She was killed in a drunk driver incident two years ago."

"Oh, that's terrible. Say, aren't you due at the Coffee Bar?"

I glanced at my phone and tried not to curse. It was five minutes after three. "I'll be back by four," I said and rushed out. The Coffee Bar was three blocks away. A misty rain was falling. I was glad for my witch's hat, but the brim funneled the water down to a spot that ran straight down the back of my neck.

I hurried into the coffee shop and took my hat off to shake it out.

"Well, if it isn't the Wicked Witch of the West," I heard someone say.

I glanced up to see my nemesis, Frankie Hillary. She was dressed as Glinda the Good Witch.

"And what," she said, "brings a serial killer to the Coffee Bar?"

Chapter 15

"Funny seeing you here," I said, not letting her comment bother me. Frankie decided to be my enemy the moment we met, which was the first day I was the new girl at Oceanview High. I never really knew why. My mom once said that some people just don't like you. It doesn't matter what you do.

Frankie had gone to Berkeley, married into money, and stayed in California after she graduated from college. She was wearing an elaborate and expensive costume, but you could still see the seventy-dollar manicure and expensive nose job. She rarely returned to Oceanview. She had made it clear on graduation day that it was too small town for her.

"Not so funny," she said. "I'm visiting my parents for the week. So, I hear you murdered the Snows. What for?

Just for the fun of it? Or did they make you angry? Should I be worried? Should I hire a bodyguard?"

"Frankly, I don't care what you do." I turned and walked over to where my aunt and an older woman, whom I assumed was Betty, were sitting having coffee. "So sorry I'm late. I was dealing with a customer."

I turned my phone recorder on in my pocket as I sat down.

"Oh, my, it's not every day I have a coffee date with the Wicked Witch of the East, is it?" the older woman said.

"Yes." I put my hat down beside me on the table. "It's not every day I get to be the Wicked Witch of the East."

"Weren't you just talking to your counterpart?" the woman asked.

"Frankie Hillary is not my counterpart," I said. "In fact, she's not 'my' anything."

Aunt Eloise sucked in a breath and looked over her shoulder. "What's she doing in town? I thought she was living in California."

"She's back for a visit and managed to bring a costume," I muttered. "I was going to order coffee, but I'd rather join you ladies. Hi, Betty is it? I'm Wren, Wren Johnson."

"Nice to meet you, Wren." Betty said. She had steel-gray hair that was cut short and warm green eyes that were rimmed in red from tears. I would not have pegged her for a murderer.

"I'm so sorry for your loss. Were you and Mr. Snow close?"

"Bernie and I were ten years apart in age. He only had

time for me when he needed a family connection for an election."

"I'm sorry to hear that."

She stirred her latte. "It's okay. Actually, I got to be an only child most of my life. He was more like an uncle to me than a brother. Still," she said, putting her elbow on the table and resting her cheek in her palm, "I'm going to miss him. It was strange to go to Agnes's funeral and now his will be so soon after hers. I'm going to have to deal with taking care of their stuff and putting their house on the market and all the things that go with it."

"We can help," I said and glanced at my aunt. "When you have to clean out the house and pack up things."

"Really? That would be amazing. I don't know how I'm going to do it. I've taken ten days off from work, but I don't know where to start."

Aunt Eloise covered Betty's hand with hers. "I can help with that. When my brother passed, I had to deal with everything. You have to do it systematically. When do you want to start? I'll set up a plan."

"Bernie's funeral is on Friday. Can we start next week?"

"Certainly."

"Can I wait to call you when I'm ready?" She looked at me as if lost.

"Yes," I said.

Betty brushed tears away from her eyes. "Excuse me, ladies. I've got to go powder my nose." She got up and went to the restroom.

I noticed Glinda the Good Witch was shooting me angry glances. I had no idea what I did to her so I ignored it.

"That was a brilliant suggestion," Aunt Eloise started.

I raised my finger and reached into my pocket to turn

off the recording. "Yes. I thought this would be our chance to dig into the Snows' secrets. By the way, Betty doesn't seem to be a murderous sibling."

"She was telling me that she would have never sued her brother except her friend, Mildred, encouraged it. She harangued Betty at every turn until Betty thought she was right and contacted a lawyer. The lawyer took it from there."

"How's Mildred involved?" I wondered out loud. "That wretched woman claims she saw me talking to Agnes. What is that all about?"

"I don't know, but maybe we'll find out after packing up the Snows' place."

Betty came back to the table with a new latte. "I got you a coffee. I hope you are good with a latte."

"Perfect, thank you," I said. "But it should be us taking care of you."

"Oh, I'll be fine," she said and sat down. "Everyone has been so nice. My friend Mildred—Mildred Wool-right—is coming over to spend the night with me. I'm going to meet her at the funeral home in an hour to go over the preparations for Bernie's funeral."

"How is Mildred?" Aunt Eloise said.

"She's okay. She turns seventy next week. Her husband, Theodore, is throwing her a giant surprise party at the Ritz in Portland. She will be so amazed. It's all very hush-hush, so please don't tell her."

"I won't," I said and sipped my coffee. "She doesn't like me."

"Why ever not?" Betty asked. "Everybody loves you—even Agnes. They think the world of your shop."

"Mildred claims to have seen Wren with Agnes the morning she died," Aunt Eloise said.

"What?"

"I don't understand it," I said. "I wasn't with Agnes. I swear to you."

"But Mildred picked Wren out of a lineup," Aunt Eloise said. "Do you have any idea why she would do that?"

"I'm sorry, I don't have a clue. You say you weren't with Agnes?"

"No, I was at home making inventory for the store," I said. "But let's not talk about it. I don't want to get between you and Mildred. You need her and we just want to help support you."

Betty sat back. "Gosh, maybe I shouldn't be seen with you two. I mean, if Mildred thinks you are involved in Agnes's murder and now you found Bernie's body . . . what will people think?"

"Oh dear," I said and pushed back from the table. "I don't want to upset you. You're absolutely right. I should go."

"Wait, wait," she said and touched my arm. "I'm sorry. I think it's the grief. I don't know what to think anymore. I didn't mean to insult you. Clearly you don't look like a killer. This entire thing has gotten me all messed up."

"Oh, no," I said. "I should go. You and Aunt Eloise can talk for a while. It's okay. I'm not insulted."

"Thank you," she said.

I gave my aunt a small hug and whispered, "Talk to you tonight." Then I turned to Betty. "Nice to meet you. Thanks again for the latte. If you need anything let me know."

"I will, dear," she said.

I left, pausing to smile at Frankie before I walked out the door. I made a mental note to figure out why she was in town.

* * *

Jim came by as I closed the shop.

"You're going to give me a bad reputation," I said. "People already think I'm guilty of killing Agnes. It doesn't help that you are here every day."

"It's a good distraction for them," he said. "Did you and your aunt speak to Betty?"

"Yes," I said. "But she seems as innocent as I am. Seriously, she's torn up inside."

"So you learned nothing."

"We offered to help her clean out the Snows' house. She agreed. We're to meet with her on Sunday. Do you think this is about what Bernie and Agnes were caught up in?"

"Why would you say that?"

"I don't know," I admitted. "Maybe because he had political ties. Maybe he didn't deliver on something and someone was upset. Then again, we think Agnes was blackmailing people."

"I told you that's a crazy theory and you need actual proof."

"What about that ledger? The one with our fingerprints on it?"

"It was a list of names and amounts paid," he said. "Not exactly blackmail evidence."

"Unless we can prove it is," I said. "Who knows, maybe we'll find more proof when we pack up the Snows' house."

"I doubt that. If she was blackmailing people and Bernie found out, it might have been enough for someone to kill him, too. Which means if you find out something, you will be next. So, why don't you drop it and let me work on that?"

"Maybe because I'm still your number one suspect," I said and narrowed my eyes. "Aren't I?"

He didn't answer me.

"Maybe I shouldn't be working with you."

"What did your lawyer say?"

I folded my arms over my chest. "Matt said I should cooperate."

"There you have it. I've made a note that you are cooperating."

"Do you really think I did it?"

He blew out a breath and leaned toward me. "It doesn't matter what I think, Wren. I'm just chasing down clues. I've got the mayor on my case to get this solved fast. It's hurting tourism."

"Funny," I said. "My store is doing very well. Linda is happy with her sales as well."

"You think this is someone trying to drum up business?"

I bit my bottom lip. "It does add a certain lure to Halloweentown."

"You're reaching."

"Yeah, I guess I am. Sorry I wasn't much help. Is that all you needed?"

"For now," he said.

"Great, I'll let you out." I unlocked the door and it cackled as I opened it. He stepped out and turned.

"Let me know if you find anything tangible in your investigation."

"Sure, my lawyer first, then you."

"I'm serious, Wren."

"Me, too," I said and closed the door.

I watched him walk to his squad car and get inside.

Then I locked the door. The shop was quiet. Everett waited for me on the counter. "Come on, it's dinnertime." I picked him up and carried him upstairs.

Aunt Eloise stopped by at seven. "What do you have for dessert?"

"I made cookies," I said. "Honey flats, I'm calling them. They are a sugar cookie made from honey. I'm trying to decide if they need icing or not. Have a seat. I'll make some coffee and bring us a plate."

She sat on my couch. "Have you heard anything from your reporter friend?"

"No," I said, as I poured coffee and placed the cookies on a plate. "She seems to be notably absent."

"You should contact her and see what her investigation is turning up."

I put the plate of cookies down on the coffee table and went back for the coffees. "Good point." I handed her a coffee with cream and sugar and sat across from her. Aunt Eloise picked up a cookie and tried it.

"These are good. Great texture. I think you can sell them without icing and with."

"Thanks. So what did we learn from Betty?"

"Well," my aunt curled up on the love seat and wrapped her hands around the mug. "I don't believe that Betty is strong enough to have killed her brother."

"I agree. In fact, I told Officer Hampton that I don't think Betty is the killer."

"The real question is, What does Mildred Woolright have to do with this?"

"Yes, her name keeps coming up and I think I know

why." I went to my desk, where I'd printed off a copy of Agnes's client list. "Remember Agnes was taking money from Mr. Woolright?"

"Yes," Aunt Eloise said. "Is he on her list?"

"Right here." I pointed to the line on the paper and handed it to her. "All told Mr. Woolright gave Agnes five thousand dollars. I think we need to visit him and find out why."

"Great idea," Aunt Eloise said. "Wait, I know Carson Edwards. He's on this list." She studied me. "We've been friends forever. I'm certain he'll tell me what Agnes was up to. If he can confirm she was blackmailing him, then we have a lot more people with motive."

"What about Mildred Woolright's false eyewitness account?"

"Eyewitnesses are notoriously wrong," she said. "I think that's why the police haven't charged you yet."

"Do you think Mildred is covering for her husband? Is that why she says she saw me speaking to Agnes?"

"Maybe," Aunt Eloise said. "I'll find out more tomorrow when I talk to Carson. In the meantime, you need to keep a careful record of everywhere you go and when."

I raised my wrist. "I bought a Fitbit. It keeps a record of everywhere I go."

"Good girl. Now I'm going to go. You lock up behind me and don't take Everett out unless you absolutely need to—and since he's a cat there is no reason for you to need to." She took a breath. "In other words, stay home."

"Yes, ma'am," I said. "Besides, I have to think up a new costume for tomorrow. There's no way I'm going to wear my zombie Glinda costume now."

"I'm sure you'll come up with something clever," she

said and gave me a quick hug and a kiss. "See you tomorrow."

"When?" I called after her.

"I'll come by after I speak to Carson. You get your inventory ready. Thursday is going to be a big selling day."

Now how the heck did she know that?

Honey Yogurt Mousse with Lemon Curd

Makes 4 to 6 servings

Lemon curd:

½ cup fresh lemon juice (3-4 lemons)
2–3 teaspoons lemon zest
1 14-ounce can sweetened condensed milk
4 egg yolks

Take a large heavy saucepan and pour in the sweetened condensed milk and the lemon juice. Heat gently, stirring until it's simmering. Simmer 1 minute. Whisk the egg yolks together in a medium bowl. Temper the eggs using the hot liquid by adding a little bit of the hot milk at a time and mixing into the eggs, then a little more until the egg mixture is nearly up to temperature. Pour into the milk mixture and simmer 1 more minute, stirring constantly. Remove from heat and add zest. Let cool to room temperature.

Mousse:

1 teaspoon powdered gelatin
2 tablespoons water
1 cup plain strained Greek yogurt
⅓ cup honey
1 cup heavy whipping cream.

In a small bowl, pour the gelatin into the water. In a medium bowl, whisk together yogurt and honey. In a cold bowl pour in cream and whip to stiff peaks.

Heat the gelatin in a microwave for 12 seconds. Quickly pour the gelatin over the yogurt and whisk thoroughly. Fold in the whipped cream until thoroughly blended.

Layer ⅓ cup mousse with 3–4 tablespoons lemon curd in glasses and repeat layers until the glasses are full. Garnish with a curl of lemon peel and enjoy!

Chapter 16

My last-minute costume included a wig change and different makeup with the same puffy pink dress. I was now Sparkle Barbie zombie. It didn't stick with my *Wizard of Oz* theme but that was okay as far as I was concerned.

Everett seemed to approve. I poured him his favorite salmon-flavored breakfast and then glanced out the back window. It was going to be a cold and rainy day, which meant my aunt's prediction of a high-traffic Thursday was out the window.

That was a good thing, as I had been up late adding to my inventory. But still, I ran out of supplies before I even had enough to fully restock the shelves, let alone create backup for a sell-out day.

I went downstairs and turned on the light. The back

door opened as Porsche let herself into the shop. I set up the cash register.

"Hello," Porsche said. "What's new today?"

"I'm no longer Glinda the Good Witch," I said and did a twirl. "I'm now Sparkle Barbie."

"Impressive. Why are you done with the *Oz* theme?"

"Frankie is in town and yesterday she wore Glinda the Good Witch."

"What is she doing in town?" Porsche asked.

I took note of her 1970s Cher costume with zombie makeup. "You look fabulous, by the way."

"Thanks," she said and flipped her hair.

"I have no idea why Frankie is in town. You have your ear to the local news. Can you find out for me? I assume she is visiting her mother, but why bring a costume? She doesn't usually want anything to do with Halloween."

"I'm on it," Porsche said and picked up her phone.

"Who are you going to call?"

She raised a finger as if to silence me, then answered the phone. "Hi, Rachel, yes, it has been a while. I'm so glad you took my phone call. I was thinking about you today. What's up?" She stepped to the far corner and paced as the conversation seemed to go on forever. I glanced at the time and realized it was time to open.

The rain was coming down in a steady stream. I figured it would keep all but the most diehard of shoppers from the store. I petted Everett and then resigned myself to straightening shelves.

"Well, that was interesting," Porsche said as she walked toward me.

"What's going on?"

"My friend Rachel Adams has some gossip about why Frankie is in town."

"Why?" I asked. "Or do I not want to know?"

"She is separated from her husband."

"Oh, dear, that's not good."

"She is in town to scope out the Main Street businesses. She's thinking about opening a gift shop."

"Where?"

"Well, you know how Mr. Gordon's been trying to lease the place next door?"

"Oh, no, no, no," I said and squeezed Everett so hard he squeaked and then leapt onto the counter to get away from me. "I can't have hateful Frankie working beside me. Knowing her, she'll deliberately dissuade shoppers from coming here. Don't we have enough gift shops in town?"

"It sounds pretty serious," Porsche said. "She's meeting with Rachel's boss, Amanda Schelling, this morning to sign the lease papers."

"Is Amanda the leasing officer? Because I'll go above her to the Hendersons."

"And do what? You can't afford to rent both spaces. You know that. We looked at it when it first went on the market."

"I can't have Frankie next door. It'll ruin me."

"Aren't you being a little dramatic?" She put her hands on her hips.

I bit my bottom lip. "Maybe. But you don't understand, Frankie mean-girled me my junior and senior years of high school. She made a big deal about how she was going to Berkley and I was going to Oregon—loser Oregon."

"You're not in high school anymore. It's been seven years."

"Tell Frankie that. She couldn't stop glaring at me at the coffee shop yesterday."

"Okay, well, we'll kill her with kindness, how's that?"

"It's not a bad idea." I said. "If we are nothing but kind to her, then she's the one who looks bad."

"Exactly," Porsche said. "Now, what about the investigation? What did you and your aunt learn yesterday when you went to get coffee with Betty?"

"We don't think Betty did it," I said.

"Oh, that's disappointing. If she didn't, then who did?"

"I am not any closer to finding out. We're looking into the names in Agnes's list of blackmail. Aunt Eloise saw the name of a friend. She's going to ask him today why he was paying Agnes. It's the only way to confirm that Agnes was blackmailing people. Once we confirm that, we've got a whole list of people with more motive than I have."

"Well, I certainly hope so," Porsche said. "I can't afford to lose my job. The boys are starting music lessons."

"Well, then I have to do my best to keep us both in business." I winked at her and she chuckled. "But on a serious note, I've put in an emergency order for supplies and paid extra to rush the shipment. We can't have bare shelves. Not during Halloweentown week."

"I agree. When the supplies come in, do you want me to tell Jason that I need to work extra hours? That way I can cover so you can make your stuff and still sleep at night."

"That would be fantastic," I said and clapped my hands. "They are supposed to come tomorrow before noon."

"I'll let him know tonight."

The doorbells cackled and our first guests came in. The kids came straight to me for candy. Porsche helped the mom find the perfect lotion for her chapped hands. The rest of the day went the same way. Aunt Eloise arrived in the afternoon after things had slowed down. I left Porsche to rearranging stock so it didn't look so bare and went for coffee with my aunt.

"How are you doing?" I asked her.

"I've decided to enter the pie making contest at the fairgrounds in two weeks. With Agnes gone, I might actually stand a chance of winning the grand prize."

"What kind will you make?"

"My famous apple raisin," she said and rubbed her hands together with glee. "This will show me whether or not I'm a true champion."

"You will always be a champion to me," I said. "So why did you come by?"

She put her arm through mine and walked in step with me. "Because I thought you would like to meet Carson. He is two years older than me and such a dear."

"Did he tell you anything about Agnes?"

"Not yet," she said. "I thought I'd wait until I had a witness."

"Me?"

"Yes," she said. "That way it can't be a he-said, she-said situation."

"Hmmm, good idea." We walked into the corner bakery and Aunt Eloise grabbed a table while I bought three coffees and a plate of petits fours. I brought the coffee to the table as a man walked up. He looked a bit like a lumberjack or a miner with long gray hair and a bushy beard. But he was wearing jeans and a T-shirt.

"Hello, ladies," the man said.

"Carson, do come sit," Aunt Eloise said. "Wren bought us coffees."

"And petits fours," I said. "Let me go back and get them. Also, I didn't know what you like in your coffee so the side bar is right over there. Help yourself."

"I like mine black, thanks," he said and took a seat.

I went back to the counter and snagged the plate of finger cakes. As I approached the table, they were both laughing. "What's so funny?"

"Oh, nothing, dear," Aunt Eloise said.

"It's an inside joke," Carson said and pointed toward one of the two spare chairs. "Sit, young lady. I'd love to hear more about you."

"More?"

"Your aunt has filled me in over the last couple of years. She's pretty darn proud of you, you know. Setting up shop and being carbon neutral."

"It's my thing," I said. "Caring for the environment."

"How did you come up with a bee shop?"

"Well, a few years ago I learned about how the honeybees were struggling and I did some research. We need bees to pollinate everything. I mean, other insects and hummingbirds do some of that, but most pollination is done by bees. We can't afford to lose them."

"So, you're selling bee by-products?"

"I wanted to help build awareness as to how beneficial bees are and why we should go organic with our food sources."

"I thought it was a virus killing the bees."

"There is some thought that industrial agriculture is one cause. Then, there are parasites and climate change. Every little bit of awareness helps."

"So you've been in business for a year and a half. How's it going?"

"Pretty well," I said. "I'm not bankrupt yet. What do you do for a living?"

"Oh, I'm a retired bookie."

"What?"

"Just kidding, although I do love to gamble. No, I was a lumberjack most of my life. As were my father and my grandfather before me. Lumber is big business here."

"Don't get her started," Aunt Eloise said. "She hates the deforestation."

He leaned toward me. "But you're drinking from a paper cup and I bet you use toilet paper and register paper and most likely paper towels."

"There, you're wrong," I countered with a wag of my finger. "I don't use paper towels. I use cloths and wash them."

"Then, you are using energy and putting soap into the environment."

"Well, I always run a full load and use natural soaps with no dyes or chemicals."

He laughed and sat back. "I can see you're passionate about it. Just be aware that a good many of your customers have parents and grandparents and great-grandparents who worked in lumber mills and paper mills."

"And I'm grateful for them," I said. I sipped my coffee, then made a face. "I need creamer."

I got up and went to the side bar and poured half-and-half into my coffee. The idea of the lumber industry had rankled me since I was a teen and saw the large swaths of deforested mountainside. But my aunt was quick to point out that they planted trees and refilled the spaces. Lumber was now harvested with care. I didn't think it made things better, but it was an Oregon way of life and Carson was right: most of my local customers had family members who worked in the industry. Who was I to say they were wrong?

They were laughing again when I sat down. "You seem to be having more fun when I'm not here," I pointed out.

"Oh, dear," Aunt Eloise said and wiped tears from her eyes. "We have been so wrong."

"What do you mean?"

"I mean about Agnes and the payments. She wasn't blackmailing people—at least not Carson."

I drew my eyebrows together in confusion. "Then why did you give her that money? The money she recorded in her book? The money that was in her secret bank account?"

"Because I ordered a handmade tapestry for my niece," he explained. "She's into all things medieval, and I knew that Agnes was a winner at handicrafts. So I went to see her and she asked me what I wanted as the tapestry scene."

"And that's what was so funny," Aunt Eloise chuckled.

"Yes, you see, I ordered a mermaid."

"Wait, are mermaids medieval?" I asked.

"Turns out they aren't," he said. "My niece thanked me for the gift and asked me who made it. Then, she took the tapestry back to Agnes. They both laughed at me and then Agnes recreated it to be more realistic."

"That was nice of Agnes." I sipped my coffee.

"It cost me an extra two hundred dollars to create a

new tapestry," he said. "Who knew my niece was into unicorns instead?"

"No! For two hundred dollars?" I nearly choked on my coffee.

"He's teasing about the unicorn," Aunt Eloise said. "Agnes recreated a lovely scene of a picnic by the stream to match one from his niece's favorite books. Tapestries are a lot of hours of work. You ask me, he got a real steal."

"Oh, whew," I said. "Why did you think a mermaid was appropriate?"

"When my niece was little, she loved mermaids. Then, last year, I went to the renaissance fair and saw there were people there playing fairies."

"So you assumed that if there were fairies, there must have been mermaids in the era as well?" I grabbed a petit four and bit into it. It was chocolate cake with raspberry filling. It wasn't bad, but I did have to wonder if it wouldn't have been better with honey.

"The joke was on me, I suppose." He sipped his coffee.

"Did all the people in Agnes's ledger order handicrafts from her? What about Mr. Woolright? Why was he paying in cash?"

"We don't know," Aunt Eloise said. "But I think it's safe for us to meet with him and find out."

"I suppose you're right," I said. "Besides, whoever killed Bernie most likely wasn't connected to Agnes's handicraft business."

"Most likely not, "Aunt Eloise said. "So much for listening to town gossip."

"I don't know if the gossip is all that far off," Carson

said. "Agnes did know a lot of people's secrets. Maybe just knowing was enough to get her killed."

"And Bernie?" I asked.

"The killer might have taken him out to cover his or her tracks."

"Let's hope no one else will suffer the same fate," I said and sipped my coffee. Another dead end in my investigation. Maybe I wasn't as good at investigating as I'd hoped.

Chapter 17

I returned to a busy shop. Normally I loved to see the foot traffic so high, but with the stock so low, I was afraid I'd sell out and have to close my doors.

"What is everyone doing in here?" I whispered to Porsche when we caught a momentary lull in people at the register.

"There's a Grateful Dread concert tonight," Porsche said. "People are flocking in from all over to be a part of the scene."

"You mean, Grateful Dead? Are they still a band?"

"No, silly, this is a cover band that is always super popular during the Halloween season."

"Is that why everyone is wearing skeleton costumes and dreadlocks?" I asked as I looked around.

"Yes and I hear the café has stocked up on Cherry Garcia ice cream."

"I guess it's good that people are buying," I said.

"They are coming in because they heard about the murders and wanted to see what you were like for themselves."

"As a store owner?" I asked.

"As a murder suspect," she said and winked. "I might have played it up a little."

"Excuse me, are these the lip balms with poison in them?" one particularly chubby skeleton asked.

"There isn't any poison in my products," I said.

"But the police said there was . . . in that murder, right?"

"Yes, that is what the police said." I sighed. "But there isn't any in my products."

"Too bad," she said. "I was going to buy a case and hand them out to mean people. I mean, what better revenge when you run into road rage, than to gift them with a poisonous lip balm?" She laughed. "Just kidding," she said when I gave her the side eye. "It's gallows humor for Halloween. I'll take two of the hand creams."

"They are buy two get one free," I said. "So pick another."

"Oh, I'll take almond honey." She grinned at me. "They say that arsenic smells like almonds."

I refused to give her silliness any more credence and rang her up. She paid and I was soon on to the next. With Halloweentown week being one of the most important weeks in the year, we had advertised that the store would be open until nine. I was glad it was so busy. Finally, at 8 p.m. the crowd quieted down.

"See?" Porsche said as she tried to make what little stock I had left look like it filled the shelves. "I told you it was the concert. It starts at nine. Most everyone is either standing in line or already in their seats. It should be a quiet last hour. What did you learn at your coffee meeting?"

"Only that Agnes wasn't blackmailing Carson and probably none of the other people on the list."

"Then why were they paying her?"

"To make handicrafts for them," I said.

"At those prices?" Porsche sounded astonished. "Someone would have killed her for gouging."

"Don't be silly," I said. "Listen, I'm going to run upstairs and feed Everett. I'm surprised he isn't down here batting me for his supper."

"I haven't seen him all day," Porsche said. "I don't blame him. A crowd like that will make anyone skittish."

"I'll be right back." I hurried up the stairs. Everett was a social cat. Even to the point of greeting me at the door. It wasn't like him to hide in his cupboard all day. I hoped he wasn't sick. "Everett?" I called when I opened the door to my apartment. I turned on a light. "Here kitty, kitty," I called and went to the kitchen. If there was anything that could get him running no matter how sick he was, it was the sound of the can opener. I buzzed the automatic can opener. "Kitty, kitty," I called.

Nothing.

"Playing hard ball, huh?" I reached into the cupboard and took out a can of tuna. Put the can in the can opener and let it open. "Got tuna."

Still no Everett. Now I knew there was something wrong. I went to his box in the closet. It was empty. I checked under the bed and in all his favorite hiding spots. Opened all the doors in the apartment in case he was shut in by mistake. "Everett?"

There was no answer. I went back to the cupboard, put

the tuna in his dish, and set it on the floor. Then I went for the bag of cat treats. Taking it out of the cupboard, I shook it. "Kitty, kitty."

Nothing. My heart raced as I went downstairs. "Porsche, is Everett down here somewhere?"

"No," she said and pursed her mouth. "I haven't seen him."

"I opened a can of tuna and he didn't come out. I think something's wrong."

"Maybe he got outside when all the people were coming and going," Porsche said.

"It's not like him to go out," I said. "He likes his leash. It's sort of a safety blanket."

"He's not declawed, is he?"

"No," I said. "I couldn't do that to him."

"Then he'll be fine. Cats are resilient. They wander off and come back."

"I don't like it," I said. "I'm going to post a picture on the neighbor app. Maybe someone saw him." I pulled out my phone and posted a picture of Everett on the social media site along with the words "Please bring Everett home."

"He's neutered, right?"

"Yes," I said. "I won't have feral cats in distress."

"So, he's not visiting a lady friend or kidnapped for breeding."

"Who would kidnap a cat?" I found myself pacing in front of the store.

"Only the worst kind of person," she said and closed up the shop, locking the door. "Come on, let's clean up the shop and then go upstairs. We can strategize how to get Everett to come home over a glass of wine."

I worried my bottom lip. "You don't seem all that concerned."

"I love cats and Everett is a particularly intelligent beautiful specimen. But I am pretty sure he can take better care of himself than you can, and you own this store."

"Fine," I said and peered out at the empty streets. "Let's close up."

Closing meant sweeping the floors and dusting the shelves. Porsche did the cleanup while I counted the cash and put most of it in a bank bag. "I'll walk the money to the bank. If Everett got out, maybe he'll be wandering around somewhere I can find him."

"I'll walk with you," Porsche said. "It's dark and damp. You shouldn't be out alone."

"Aren't you ready to go home?"

"Yes and the bank is on my way," she said and grabbed my bright green raincoat from the hook near the back door. I'd gotten the coat in high school when I was going through an everything-must-be-green phase. It's never worn out and now it's nostalgic. "Here, put this on."

"Yes, Mom," I teased her and put on the coat. We stepped out to a chilled mist. Fog had rolled in and the streets were that strange quiet that fog creates, as if you are wrapped in a shroud. "Everett must be cold and hungry."

"He's a big boy," she said. "If he's out here, he'll take care of himself."

"How do you think he got out?" I asked, as water dripped from the hood of my raincoat.

"He could have slipped out when people were coming and going."

"He's never done that before," I pointed out. "Why now?"

"I know you want to think someone took him," Porsche said.

"I don't want to think that," I disagreed.

"That means he wandered out of the store and when you find him, you'll have to ensure he is upstairs when the store gets crowded or he'll do it again."

"I suppose so," I said. We arrived at the bank and I made the deposit. Then I slipped the receipt in my pocket. "Have a good night and thanks for all your help."

"My pleasure," Porsche said. "Materials for more inventory should be here tomorrow. I'll stay late so you can make more products."

"I really should outsource some of it. Do you know anyone who might be good at candles or homemade lotions?"

"I'll make some calls."

"Thanks. Have a good night," I called and watched her head toward her van with a black umbrella over her head. In the distance I could hear the roar of the ocean and the call of gulls. I kept my eye open for Everett as I walked back. "Everett, here kitty, kitty."

A half a block from my shop I was still calling my cat's name when a figure stepped out of the fog, startling me. "Wren?"

It was Conrad.

"Oh, hello," I said. "You gave me a scare. What are you doing out this late in the fog?"

"I was going to ask you the same question," he said.

"I made a bank deposit. We had a banner day."

"That's good, right? Do you mind if I walk with you?"

"Yes . . . er, that 'yes' was to having a good day, not minding if you walk with me. What I mean is, I don't mind if you walk with me."

His expression warmed. "Thanks, I was on my way to see you anyway."

"What about?"

"I wanted to make sure you were all right."

"I am," I said. The only sound in the fog was our footsteps and my voice.

"Did I hear you calling for your cat just now?"

"Yes, I think he got out. I can't find him."

"My mom had cats when I was growing up. They can disappear and still be in the house. I wouldn't overworry."

We reached my back door. "Wait, aren't you watching your son?"

"He's at his grandma's for the night. Can I come in?" he asked.

"Okay, um, sure." I unlocked the shop and flipped on the lights. The only sound was the patter of rain on the ground behind us. We shook off our coats and hung them to dry. Then, we left our shoes at the door and padded through the shop to my apartment upstairs. There was no sign of Everett. "Can I make you some coffee?"

"That would be nice," he said and wandered my apartment looking at my art collection. "These paintings are wonderful. Who did them?"

"My aunt, Eloise," I said. "She's pretty talented."

"So are you," he said. "I've seen it in the way people respond to your products." I handed him a coffee. "You should really think about opening an online store."

I curled up on my couch. "I do have a website, but I'm not quite ready to allow people to order online. That's next in my business plan," I explained and sipped the warm brew. "I don't think you came all this way to hear about my business plans."

"No," he said with a half-smile. "I wanted to see you."

"Okay . . ."

"Frankly these murders have me worried. I thought I would invest in a business in Oceanview, but now I'm on the fence."

"I for one am not all that concerned," I said. "I went to high school here and my mom's family has been here since it was founded. It's hardly a hotbed of murder." I sent him a wry smile. "I think you'll be safe to invest."

"You seem pretty confident."

"There are murders all the time in places like New York, Chicago, San Francisco. No one seems to think twice about moving there and owning businesses."

"I guess when you think of it that way . . ." He studied me.

"What?"

"You seem to be intimately involved in the deaths."

"Not on purpose," I said. "Does that bother you? Because if you're thinking about canceling our date, I would understand." I stood. "You have a son to think about."

He stood as well and put his mug on my counter, then shoved his hands in the front of his jeans. His expression was sheepish. "Look, I know the local district attorney."

"How? I thought you lived in Portland."

"He's an investment partner."

"Okay, well . . ."

"I'd really like to get to know you better, but . . ." He hesitated. "It's not good for business." There was a pause. "I wanted to tell you in person."

"Great," I said and opened the door. "Thanks." I walked him down the stairs and to the back of the shop. I made a mental note to look into having a regular door with stairs installed for the apartment. It was awkward to walk someone out the long way when they were breaking up with you.

He grabbed his coat, slipped it on, and stopped just outside the door. "They're building a case against you."

"Conrad, I'm not a murderer."

His mouth became a grim line. "Good night, Wren."

"Goodbye, Conrad." I closed the door and locked it. Everett was missing and now this. My life was a nightmare.

Chapter 18

I had trouble sleeping without Everett. Finally giving up around five in the morning, I threw on jeans, a T-shirt, and a dark hoodie and went out into the cool morning fog to see if I could find him. I walked the back alley, calling his name softly so I wouldn't wake the neighborhood. This time I brought a flashlight because it was stronger than my cell phone flashlight.

It didn't help. Everett was nowhere to be seen. I covered the entire town before circling back to the coffee shop. The bells rang as I entered the shop. It was busy with fishermen and people stopping by before work.

"An Americano to go, please," I said.

"What brings you in so early, Wren?" The barista, a young man with bleached dreads and a tattoo on his neck, had worked at the coffee shop for three years now and was likely to spend his entire life there.

"Hi, George. Everett is missing," I said.

"Your cat?"

"Yes."

"Too bad, he's a cool guy."

"You haven't seen him, have you? I know you get here early. Everett likes to walk to the beach. Did you come from the beach this morning?"

"I did but no, I haven't seen Everett," he said. "I promise I'll be on the lookout for him."

"Thanks." I stepped over to the pickup counter and George went to work on the order.

"I'm an Everett fan," a woman said.

I turned to see Sally Hendrickson stirring something into her coffee. "Have you seen him?"

She snapped a lid on the cup. "No, but I saw the note you put on the neighborhood app. I've been keeping an eye out."

"Thanks."

"Wren." George put my large coffee on the counter. "Did you try opening tuna?"

"I did," I said. "It was untouched this morning. So I know for sure he's not in the shop."

"You don't think he was snatched, do you?" Sally asked.

I picked up my coffee and added creamer. "Why would someone take him?"

"He's a gorgeous cat," Sally said. "Very sweet."

"Yeah," I said and put the cover on my coffee. "He's a doll."

"Have you tried the animal shelter?"

I shuddered. "He's chipped. I don't think they would keep him without checking."

"Well, good luck," she said as we left the shop and she

headed down Main Street. I headed back toward the beach when Barry Ziegler popped his head out of the coffee shop.

"Are you looking for your cat?"

"Yes." I stopped. "Have you seen him?"

"Havana Brown?"

"Yes, his name is Everett and he's wearing a green collar."

"Someone mentioned seeing one at the Perrys' place near their shed just off the alley."

"That's pretty specific."

He shoved his hands in his pockets. "They were riding a bike down the alley and didn't normally see that type of cat."

"Where's the Perry place?"

"Next to the Woolrights' place on Beech Street."

"Thanks, Barry."

"Best of luck," he said and popped back into the shop.

I headed toward Beech Street and tried to keep my hopes in check. Just because someone thought they saw Everett didn't make it true. I tried not to think about how close I'd be to the Woolrights' place. They didn't like me. I got that. Or at least Mildred was convinced I was a killer. It didn't mean I wasn't going to follow every lead to find Everett. Although what he'd be doing on Beech Street was a question all unto itself.

I power walked that way calling Everett's name. I passed some kids on the sidewalk waiting for the school bus. "Hi, I'm looking for my cat. His name is Everett?"

One little girl screamed, "Stranger danger! Stranger danger" and took off down the street.

"Sorry," I said and power walked away. This was not my morning.

A few blocks later I reached the Woolrights' place on the corner of Beech and 10th Street. It was a massive two-story house with a large front porch. I sighed and then lifted my chin and powered forward to the alley that ran behind the house. Then, I turned and looked for a shed that might be reachable from the alley.

The shed was in the back of the house behind the Woolrights'. I looked around but no one was there. So I called Everett's name. "Everett, here kitty, kitty."

I thought I heard a meow and rushed to the shed. The door was cracked. It was dark inside so I pulled my flashlight out of my hoodie pocket and turned it on. Then I stepped inside. "Everett?"

A definite meow came from behind some boxes. I stepped over the lawn mower and went deeper into the shed. The door slammed shut from a gust of wind. I looked around—the place was dark and spooky. If someone on TV would have come inside such a place, they would have found a dead body—for sure. I tried not to think like that. "Everett, is that you?"

I unstacked the boxes and discovered a set of shelves. I flashed my light on the second to the bottom shelf and an orange tabby cat hissed at me. Startled, I jumped back. The cat leapt away from me and into a dark corner. "Great. You are most definitely not Everett."

The meow sound came again from the same place. Frowning I turned my flashlight onto the spot, but all I could see was a wooden box. "Everett?" I knelt down and pulled the box off the shelf. Something was inside and it sounded like Everett. The box was nailed shut. Whoever put a cat in this box should be shot. "Everett, if this is you, I'm going to be so mad at the person who did this. I just might hunt them down and shove them in a box."

There was a meowed response. Even if it wasn't Everett, I was hopping mad. "Hold on, kitty," I said. Standing, I searched the shed. The orange tabby was distressed by my frantic movements and squeezed out of a hole in the side wall. "Well, you were a big help."

It took me what felt like forever to find a flathead screwdriver. There wasn't a hammer or a crow bar in sight. But I thought I could try to leverage the screwdriver.

I propped the flashlight on the floor beside me to shine a light on the box. I could see a few small air holes drilled into the box. "Hang on, kitty."

There was another meow.

"This might scare you. Try to remain calm." I didn't know if the "remain calm" was for me or the kitty. My hand trembled as I dug the screwdriver between the top and the side of the box and pressed my entire body weight. It gave about an eighth of an inch. The meow was louder.

"I know. Hang on." I turned the box and tried to leverage another side. It moved an eighth of an inch. That was all I could do. "There's got to be something better."

Meow.

I jumped up and grabbed the flashlight and checked the shelves again. But there was nothing. This time I checked in the cardboard boxes that had hidden the wooden one, tearing them all apart for anything I could use to leverage the lid off. I took a deep breath and tried to slow my heart rate and be less frantic.

Then, I decided I'd just take the box—cat and all—and go home and get a hammer. I picked up the box and stumbled toward the door. The box was pretty big and heavy and the flashlight rolled around on top. I hit my shin on something and tried not to curse before I realized only the cat could hear me. I made it to the door, but it didn't open. I pounded on it, but it didn't budge.

Great.

Meow?

"The door," I said to the box. "It's stuck." I put the box down and grabbed my phone. There was no signal in the shed. "What is going on? Is this place made of lead?" I tried all over the small space. It couldn't have been bigger than six by eight. I got desperate and got down on my knees and held the phone through the hole that the tabby had gone out. The problem was I couldn't see if there was a signal.

Meow?

"I'm trying," I said. Then I pulled up Porsche's number, put my phone on speaker, stuck my hand out and hit Send.

"Wren, where are you?" I heard her say.

"I'm stuck in a shed."

"Wren?"

I shouted, "I'm stuck in a shed."

"I can barely hear you . . . Wren?"

I pulled the phone in. It went dead. Okay. So. I set up a text telling Porsche where I was and to bring help. Then, I stuck my hand out and hit Send. At least I hoped I hit Send.

Meow?

"I'm trying." There had to be a way to get one of us out of the box we were in. I continued to search for something to open the cat's box. Finally, I discovered a rusted axe head in the far corner of the shed. I wedged it into the crack in the box and was able to open the lid up enough that the nails squeaked. Then, I dug my fingers inside and pulled and pulled.

The lid popped open. I flew back and the cat jumped out of the box, streaked for the hole in the shed, and disappeared. "Well, that just happened." It's not crazy to talk to yourself. At least not when locked alone in a shed.

There was no way to know if the cat I'd rescued was Everett. My phone was on the ground beside me and the flashlight off. The shed was far too dim and the cat too fast to have seen the color.

Not that I blamed the cat. If I could fit through the hole, I'd be gone in a flash as well. Maybe if I tried getting a hold of Porsche again . . . I brought up her number in my contacts and stuck my hand out of the hole and pressed the button. I heard Porsche answer.

"This isn't funny, Wren. Where are you?"

"Help," I shouted.

"Did you say help?"

"Shed beside Woolrights'."

"You're at Walgreens?"

"No," I shouted. "Stuck in shed behind Woolrights'."

"Okay, I got 'stuck,'" she said. "Stuck in traffic? What are you doing at Walgreens?"

I eased the phone as close to the hole as I dared. Put it on the ground and shouted, "Locked in a shed by Woolrights'."

"Well, that I heard," she said. "How did you get locked in a shed?"

I rolled my eyes. "I'm not your child. Please get me out."

"Okay, okay," she said. "I'll call nine-one-one. Why didn't you call them?"

I reached out and hung up on her. Then sat with my back to the shed and waited for the sirens. Calling the emergency responders was the last thing I wanted. It would mean everyone would know I was this close to the Wool-rights' house. Some people might think I was breaking the law.

Which I wasn't.

I shivered. The ground was cold so I stood up and paced. Telling the truth was the best thing, no matter what people thought. After what felt like hours, I heard voices outside and thankfully no sirens. Pounding on the door, I shouted, "Help! I'm stuck!" Then rattled the door and pounded again.

"Hang on."

The shed muffled the voice so I didn't know who it was, but at least someone was there. There was an attempt to open the shed.

I heard "locked" and some more muffled conversation. Then silence.

"Don't go away. Please don't go away," I shouted and tried hard to tamp down a sudden feeling of claustrophobia.

"Wren?" It was Porsche's voice coming from the hole in the wall. I got down on my knees and peered out. A flashlight shone in my eyes and blinded me.

"Yes, Porsche, it's me. Can you get me out?"

"There's a chain and a lock on the door. Jason is getting some bolt cutters."

"You have bolt cutters?" I know it was a random question considering the circumstances, but I was cold and scared and not in my right mind.

"How did you get locked in there?"

"Do you have any water?" I asked.

"Oh, no, shoot. I can go get some."

"No, no, no," I said and stuck my hand out. "Don't leave me."

She grabbed my hand and squeezed. "I'm not going anywhere." I heard a commotion and Porsche muttered, "Oh, crap."

"What?"

She let go of my hand. Someone else kneeled down and shone a light in my eyes. "Wren Johnson?"

"Yes," I said and rubbed my eyes.

"We're going to get you out." It was Jim and he was not amused.

Within minutes there was the sound of a chain hitting the door and then two men grunting as they pushed the door open. I got out of the shed as fast as possible.

A spotlight illuminated the front of the shed and a cop car was parked next to it. Flashes went off as people took pictures.

Great. There was nothing like public humiliation.

"Thanks," I said to Jason and Jim.

Porsche put a blanket around my shoulders as I shivered hard. "Are you okay?"

"Yes," I said. "Just cold. What time is it?"

"It's nearly four p.m. You've been gone for hours," Porsche replied.

"What were you doing in the shed?" Jim asked.

The small crowd that had formed hushed for the answer. I winced and my jaw shivered. "Can we go someplace else and talk about it?"

"What's going on here?" Theodore asked as he pushed through the crowd. "What are you doing?"

"Someone locked Wren in this shed," Porsche said and put her arm around me. She glared at Theodore. "You wouldn't happen to know who?"

"What are you implying?" he asked and crossed his arms over his chest. "Clearly you all are trespassing. The Perrys are out of town and they asked me to keep an eye on their house. Now, I'm going to have to report . . . this."

"I've got this covered," Jim told him. "You can all go home now. There's nothing more to see."

"Great," I said to Porsche. "I'm ready to go home. You didn't happen to see Everett, did you?"

"Is that how you got stuck in the shed? Looking for Everett?"

"Yes," I said.

"There doesn't seem to have been anything more than a prank here," Jim said. "Are you okay?"

"Yes," I said and tried not to shiver. "Just cold and a bit scared."

"Why don't you tell me what happened?"

"I'm not sure what happened," I said.

"Well, start at the beginning."

"Everett is missing," I said and Porsche hugged me. I went on to tell him about the coffee shop and the sighting of Everett. Then the cat in the box and being locked in the shed.

"Do you think the cat that was in the box was Everett?" he asked me as he took notes.

"I don't know," I said. "It was dark and I didn't get a close look at him. But why would anyone trap a cat in a box?"

"Why would they lock you in the shed?" he asked. "Probably teenagers pulling a Halloween prank. I'll take the box in and see if we can't lift some prints. Otherwise there's little we can do." He pushed his hat up with the end of his pen. "Rain's coming. Why don't you two ladies let Officer Jones take you home." He turned to another officer. "Jonesy, see that they get home safe."

"Call me if you think of anything else," Jim said.

"Thanks for getting me out," I said to Porsche as I slipped into the back seat of Officer Jones's squad car. Porsche got in beside me.

The ride back was short and very quiet. The officer parked outside the front of the shop. "Would you like me to go in and make sure you're safe, Wren?"

"I'm sure I'll be fine," I said and gave Porsche a quick hug. "Thanks for giving up your evening with the boys to come rescue me."

"It was my pleasure," she said and hugged me back.

I got out, unlocked the shop, closed and locked the door behind me before I waved them on. Officer Jones headed out to take Porsche home. It had been a long day. Porsche was right to close the shop early, even though I lost revenue. I blew out a long breath. All I could do now was hope that Everett came home.

Raw honey can help repair and prevent acne breakouts. It not only heals the inflammation but keeps the skin from producing too much oil. Rub a small amount of raw honey on your breakout. Wait ten minutes and wash it off with warm water.

Chapter 19

Pounding rattled my door. I opened one eye. It was still dark out. I glanced at the alarm. The clock read 6 a.m. I had trouble sleeping because I was worried about Everett and had only been in bed a few hours. The back doorbell rang. I put on my cozy, knee-length, plaid flannel robe and tied it around my waist, then stuck my head out the window to see who was making all the noise.

It was Jim and Officer Jones.

"I'm awake," I called from the window. "I'll be right down."

I hurried out the apartment, down the stairs, and into the back of the shop. I paused and checked the peephole. A girl could never be too safe with a murderer on the loose. It was the two officers, all right, and no one else was with them. I opened the door. "Good morning, gentlemen."

"Can we come in?" Jim asked.

"Sure," I said. The rain had slowed to a fine foggy mist, which left everything dripping. You could smell the salt air off the ocean. The clouds were low enough to reflect the light from the back alley.

The two men entered. I turned on the hall light and closed the door behind them. "What's this all about? Do you ever sleep?"

Jim's mouth was a grim line. "We found arsenic in the shed."

"I'm sorry?" I wasn't understanding what he meant.

"There was arsenic in the shed where you were locked inside," Jim said. "We need to ask you a few questions."

"Should I get my lawyer?" I pushed my uncombed hair out of my eyes.

They didn't answer my question and I felt the spit dry up in my mouth.

"I'm going to get my phone," I said. "You can follow me."

I went upstairs and grabbed my cell phone from my nightstand. Jim stood in the doorway watching.

"It's just my phone," I said and wiggled it. "I'm not trying to escape out the back door or grab a weapon. I'm calling my lawyer now. See?" I dialed Matt's office number. I got the answering service. Sighing, I dialed the cell phone number he'd given me.

"Hello? Wren?" came the grumpy voice of a man who was woken out of a sound sleep.

"Hi, sorry to wake you, but the police are here again, and they want to talk to me. You said to call you first."

There was a mumbled curse and the sound of a man getting out of bed. "Where are you?"

"I'm at my apartment above the shop."

"Don't say anything. I'll be in there in fifteen minutes."

I hung up the phone. "He said he'd be here in fifteen minutes. In the meantime, can I make some coffee? Maybe get dressed?"

"Officer Jones, make sure there's no other way out of the apartment," Jim said.

I rolled my eyes. "Just the fire escape through my living room windows." I went to the window and threw it open. "See?"

"Clear," Officer Jones said. "There's no exit from her bedroom."

It didn't take long to go through the apartment. It was a two bedroom and one bath with a living room and kitchen combined. "Can I get dressed now?"

"Sure," Jim said.

I scooted off to my room and closed the door, then changed into yoga pants and a long shirt. I brushed my hair and put it into a high ponytail, then stepped out to catch the smell of coffee.

"I hope you don't mind that we made some," Jim said.

"No, I don't mind," I said and got down three mugs then poured the coffee. "Milk or sugar?"

"Black," both men said at the same time.

I poured half-and-half in mine. "Suit yourself."

More knocking was accompanied by the ringing of my back doorbell.

"I'll get it," Officer Jones said and left the apartment.

I took down another coffee mug and poured a fourth cup. "You must think this is pretty important to come here so early. Did you get any sleep?"

His mouth twitched. "Please sit."

"This is my home. You should sit first. You have coffee." I pointed at the couch. "Make yourself at home."

He seemed to blush and sat down. I sat across from him.

"Why did you go to the shed yesterday?"

"I told you yesterday, I went there because a guy from the coffee shop said someone saw Everett there. I miss my cat and I'm worried about him."

"Why go into the shed?"

"I heard a cat inside." I sipped my coffee. "I told you that, too."

"But that cat wasn't Everett and it ran out of the shed through the hole."

"That's right, the first cat I saw was a large orange tabby. It left through the hole in the shed."

"So you saw a cat run out, discovered it wasn't Everett, and yet you didn't leave the shed?"

"No," I said and leaned toward him. "Like I said, I heard another animal in a box."

"A wooden box with the lid nailed shut."

"Yes."

"Don't say another word!" Matt stood at the door with Officer Jones behind him. His eyes were red and his usually well-groomed hair was mussed.

"I wasn't saying anything I didn't already tell him last night. I don't know why repeating what I said could—"

"Don't say another word," he repeated and unbuttoned his coat. "Until we know why they are questioning you."

"He said something about—"

"Please don't be a difficult client." He stepped between Jim and me. "Why are you here?"

Jim stood. "I wanted to verify the reasons Wren was locked in a shed last night."

"You were what?" Matt turned to me.

"At first I thought it was an accident and then I learned someone purposefully locked me in. But I didn't think I needed to call my attorney," I said.

He turned back to Jim. "Why is my client's getting locked into a shed important enough to get us both out of bed early on a Saturday?"

"Because we found arsenic in the shed," Jim said.

"It appears to be the same stuff chemically as what we found in the lip balm that killed Agnes Snow," Officer Jones said.

"I didn't know anything about arsenic in the shed," I said and stood. Adrenaline shot through me. My heart pounded in my chest.

"Don't say another word!" Matt put his hand on my shoulder. "Are you charging my client?"

"No."

"Then you need to go."

I bit my bottom lip to keep from talking. The two policemen put on their hats and stepped out of my apartment.

"I'll see them out," Matt said. "You sit and don't move."

I sat down.

This was bad. Very bad. Had I touched the poison while I was in the shed looking for something to open the box? Did they have my fingerprints? They probably had them all over the shed . . .

Matt came back in and closed the door to my apartment. He took off his coat and poured himself a cup of coffee. He wore jeans and a black T-shirt that outlined his well-muscled chest. I'd never seen him so casual. I kind of liked it.

"I have some whiskey if you want something stronger in your coffee," I suggested.

"This isn't funny," he said. Then he took the seat across from me. "Why were you in the shed?"

"Everett is missing."

"Your cat."

"Yes," I said. "It's not like him to be gone so long. I spent a couple hours yesterday looking for him. I put signs up all over. When I was at the coffee shop, Barry Ziegler came out and told me that a friend of his had seen Everett around the Perrys' shed."

"So you went to the shed without a second thought."

"You make that sound bad. I was looking for my cat."

"And was there a cat?"

"There were two actually, but I don't know if the one in the box was Everett or not."

"The cat in the box?"

I told him the entire story. He sat back and studied his

coffee cup. Then, he looked at me with sincere brown eyes. "You were set up. They locked you in so that the cops had to come and let you out. People saw you leave the shed. Now that they found poison, everyone will assume you went to the shed to hide the poison."

"But I didn't. I can't even tell you where the poison was. The inside of the shed was dark."

"Okay, look, I hate to say this, but I think someone needs to be with you twenty-four-seven until we get through this. You need a witness who knows your exact location."

"Well, that's silly. I'm not going to be followed into the bathroom. Plus, I'm wearing my Fitbit. It watches where I go."

He ran his hand over his face. "Fine, don't listen to me. Give the person who is framing you another opportunity to make you look bad."

I chewed on my bottom lip. "I suppose I can ask Aunt Eloise to come and stay with me. The window in my bathroom is small and there isn't any way to get out through it. So, whoever stays with me should be able to let me go alone."

"I'm not sure your aunt is the best choice," he said.

"Why not?"

"She's biased and I wouldn't put it past her to lie for you."

"She would not!" I protested and then thought about it. "Fine. What about Josie?"

"Josie?"

"Josie Pickler, the new nine-one-one dispatcher. She's friendly enough that I wouldn't mind her staying with me, but she works for the cops."

He picked up my phone. "Call her."

"Now?"

"Yes, I can't stay with you. I charge by the hour."

"I thought you were pro bono."

"Not if you keep making yourself look bad."

"Fine."

"Good."

I made the call and Josie agreed to help out. Then I turned on the TV and we both pretended to watch it intently, to avoid further conversation.

Thirty minutes later, Josie showed up at the back door to the shop with an overnight bag. Her red hair was flying all over in the wind and her freshly washed face made her freckles stand out even more.

"Oh, Wren, what happened?" She gave me a big hug. She wore yoga pants, a T-shirt, and an open hoodie.

"Stay with her from now on," Matt said. "Don't let her out of your sight no matter what. She might have a Fitbit but it doesn't know why she went where she went, and right now, Wren needs witnesses."

"Okay, I won't let her out of my sight," Josie said.

"I'm still going to open the store," I said. "I have to make money."

"I can't stress enough how important this is," he said. "Wren will go to jail unless she has an alibi, and the store will be closed forever if she goes," he warned us both and left the building.

"Well," Josie said. "Seems like you've had an interesting morning. Let's make some pancakes." She put her arm through mine and dragged me upstairs. "What costume are you wearing today?"

"I was going to be the Wicked Witch of the West, zombie of course, but now I think I'll just wear prison orange."

"Stop it," she said. "I like the Wicked Witch of the West. Now let's think this through over breakfast."

Two hours later I wore my witch costume with zombie makeup. Josie had talked me down. If I was going to go to jail for a crime I didn't commit, then I would live my remaining days of freedom like I was truly innocent.

We opened the door and a costumed crowd flooded in. Aunt Eloise came in to help out. She was dressed as a vampire princess. I laughed at her sparkly skin makeup. "What?" she asked and blinked innocently. We both knew how much she didn't like the sparkly kind of vampire. I handed her a bowl of candy.

"Help a witch out," I said. We stood on opposite sides of the door ready for the trick or treaters. Lucky for us, a few of the grown-ups stayed to look around and buy things. Porsche wasn't scheduled to come in until afternoon. She had put in a lot of extra hours, and I was trying to give her more family time. Besides, with Aunt Eloise at my side, I didn't need a second helper.

"You should put cameras in the shop," Josie suggested.

"What?" I handed candy to a second grader in a demented bunny costume.

"Surveillance videos," Aunt Eloise repeated. "You should have them. That way you have proof you are where you say you are."

"Tired of me already?" I teased Josie.

"If you had put them in earlier, you might have seen who took Everett," my aunt said.

"You think he was taken." I thought so, too, but hearing her say it made it sound more definite.

Her mouth became a firm line. "Yes, he is a beautiful cat and smart and well-bred, if I say so myself."

That made me smile. "You're prejudiced toward him."

"I loved his grandfather, such a beautiful cat."

I left the door and moved to the counter. "I was hoping the cat I rescued from inside the box was Everett."

"How do you know it wasn't?" Josie asked

"He would have come home by now," I said.

"Are you sure it was a cat?" Aunt Eloise asked as she followed me to the counter.

"What?" I straightened.

"Well, locked in a box, it could have been a raccoon or a possum."

"That's reaching," I said. "I heard a cat meow." It was my turn to frown. "In fact, it talked to me like Everett does."

"They say that cats talk to their owners," Josie offered.

"Then why hasn't he come back?"

"He might have gotten spooked. He's been gone a couple of days. If whoever took him, put him in that box, then he was probably a little out of his mind," Aunt Eloise said.

"Wouldn't you be?" Josie asked.

"Indeed."

The doorbells cackled and Alicia Lankson walked in, trailed by her photographer, Mitchell, a lanky young man with a straggly goatee. "Oh, good, you're here," she said to me. "I understand that you were locked in a shed last night and that the police found arsenic in the same shed. So is that your murder lair?"

"Are you kidding right now?" I asked.

"No pictures without permission," Aunt Eloise said. She grabbed the photographer by the ear and tossed him out.

"Can she do that?" Alicia asked.

"It's my property," I said. "Technically you're trespassing. I doubt he's going to press assault charges for having his ear tweaked."

The door cackled and Aunt Eloise walked in, dusting off her hands. I could see Mitchell through the glass. He was frowning and rubbing his ear.

Alicia laughed. "Sorry to make a fuss, but I have a job to do."

"Where have you been?" Aunt Eloise asked. "I thought you were one of Wren's friends."

"More like frenemies," I muttered.

"Oh, of course, we're friends," Alicia said. "I've been investigating the Snow murders."

"Then you should go," Aunt Eloise said.

"No, no." Alicia held up her hands. "I'm on your side. I don't think Wren did it."

"Then why did you ask about a lair?" I asked.

"Because that's the angle the paper wants to take," Alicia said.

"Who do you think did it?" Aunt Eloise asked.

"Well, if I give that away, then I blow my whole story," Alicia said. "So why don't you tell me about your adventure yesterday?"

"My lawyer advised me not to talk to anyone without him," I said.

"That's too bad," she said. "Don't you want to tell your side of the story?"

"Only if it keeps me out of jail. Right now, I'm not sure it will."

The door cackled again and the mail carrier walked in. "Love your costume, Wren," she said.

"Thanks, Beverly," I replied. Beverly had beautiful cocoa skin and wide dark eyes. "Sorry they won't let you wear a costume for Halloweentown week."

She laughed. "My uniform is my costume. I'm a mail-man."

"I won't say 'man,'" Aunt Eloise said. "There's no hiding your lovely figure."

"Aunt Eloise!"

"What?" she asked. "It's true. I would have killed for a figure like hers."

I hoped no one would notice her casual use of the word "kill."

Beverly handed me my mail. "I love you, too, Eloise. Happy Halloween, everyone."

"Happy Halloween!" we all chorused.

"There's a story," Aunt Eloise said to Alicia and pointed toward Beverly. "That woman is an ex-marine. Did two tours in a war zone."

"I've got a story slated for her around Veteran's Day," Alicia said.

Half listening, I glanced through the mail and stopped on an envelope with no return address. It was addressed to me care of the store. I opened it and a white powder puffed out. Choking, I glanced up to see that everyone else had frozen in their spots and stared at me with terror.

"Don't move," Aunt Eloise said softly. "Alicia, call nine-one-one."

Alicia took a careful step back. She dialed her phone.

Josie stood closest to the door. "Oh, I know what to do," Josie said. "We need to evacuate. Sorry, not you Wren." Josie turned to the room. "Everyone please leave immediately. This is not a drill." She carefully ushered customers out.

I wanted to say something. I wanted to breathe, but I was afraid. I looked at Aunt Eloise. She reached inside a drawer and removed linen napkins with bee motifs. Then, she slowly went over to the back room and then came back in wearing one as a face mask. She handed me another. I realized it was wet and wrapped it around my head slowly so as not to disturb too much of the fine dust covering me.

The three people inside left with Josie. Alicia spoke to the dispatcher a yard or so away from me. The photographer pushed the door open with concern on his face. "What's up?"

"We have a mysterious powder in an envelope," Aunt Eloise said. "Please stay out and don't let anyone in."

He shut the door, then turned to guard it.

I wanted to tell Aunt Eloise and Alicia to run. To leave while they could. But if I spoke I would disturb more of the powder. My nose itched. My eyes watered.

"Yes, we've cleared the building," I heard Alicia say. "It's only Eloise, Wren, and me left. We are the closest to the powder." Her voice was low and careful.

In the distance sirens sounded as I tried to remain calm. It's hard to slow your breathing and your heart rate when you're in a deadly situation. I thought I'd close my eyes, but that only caused me to sway.

If this was poison, I'd be dead soon. But if I moved and spread it, then Aunt Eloise and Alicia could be dead, too, and that was something I didn't want to happen. I simply had to remain as still as I could and hope I didn't pass out. I had a sudden memory of marching band practice where the band leader coached us all to keep our knees bent to keep us from fainting. I bent my knees slightly and prayed he was right.

*A teaspoon of honey mixed with pink Himalayan
salt every night helps with insomnia. Mix five parts
of honey into one part of salt and keep in a tightly
closed container.*

Chapter 20

"Don't move," the guy in the white hazmat outfit ordered. I shot him an evil glare. I hadn't been moving for what felt like eternity while they tented the door to my shop, suited up, and took Aunt Eloise and Alicia out one by one. I noticed they made them strip and shower. They now stood on the other side of the glass wearing scrubs and staring at me.

I would have talked but I'm pretty sure there was powder on my face, and I didn't want to move it into my nose or mouth.

"I'm Calvin Holmes, and this is Greg Smith," he said.

"We're going to collect the dust." Then he and another hazmat outfitted man used a handheld vacuum to slowly, methodically collect the fine powder. I felt like if I was going to die, I probably would have done it by now. I guess that was a positive way of thinking.

"Walk now," Calvin said after taking away the make-shift mask and vacuuming off my face. He put the envelope in a collection bag and helped me shamble to the door. My muscles had grown stiff. I stripped and showered the powder off me as best I could. The water was freezing, but I guess when you were in a hazmat shower, comfort was the last thing on your mind. My green makeup dripped down with the water. I sudsed up as told and then let the water rush over me for fifteen minutes.

By the time I was finished, my teeth were chattering. I dried off and they put the towels in separate bags. I stepped through plastic strips, got hit with a blast of air, and finally was able to climb into scrubs and step out into the fresh air.

I took my first deep breath and then was handed off to an EMT, Ritter, who took my vitals. She was all business and I felt both comforted and like she was judging me.

"Wren, how are you feeling?" Aunt Eloise asked as she rushed up. "Do you feel any symptoms?"

"No," I said and thought about it. "I feel fine."

"Maybe it was a prank," Alicia said. "Was there a note with the powder?"

"I think so," I said. "I didn't pull it out. I didn't want to make things worse."

"It could have been arsenic," Josie said. "That's what the killer has been using, right?"

"If it was arsenic, you probably inhaled enough to make you quite sick," Aunt Eloise said.

"Thanks," I said. I looked at Ritter, who was listening to my heart. "When will they know what it was?"

"How's your stomach?" she asked.

"Okay," I said.

"I'm going to take some blood to see if you have any metal poisoning."

"What if it was ricin?" Alicia asked.

I looked at Ritter in horror. "Could it be?"

"I can't make any guesses. If it was ricin, we may not know the extent of your injuries for a few days." She pulled the stethoscope out of her ears. "Your lungs are still clear so that's a good sign. Still, you could feel the effects six to ten hours after exposure."

"Awesome." A shiver ran through me.

The hazmat guy came out. He was tall, about six foot two, with black hair and copper skin. His hair was wet. They had made him shower after taking off his suit as well. "Initial testing of the substance shows it was powdered sugar."

"Seriously?"

"Seriously," he said.

"And they made you shower?" Alicia asked.

"I was out before they figured it out," he said and stuck his hand out. "Mike Hanes."

"Nice to meet you," I said. "Wren Johnson." I shook his hand and he shook Aunt Eloise's and Alicia's as well.

"Well, ladies, thanks for the practice. We like to keep our skills up."

"Does that mean we can go back into my shop?" I asked and hopped down off the ambulance. "I've missed about four hours of sales."

They took down the police tape and Porsche came running up and hugged me. "Oh my gosh, are you okay? Sheesh, I can't take one morning off without you getting into trouble."

"I'm fine," I said.

"It was powdered sugar," Aunt Eloise said.

"Likely a prank," Mike said. "The police will take the envelope and try to figure out who sent it and why. Good call on the wet napkins as a mask."

"That wasn't me, that was all Aunt Eloise," I said and hugged my aunt.

"Smart," Mike said.

"Thanks. I used to be on the city council emergency preparedness committee," Aunt Eloise said.

"It's such a terrible thing to happen, especially after last night," Porsche said.

"What happened last night?" Mike asked.

"I got locked in a shed," I explained.

"Wow, you must really be on the kids' hit list this year. What happened? Did you fire a teenager?"

"No," I said.

"She found Agnes Snow dead," Aunt Eloise said.

"And my life has been crazy ever since."

"Wait," he stopped and stared at me. "You're the serial killer?"

"I am not a serial killer."

"So you only killed one of them?" he teased, his brown eyes twinkling.

"I'm not a killer." I put my hands on my hips. It was then I noticed that Porsche was wearing pink hair and a witch's costume. "Oh, man, my costume is ruined."

"You can go as a freshly scrubbed poison survivor," Mike suggested.

"Right." I noticed that they were cleaning up all the heavy-duty plastic and hauling away the gear. "Guess you have to go back to work."

"It was nice to meet you ladies," he said. "Next time, try not to open any odd envelopes."

"Deal," I said. The EMTs closed up the ambulance and drove off. The last of the firefighters left as well. "Come on, let's go inside."

"Feels weird," Josie said as we walked back into Let It Bee. "Less than an hour ago we thought we were dead. Now it's business as usual."

"Maybe," I said. "There are a lot of people on the street, but no one's coming in." I looked out at the busy sidewalk.

"It's early yet for Halloween," Porsche said. "It looks like they cleaned up pretty well. Why don't you folks go get changed. I can handle things from here."

"After I get my own clothes back on, I'm going to hit up the police and see what they know about the envelope," Alicia said. "This is a story for tonight's paper."

"It was a prank," Aunt Eloise said.

"Maybe, but they broke a federal law," Alicia said. "I have to tell you, I've never been so afraid in my life. That means I'm going to see they find whoever did this and sue. Think about it. If one of us had been older and had a bad heart, they could have murdered us."

"I guess you can kill someone with powdered sugar," I said without sarcasm.

"Listen, I'm going to head home and put my own clothes on," Aunt Eloise said. "These scrubs they loaned us are paper thin."

Josie and I went upstairs, leaving Porsche to run the shop. For good measure, I showered again and blew out my hair. If I wasn't going to be wearing a costume on Halloween, then I might as well not look like something the cat dragged in.

"I'm glad you packed a bag," I said to Josie. "Now you can shower, too. I hope to never feel water as cold as what we showered in outside ever again."

"It will be nice to use my own products. They are certainly less harsh." She went into my den to gather her things. I put on a kettle to make calming chamomile tea. It was dark out and the trick or treaters filled the streets, even though it was only 5 p.m. The wet weather and fog helped create the fall darkness.

I opened the window and stuck my head out. The fire escape was large enough to sit on. One of the old owners designed it to be more of a balcony that ran the length of the building. Everett and I often climbed out through the window onto the platform. It was nice because we could see the beach from there. Hear the waves. When the fog came in, it wrapped us in a chilly blanket and made me feel safe.

The sound of children running through the streets and calling out "Trick or treat!" made me smile. I'd been through a lot in the last twenty-four hours, but it didn't stop me from loving the holiday. I heard a sound that made me turn to my left. *Meow.*

"Everett?"

Meow.

"Oh, my kitty," I called as he ran across the fire escape to my window. I picked him up, brought him inside, and gave him a cuddle. "Are you okay?" I asked as I carried him into the kitchen. "You must be starving." I found a can of tuna and opened it. He paced, rubbing up against me and telling all about what happened while he was gone. I put the bowl down on the floor. "Don't ever do that to me, again, okay? I was so worried."

He jumped down and gobbled the tuna. I petted him while he ate and then drank water from the bowl. The teapot whistled. I had forgotten I'd put it on. I grabbed two mugs and put herbal tea bags in and poured the water to let them steep until Josie came out of the shower.

Everett weaved between my legs. He had not stopped talking since I brought him in. I picked him back up. "Was it you in that wooden box?"

Meow.

"I thought it was you. Who would do such a thing?"

Meow. Meow.

"Yes, a killer of old ladies would."

Meow. Meow. Meow.

"Oh, that's my friend Josie," I said. "She's staying with us for a while. Lawyer's orders." I looked into my cat's eyes. "Would you testify that it was you in the box in that shed?"

Meow.

"Wait, if it was the killer who took you, then you can also testify as to who killed Agnes Snow, right?"

Meow. Meow.

"You are such a clever kitty."

"Wren, I'm starving. I know it's before six and you normally eat at eight but do you have any ideas for dinner?" Josie said as she came around the corner. "Oh, is this Everett?"

Meow.

"Oh you found him! Where? How?" She came over and petted him. "Everyone missed you. Don't ever do that again."

Meow.

"That's right, you won't." She scratched under his chin.

"He came in from the fire escape," I said and shut the window.

"How? The ladder isn't pulled down, is it?"

"No, but it's easy enough for him to go from roof to roof to get here," I said. "I've seen him do it before when he was young and full of mischief."

"Do you still think he was taken?"

"He tells me he was," I said, "and Everett doesn't lie."

"Of course he doesn't, why would he?" She picked up her mug of tea, poured honey into it and stirred. "What are we going to eat?"

"I'll order pizza. We should go downstairs and let Porsche know Everett is back. She might want some pizza, too. Besides, I think I know how to catch the killer."

"How?"

"Everett is going to testify," I said. "He tells me it was the killer who took him and stuffed him in that box. I'm going to prove it."

"Well then, order an extra-large pepperoni with a side of anchovies for Everett."

*Honey makes a great bath soak. Mix two large
tablespoons of raw honey into a cup of warm
water and add it to your bath with two cups of
Epsom salts. Soak for fifteen minutes and enjoy the
pleasure of smoother skin.*

Chapter 21

"I'm so glad you guys came down," Porsche said. "No one's come in and the kids aren't even coming in for candy." She paused, spotting my kitty snuggled securely in my arms. "Is that Everett?"

"Yes," Josie said as Porsche walked over and scratched behind his ear.

"He was on the fire escape," I explained.

"You're right, the street is packed," Josie observed. "But no one's coming in."

"They all might be freaked out because of the poison scare," I said.

"We can open the door and let people see it's safe," Josie suggested.

"But I don't want Everett to run out," I said. "And I don't want to put him upstairs. There's no way he's leaving my sight for a while."

"Especially since he's going to testify for you," Josie said, teasing. She studied the crowds walking by laughing. "Look at that cute teddy bear costume and ballerina. Maybe if we dressed up they would come in."

"What am I?" Porsche asked. "Stuffed pepper?"

"Maybe you should stand at the door with the bowl of candy," I suggested.

"I can do that," she said. "Then I'll keep an eye on Everett."

She grabbed the bowl of honey candy and went to the door.

"That might get the kids to stop," I said. "But it's not going to get their parents to come in. I swear whoever is doing this is trying to run me out of business."

"I don't know who would want to run you out of business," Porsche said. "You already proved your worth to your only competition."

"And I don't know enough people in the community for anyone else to want to blame me for anything."

"What if," Josie surmised, "that's the reason why they are targeting you. Maybe they figure people will care less about you than a long-standing member of the community."

"That might actually make sense. I was here for high school, then went away for college, and I've only been back a little more than a year. Not really long enough for anyone to get attached."

"That makes you an easy target," she said.

"The killer is someone who has been in the community their entire life," I said and looked at the crowds outside. The kids were coming up to Porsche and the open door for candy, but the parents weren't coming in.

"That narrows it down to about twenty thousand people," Josie said. "You said that Everett was going to testify for you. What did you mean by that?"

"I have an idea," I said. "The chamber of commerce has a coffee on Monday morning."

"Oh, I see, take Everett and he will recognize whoever stole him. You can confront that person and maybe get them to spill their guts."

I scrunched up my face. "I don't think it's as easy as a television show would lead you to believe."

"But the police will be there."

"They usually have a representative," I said.

"Should someone confess, you'll have witnesses."

"All we have to do is stay alive until then," I said.

"That's where I come in." Josie patted my hand. "I'm keeping you within my eyesight for the next forty-eight hours."

"Let's hope we figure this out by then."

Alicia had a front-page story in the *Oceanview Gazette* the next morning. Josie sat at the breakfast table and read it while I made eggs and bacon. Everett was a fan of bacon so I slipped him a piece before taking the food to the table.

"Any other pranks happen yesterday, or was I the only subject?"

"Someone was smashing pumpkins against curbs and

a few cars got egged and soaped. The Mulligans were toilet papered, but other than that, no further mischief." Josie folded the paper and set it on the table so she could dive into her breakfast. "I can't believe you get the real paper and don't just read it online."

I sipped coffee and watched the sky lighten as the fog rolled off. "My mom used to get it so I kept up the tradition.

"Say, it's Sunday. Aren't you going to church?" I asked and sipped my coffee.

"Only if you're going," she said, giving me a look.

"Fine, we'll go to the ten o'clock service. I just have to be back before eleven, if that's possible. I gave Porsche the day off. She's been working a lot lately and her boys miss her."

"She's a good employee," Josie said. "I'd love to help, but I'm back on shift tomorrow."

"You are both good friends," I said. "I hate to leave Everett while we're away at church."

"There's no way Pastor Harold will let you bring a cat to church."

"Yeah," I said. "We'll have to make sure we lock him in the shop."

"Who else has a key to this place?"

"My landlord," I said. "Rosemary Greer with Greer Realty. Why?"

"Maybe she has something to do with Everett going missing in the first place."

"What? Why?"

"I don't know," Josie said. "She has a key. Maybe the killer is blackmailing her or maybe she lost the key and didn't tell you."

"Or a million other things," I said. "I'll call her. Let her know I want to change the locks. That might get her attention."

"Good idea." Josie got up and picked up her empty plate. "I'm not sure I packed anything fancy for church. But that's okay, I'm sure I can make something work."

I watched her disappear down the hall to the second bedroom that I had made up like a den or office. Luckily, I had a futon in there for guests to sleep on. Everett jumped on the table and meowed at me expectantly. I fed him my breakfast. My stomach wasn't happy. Then again, the rest of me wasn't too happy, either.

It was time to go back to the beginning. Things had gotten a little off track. My favorite TV detective always said that the simplest explanation was often the best one. So, who was the simplest person to have killed the Snows? It had to be the Woolrights, right? They did live by the shed where I got locked in, and Mildred did lie about seeing me talk to Agnes. Now, how do I prove it?

An hour later I was no closer to my answer. Josie and I were both dressed for church and walking the few blocks. The rain had let up for the moment and the crisp air smelled of autumn. The route took us past the Snows' house. It was silent and looked creepy with the crime scene tape still half strewn across the yard.

We approached the church as people straggled in. When we entered, we took a middle pew, and I felt the heat of people's stares at my back.

The service was uncomfortable. I felt like a pariah but I knew an innocent person should never hide no matter how uncomfortable things get.

Finally, the uncomfortable hour was over.

"Wren, I'm surprised to see you," Kathy Abernathy

said as she exited the church. I had stepped out of the church and onto the sidewalk. Josie had stopped to talk to Nell Oppermeyer.

"Good morning, Kathy," I said and smiled brightly. "Nice sermon this morning, wasn't it?"

"Certainly," she said. "'Love your neighbor,' wasn't it? Did you learn anything?"

"That's one of my favorites," I said. "I don't see the Woolrights here this morning."

"Oh, they haven't been in for a few months now. I think they started going to brunch at the country club instead."

A mist started to come down. I excused myself from Kathy, put the hood of my jacket up, and went to collect Josie. She said goodbye to her friends, put up her hood as well, and put her arm through mine. People in Oregon didn't shrink from a little rain. Rather, we embraced it no matter how cold. Besides, the walk home wasn't very far.

I unlocked the shop and found Everett sitting in the window watching people walk by. Josie and I stepped in, stomping the water from our shoes. We hung our coats on the rack beside the door. I kept an assortment of umbrellas near the door as a treat for my patrons. Anyone could take one at any time. It was an honor system. I trusted them to bring them back, and so far, no one had ever let me down.

"Day after Halloween," Josie said, "People might be slow to get started. Do you have coffee?"

"There's a pot in the back room. I can make fresh."

"No need," she said. "I can figure out how to make it."

While she made coffee, I opened the register and counted the drawer to start the day. Slow or not, we needed to be open. This murder case was not helping my business.

"I bet that between that and the rain, a lot of people will be staying home today."

"Oh, I don't know," I said. "Cold rain makes me think of football and turkey and that makes me think of shopping."

"Oh, so true," she said and handed me a cup of coffee. I poured some half-and-half in and stirred before I took a sip. Just then Everett jumped up, arched his back, and hissed. It startled me. I'd never seen him do that.

"Everett!" I said his name sharply because he startled me. He ignored me and attacked the window. "Everett!" I put my coffee down and raced to the front. I grabbed my cat and glanced outside. A man walked passed. He wore a fedora and a dark tweed coat. Running outside, I lost him around a corner. Everett and I checked a few blocks, but I didn't see him again.

"What was that all about?" Aunt Eloise entered the building with us. "Are you okay?"

"I think so," I said and petted Everett, doing my best to calm him down. I could feel his heart pounding. "He didn't like that man who walked by. I have a suspicion he was the person who took Everett and locked him in that box."

"That means he might be our killer," Aunt Eloise said. She stroked Everett's head. "It's okay, kitty. We're going to find him and make sure he goes to jail."

"I told you Everett can testify," I said.

"Did you recognize this man?"

"No, all I saw was his back. He was too far away and I couldn't go far," I said. "He was wearing a fedora and a tweed coat."

"Could you see his hair?"

"No, all I saw was his hat. It's misting out and cold. He was moving fast."

"What direction was he going? Should we call Officer Hampton?"

"And say what? That Everett didn't like a man in a fedora? I think we'll have to take Everett out for a walk later. We might be able to find out who he hates so much."

"The streets are empty and so is the store," Aunt Eloise noted. "Not the best day, I imagine."

"No, sales are down," I said. "After Halloweentown, the next big celebration doesn't come until Thanksgiving. It's a good thing. I'll be able to rebuild my stock."

"The bees seem to be huddled in the hive today," Josie said. "I've been watching. Only a few have left."

"There's a cold front coming through," I said. "I think the rain is going to take out any remaining flowers."

"That's not true," Aunt Eloise said. "We'll have mums and pansies until the first snowfall."

"They'll only send a few worker bees out. They have most of the honey already to make it through the winter," I said. "It's easy for them with the hive in the building. I keep this side warm and they don't have to huddle so much and burn off a lot of energy. It's actually why bees like to build hives between the walls inside houses."

Four hours later, Josie sat in a lounge chair near the hive, reading a book. No one had come in all day.

"I say we've been through a lot this week," Aunt Eloise said. "The town is dead. Let's take the rest of the day off."

I chewed on my lip. "You know, you're right. I'm sure it will be fine if we close a couple of hours early."

"Oh, good call," Josie said as she got up. "I can help close."

Aunt Eloise turned the sign over to CLOSED and locked the front door. "Why don't we clean up here and then go out for dinner? The diner has a nice pot roast on Sunday evenings."

"I prefer your pot roast," I said. Everett sat on the counter next to me as I counted out the cash for deposit. He was calm now that the man was gone. I stopped counting the cash. "What if we take Everett for a walk first?"

"You think we'll run into his kidnapper?"

"I don't know," I said. "But we all agree his kidnapper might be Mr. Woolright. It couldn't hurt if we went for a walk to see if Everett can identify him."

"I'm not sure that's such a good idea," Josie said. "Since Matt asked me to look after you, I think you should let him know what you're going to do."

"It's just a walk," Aunt Eloise said. "There really isn't a good reason to call a lawyer. Is there?"

Josie thought about it. "I guess not, if it's just a walk."

"Good," Aunt Eloise said. "You girls finish up here and I'll get Everett's leash."

Within minutes we were on Main Street walking Everett. I wore my green raincoat, Josie wore her church coat, and Aunt Eloise struggled with an umbrella against the wind. Everett seemed unphased by the weather and enjoyed the walk, as I purposely moved us in the direction the man took. Soon, we came to the end of the block and the ramp where the road veered off into Highway 1.

"End of the road," Aunt Eloise said as she turned to me. Her clear rain hood was plastered to her head.

"Isn't it strange that Everett doesn't seem bothered by the rain," Josie mused. "Most cats hate water."

"Everett loves the beach," I said and looked down to see that he had stopped under an overhang and was licking his paws. "Maybe it was nothing," I said thoughtfully. "I only assumed it was the man who made Everett angry. It could have been a fly or a bee in the window. We should head back."

"Now you're being silly," Aunt Eloise said. "Of course it was the man. I know you were trying to follow him, but we should take Everett walking by the Woolrights' house."

"I'm not taking him anywhere near that shed," I said. "No, only the beach and Main Street from now on."

"Fine," Aunt Eloise said. "Then I'll bring Theodore to you."

"How are you going to do that?" I asked as we walked back to the store. "It's not like he'll be coming out after closing to buy candles or honey."

"I have my ways," she said mysteriously. We made our way back to the store and Aunt Eloise disappeared up the stairs.

"I think we're in trouble, Everett," I muttered as I took off my raincoat.

"I'm sure everything will be just fine," Josie said.

Use raw honey for your next manicure. Soak your cuticles in it for ten minutes, then rinse with warm water. They will be moist and peel-free.

Chapter 22

"I'm going to run to the bank," I said to Josie.

"I don't think that's such a god idea," she replied.

"I just really need a moment alone to breathe," I said and tried not to beg. "I'll take the deposit bag and come right back." I looked at Everett. "Look, I'll take Everett. You know I won't veer off Main Street with him. Seriously, it's only the bank. There's no reason to babysit me. Don't you want a minute alone?"

"Well, I do need to pack up. I have an early shift in the morning."

"See, what could go wrong?" I picked up Everett. "We'll be fine."

"Okay," Josie said. "But if you're not back within ten minutes, I'm calling the cops."

"Deal," I said. I was so happy to get a moment alone that I grabbed a raincoat and put it on, lifting the hood around my head to keep my hair dry. Hoodies were a necessary Oregon thing as most people chose hoodies over umbrellas—even if my aunt used both. I put Everett on his leash and we went out the front.

Main Street was deserted. The rain was misty and dripping, and the ocean crashed as the tide had come in. Oregon beaches are flat and wide because the tides make them so. People not used to the beaches occasionally park their cars on the sand, and the tide comes in, sinking the cars. Then, it takes a lot of work to dig them out.

The bank was a few blocks down Main Street between Let It Bee and the promenade. I could hear my own muffled footsteps as Everett trotted beside me as if he were on a mission. The remains of Halloween were scattered everywhere. An occasional ghost hung from a rafter. Smashed pumpkin bits littered the curbs, along with candle wax-filled jack-o'-lanterns. The sky was dark, reflecting the streetlights and the fog.

I stuffed the deposit bag into the bank deposit slot, and Everett and I turned to head home. As we rounded the corner a man stepped out of the fog, startling me. "Oh! What are you doing out here?" I asked.

"Foot patrol," Jim said. "It's a little late for you to be out isn't it?"

"Well, it may seem like the streets of our small town roll up at seven p.m. on a Sunday, but they don't," I quipped. "Everett and I were putting a deposit in the bank slot."

"Then I'll walk you home," he offered. "Since Josie

was supposed to be with you every moment of the day, and I don't see her."

"How did you know that?"

"Your lawyer made it a point to call me, and yet here you are, outside alone."

"I don't need to be babysat. Besides, she went upstairs to pack. She has to work in the morning. Aunt Eloise will stay with me tonight, and I was just depositing the cash," I said, feeling the heat of a blush rush up my cheeks. "I always go to the bank at the end of the night. I just wanted a moment to myself."

"You found Everett," he said and glanced toward the cat. I swear Everett studied him back. Not a single hiss came out of my cat. It was as if the arching and hissing had never happened.

"Yes, he was on my fire escape last night. I think he's the cat who was nailed in the box. I'm going to prove it."

"How?"

"Everett is going to testify," I said with full confidence. Everett meowed up at me.

"And how is he going to do that?"

"Whoever took him wanted to lure me into that shed. I don't think it's a coincidence that you found poison in there along with my fingerprints. I was looking all over the shed for a crowbar of some sort to pop the lid off the box."

"You think someone is trying to frame you and used Everett?"

"Yes."

"And Everett is going to testify to that?"

"That's right," I said. "I'm certain Everett saw the killer tonight."

"Why?"

"A man walked by the shop and Everett was sitting in the window. Suddenly, my sweet kitty jumped up and hissed and arched his back. Nearly scared the daylights out of me. I went out to see what Everett would do to the man if we confronted him, but the guy was lost in the crowd."

"What did he look like?"

"Oh, gosh, maybe your height with a tweed coat and a dark fedora. I didn't get a look at his face, but I'd recognize the coat if I saw it again."

We were almost back to the shop. "Let me get this straight. Everett reacted to some man walking by and you think that will make for good testimony in court?"

"Everett is gentle by nature," I said and picked up my damp kitty. "He would only react that way to someone if they scared him."

Jim reached over and petted my cat. "You really think he'll hiss at the person who stole him?"

"And locked him in a box," I said. "Wouldn't you pitch a fit if you saw someone who did that to you?"

"Who do you think the man was?"

"I don't want to say without proof," I said and unlocked the front door to Let It Bee. "I know what it's like to be falsely accused. Well, this is my stop. Unless you want to come in?"

"No," he said and tipped the brim of his hat. "I've got rounds to make. Please let Josie and Eloise know that I'm not happy to have found you wandering the streets at night alone."

"First off, I wasn't wandering, and second, I wasn't alone."

"No?"

"No. Everett was with me."

"Right. Good night, Wren."

"Good night, Jim." I closed the door and locked it behind me. The shop was strangely quiet. I could hear the *tick, tick* of the clock on the counter. "Josie? Aunt Eloise?"

I unleashed Everett and hung up my raincoat. He dashed up the stairs and I wasn't far behind him.

The door to my apartment was wide open. "Aunt Eloise?" She didn't answer and I started to get a very bad feeling. "Josie? Maybe they're in the bathroom or the back bedroom," I reassured Everett.

Meow.

"Aunt Eloise? Josie?" But there was no answer. My aunt was gone and so was Josie. "Now, where did they go?"

Meow.

"You think Aunt Eloise panicked and they went out looking for us?"

Meow.

"I'll call her." I grabbed my phone out of my pocket and dialed her number. I could hear a faint buzzing sound and searched until I found her cell phone. It was under my couch. "Well, this isn't good."

Meow.

"I hope she's okay. Do you think we should call the police?"

Everett tilted his head at me.

"Yes, I suppose that's a crazy question seeing as we just saw her not more than forty minutes ago. I'll call Josie." I dialed the number but it just rang and rang, and finally went to voicemail.

"You've reached Josie. Please leave a message at the beep." *Beep.*

"Josie, I'm home. Where are you? Aunt Eloise isn't

here. I found her cell phone and I'm worried. Please call me when you get this and let me know you are okay." I hung up and tapped my phone. Everett jumped up on the counter and rubbed his head against me. I reached over and stroked him from head to tail.

Then, I made a decision. I called Jim.

"This is Hampton," he said, his voice gruff.

"Hi, this is Wren Johnson."

"I just left you."

"I know, but Josie and Aunt Eloise aren't here. I thought perhaps you should come and be my witness until one of them gets back."

"I'm heading on back to you. Where did they go?"

"I don't know. Josie's overnight bag is gone, but Aunt Eloise's purse is on her bed and her phone was on the floor of the living room."

"Did you try calling Josie?"

"Yes, but she didn't answer."

"What about Eloise? What was the last thing she said to you?"

I thought about it. "She was going to bring Mr. Woolright here."

"Why?"

"So that Everett can rule him out as his captor." I tucked my hands behind my back and crossed my fingers. It wasn't a lie exactly, just a different way of saying the truth.

"Why would Everett say Theodore captured him?"

"I'm sorry? I never said—"

"You and your aunt think Theodore took Everett, locked him in a box, and then lured you to the shed to lock you inside."

"My aunt is missing," I said very carefully. "You

asked me what her last words to me were, and that's what I remember. Does it help? Call Josie. She can help."

"I'm sending people over to Josie's and Eloise's houses." he said. "They might have gone home for something. Listen, I'm downstairs. Please let me in."

"Right." I hung up and ran downstairs. He stood outside the front door and I unlocked it and let him in. "Shouldn't you be checking the streets for her? It's foggy."

"And she is in great health, correct?"

"Yes."

"She wasn't on any new medication?"

"No."

"Then, I suggest you make yourself some tea and we wait until she shows up." He gestured toward the stairs. "After you."

"I know I asked you to stay with me, but I have a bad feeling about this. You need to be looking for Josie and my aunt."

"Someone needs to stay with you," he said. "I can't be in two places at once."

"I'll call my lawyer and get him to come over," I said. "He won't like you spending time alone with me. I'm still under suspicion, right?"

"I'm afraid so," Jim said.

I phoned Matt and gave him the rundown. He was not happy and told me to not say anything until he got to the shop. "Fine." I hung up. "We should stay here until he gets here."

"Okay." He wandered over to the far corner and said something into his radio. I couldn't hear what he said, but I hoped it was getting someone to check for Aunt Eloise.

Maybe I should ask him to go over to the Woolrights'

house and see if she was there. I mean, knowing my aunt she probably got herself invited in for a piece of cake and a cup of coffee. Then, I remembered that Matt said not to say a word to Jim. I decided to take his advice.

It was a long and awkward twenty minutes, but finally the back bell rang. I hurried off to open the back door.

"Well, it's cold and raining, but I'm here," Matt said. "Anything new happen?"

"I just got off the phone with Josie," Jim interjected. "She said Eloise sent her home. She asked if she should come back, but I told her to stay and get some rest since she has to work in the morning. As for Eloise, we don't know if she dashed home for something or went out looking for you."

"Why would she be looking for you?" Matt asked.

"Because I ran to the bank to make a deposit by myself. Well, Everett came with me."

"Why would you do that?" He crossed his arms.

"Oh for goodness' sakes, can't a grown woman be alone for a few moments?"

"No," they both said at the same time.

"Fine, I was wrong. Come on, gentlemen, let's go upstairs."

We all went up and I opened the door. Jim went in and looked in every room and even under the beds and in the closets. I rolled my eyes. "That's a bit dramatic, don't you think?"

"I'm doing my job," he said solemnly. "Walk me through what happened."

I did and even dialed my phone so he could hear her phone ring and see where I found it. "So, do you see how this is suspicious?"

"It does look a bit off," Jim agreed. He turned to Matt. "Can you stay with her? I'm going to help the patrolmen see if they can't locate Eloise."

"You tried her home?" I asked.

"They did," he said. "The lights were out and it didn't appear that anyone was there."

Concern filled me. "Please find her."

"I will," he said. "You stay here." He turned to Matt and reiterated, "Don't let her leave your sight."

I heard the cackle of the doorbell when he exited. "Should we go down and lock the door?" I asked.

"Does your aunt have a key?"

"Yes."

"Then fine, let's go down." Everett ran down the stairs ahead of us. "I see you have your cat back."

"Yes," I said. "He showed up on the fire escape yesterday. I am pretty sure he was the cat I freed from the wooden box. I also think he can identify the killer."

"Why?"

I explained how Everett hissed and put up a fuss when the man in the fedora walked by. "We think it might have been Mr. Woolright."

"Why?"

"He has the key to the shed," I said. "That's where they found the poison, right?"

"You think he killed Agnes and Bernie and set you up. Why would he do that?"

"I don't know," I said. "I barely know him. That's why it's so odd that he and his wife are so bent on seeing me go down for a crime I didn't commit."

"It's certainly an interesting theory."

I paced for the next thirty minutes but still there was no call from the police. "Can we go out looking?"

"You want to wander around the streets looking for your aunt as if she were a lost pet?"

I winced. "No, but I was thinking we could go by the Woolrights' and—"

"No," he said with a grim expression. "You are not to go anywhere near their place."

"But what if they took Aunt Eloise?"

"Then you have an even bigger reason not to go there."

"Ugh!" I paced some more. Everett watched me from his perch on the cat tree in the corner.

My phone rang and I rushed to get it. "Hello?"

"Wren, it's Porsche. What's going on?"

"What do you mean?"

"I just had a visit from a police officer. He said they were looking for your Aunt Eloise."

"You haven't seen her, have you?"

"No," Porsche said. "What happened?"

"Um," I glanced over my shoulder and Matt shook his head. I put my hand over the receiver. "She's family," I said.

"No," he said.

"I'm coming over," she said and hung up.

"I think she's coming over," I said. "You can't stop my friends from coming and helping me. Besides, she said that a police officer came to her house and asked her if she's seen my aunt. That means the entire community knows Aunt Eloise is missing."

"It also means the community will be looking at you as the reason she's missing," Matt said and crossed his arms.

"What? Why? I love my aunt."

"They'll say that she discovered you were the killer

and so you killed her in cold blood and then went to the bank to make a deposit, alone, to establish your alibi."

"Now that's ridiculous," I said. My heart pounded in my chest so hard I thought it would burst. "I didn't kill anyone, least of all my aunt."

"Relax, I'm not saying it's true," he said and patted my shoulder.

I jerked away from his touch.

"I'm simply telling you that anything you say and do right now can be seen in a negative light."

The door cackled and I rushed to the top of the stairs. "Aunt Eloise?"

"It's me, Porsche," she said and hurried up the stairs. Her jacket dripped with rain. She pulled the hood off. "Are you okay?"

"I'm scared."

Porsche hugged me.

"I've advised my client not to talk to anyone," Matt said. "Not to have any visitors at this time."

"Why?" Porsche kept her hands on my shoulders and looked me in the eye. "Why do you need a lawyer?"

"He seems to think they might make a case against me in my aunt's disappearance."

"Well, that's ridiculous," Porsche said and hugged me to her side. She faced Matt. "I will fight every person in the town if they so much as look at Wren sideways." She walked me into my living area and sat me down. "Now, let me get you some tea. You're positively frozen with worry." She gave Matt the stink eye.

He pulled out his phone and studied it.

Everett jumped into my lap, did a patty-cake, and lay down. I stroked his fur while Porsche tried to distract me by chattering on about the boys and Halloween and how her house was a mess and she was glad for the day off but not if it meant Aunt Eloise was missing. She brought me a steaming mug of apple cinnamon tea and sat down next to me. "Do you have any idea what happened?"

I refused to look at Matt. I told her about Everett's reaction to the man and Aunt Eloise's notion that maybe it was Theodore. "The last thing she said to me was that she was going to bring Mr. Woolright over to see if Everett would testify that it was Mr. Woolright who locked him in the box and killed the Snows."

"I guess I can see why you would worry about Theodore Woolright," Porsche said. "After all, his wife picked you out of a lineup. Why would she do that if she wasn't trying to cover something up?"

"He said he had a key to the shed where they found poison that matched the poison that killed Agnes."

"It all sounds perfectly logical," Porsche said. "Why haven't you gone over there and asked him what he's done to your aunt?"

"Because she has no reason to," Matt said. "If she confronts anyone at this point, it only makes her look guiltier."

"Then I'll go and confront him."

"For what? What is Theodore's motive for killing the Snows?" Matt asked. "You have no proof. If you go over there, you're no better than the people who are framing Wren."

Porsche crossed her arms in silent protest.

"He's right," I said. "Listen, Matt, Porsche's here now. You can go home. All I need is someone with me all the time, right? I mean as witness to my whereabouts?"

"Yes, but—"

"I promise you that Porsche won't do anything to put me in jail. Will you?"

"I won't," she said. "We'll stay here and sip tea and wait for the police to act."

"Why is it that I don't believe you?" He narrowed his eyes at us. "That said, I do have a meeting with a paying customer very early tomorrow."

"Go," I said and stood. "I'll walk you out."

"We'll walk you out," Porsche said. "I'm not going to let Wren out of my sight."

"Fine." He picked up his coat and went downstairs. We followed him to the back door.

"Thanks for coming over and for all your time," I said.

"Just do yourself a favor." He looked from me to Porsche and back. "Stay home and wait for the police to find your aunt."

"That's good advice," I said and put my hand on the door between us.

"Take it," he said, putting on his hat. "Good night."

"Good night," we both said and closed and locked the door. It was a silent walk back to the apartment. Porsche looked out the windows.

"He's gone." She turned to me. "Well, let's go."

"Where?"

"To the Woolrights', of course." She put her hands on her hips. "We need to check the shed and the basement and anywhere else he might have stuffed your aunt."

"What do you mean 'stuffed' her?" I asked a bit horrified. "Do you think she's dead? She can't be dead." I sat down hard. "I just saw her. She was just here with me." Tears welled up in my eyes.

"Oh, honey, I'm so sorry," she said and hugged me. "I mean 'tucked her away to hide her.' I didn't mean to imply she was dead."

Everett meowed and rubbed against my leg to comfort me.

"If we go, we all go," I said and got up.

"That's my girl." Porsche got my coat while I leashed up Everett.

We got as far as the back door when we ran into Officer Sanford. "Sorry, ladies," he said. "I've been given strict instructions to not let you leave."

"You can't make me a prisoner in my own home," I said. "I'm not under arrest."

"Yeah, she hasn't been legally charged with anything," Porsche said.

He crossed his arms and studied us with his cop expression. Rain softly dripped off his hat. I realized he was charged with standing out in the rain for the foreseeable future, and that would make anyone cranky.

"We were going to take Everett for a walk," I said.

"Who walks a cat in the rain at ten o'clock at night?" he asked.

I winced.

Porsche gave him the stink eye. "We do."

"For your own safety I'm going to instruct you to go back inside," he said. "We're here for your protection, whether you like it or not."

"We?" I asked.

"Jonesy is working the front of the building."

"Right." I looked at Porsche. "Let's go in and let these guys do their job."

"But—"

"Wait," I said as I put my hand on the door. "When did you guys get here? Porsche just came over. She didn't see you then, did you?"

"No," Porsche said her eyebrows drawn. "They weren't here."

"Look," he said. "This is costing taxpayer dollars so if I were you, I'd go inside."

"What does that have to do with anything?" Porsche asked and crossed her arms and jutted her chin out to mirror him.

"Come on," I said and grabbed her arm. "Let's go in. All we're doing here is getting wet." I pulled her into the building.

"Why are you giving up?" she asked as Everett and I power walked straight to the front door.

"Who said I was giving up?" I opened the front door and the sound of cackling reminded me I needed to change the sound back to the normal bells.

"Ladies, please go inside," Officer Jones said. He had blue eyes that twinkled in the damp streetlight.

I closed the door and locked it. "Darn."

"You were hoping Officer Sanford was kidding about Jonesy?" Porsche said and looked out the window.

"There was a chance," I said. "So really, they weren't here when you came over?"

"No," she said and turned to me. "They must have just come. Maybe your lawyer asked for protection."

"I don't think so," I said. "I think this is Officer Hampton's way of keeping me out of things."

"Do you want me to go? I mean, I can say I'm going home to the kids and then double back and go to the Woolrights'."

"No," I said and put my hand on her shoulder. "I wouldn't be able to bear it if I lost you, too. Besides, someone needs to be my alibi."

She wasn't happy but she agreed. "Now what?"

"I have no idea. All I know is that I can't sit here and drink tea while who knows what is going on with my aunt." My phone rang and we both jumped. Startled, I looked down and saw it was a number I didn't recognize. "Hello?"

"Wren! Help me," the phone crackled.

I put it on speaker. "Aunt Eloise! You're breaking up."

"Help me." This time it was weaker.

"Where are you?" My heart pounded in my chest. "What phone are you calling me from?"

"Beach . . . hurry."

"Stay on the phone," I said and we rushed out the front door. Officer Jones scowled at us. "It's my aunt, she's on the beach and needs help." I pushed past him and ran down Main Street.

"This better not be a lie," he shouted and chased after us. I heard him call over his radio that we were running.

Porsche had scooped Everett up and ran with me. The pavement was cold and wet. I rushed through the puddles and the sound of my breathing was heavy in the fog. The beach was about five blocks from the shop. I arrived to realize that it was dark. The promenade shot to my left and to my right for a mile or so in each direction. The beach beyond was cold and damp and wide.

"Where?" I asked, trying to catch my breath. "Where are you?" The coast stretched out in front of me. The surf pounded. There was crackling in her phone.

"What do you think you're doing?" Officer Jones said as he caught up to us.

"It's Aunt Eloise," I said and held up my phone. "She needs help. She said she was on the beach."

He grabbed the phone from me. "Ma'am, this is Officer Jones. Where are you?"

The phone crackled. "Beach . . ."

He looked at me and then scanned the ocean. "Ma'am, it's a big beach. Where are you? Close to First? Close to Sixth?

"Park . . . hurry."

"Park," I said. "She said Park. But Park isn't near the beach."

"Maybe she means the parking area," Porsche said.

"There are two," I said. "One on each side."

"I'm sending a patrol out to the south side," Officer Jones said.

"We'll go north," I said. I grabbed my phone from him and raced down the promenade. The rain picked up. The surf was close and loud and I shouted my aunt's name. "Aunt Eloise! I'm coming. Where are you?"

Porsche had stuffed Everett into her jacket and ran with me as we stopped every few yards and searched the coastline. I was at the north parking lot and tore down the stairs to the beach. The promenade was a few yards higher than the sandy beach.

"Aunt Eloise," I called into the darkness. I stopped and looked at my cell phone. I'd lost her call. I took a shot and called back the strange number, listening to see if I could hear the phone ring. There was a faint chirp off to the right. I plunged into the darkness, my eyes adjusting rapidly. "Aunt Eloise!"

"Aunt Eloise!" Porsche called beside me.

"Shh," I said and tried calling again. This time the sound of the ring was closer. We both ran toward the sound. Officer Jones was with us.

Aunt Eloise was tucked up against the edge of a cement pillar. I got to her first. "I'm here. What happened? Are you hurt?"

"Wren," she said in a low whisper. I leaned in and she grabbed my hand and passed me something metallic. "This is the key to everything."

"Let me in here," Officer Jones said. "Ma'am, are you all right?"

"No," I said. "She's hurt. It could be her heart. My mom died of a heart attack. Call an ambulance."

"The ambulance is on the way," he said. "Please stand back."

I pushed away and stuck the metal object in my pocket.

"Ma'am, can you tell me where you hurt?"

I heard her moan. "Don't touch her!" I was back beside my aunt holding her hand. "She's freezing. She might have been out here in this rain for the last hour or two." I went to take my coat off when the officer stopped me.

He took his off instead and covered my aunt. "I have more body heat."

"I hear the sirens," Porsche said. "I'll go flag them down."

"Ma'am, what happened?"

She moaned again.

"Tell them to hurry," I called.

"Are you bleeding anywhere?" he asked.

I held her frozen hand and tried to warm it with mine. The rain pelted us and we tried to block it from her with our bodies. I was certain Officer Jones was getting soaked through.

The EMTs arrived with a backboard because a wheeled stretcher would have been impossible to maneuver through the wet sand.

They pushed me away and went to work on my aunt. Jim and Officer Sanford hurried over. Jim told Officer Jones to go to the ambulance and get a blanket. Then, he turned to Porsche and me.

"What happened?"

I explained about the phone call and finding my aunt. My teeth began to chatter. Porsche was wisely covered and had Everett to keep her warm. A small crowd formed on the promenade as neighbors poured out of their homes, drawn by the police lights. The EMTs took my aunt up through the sand and we followed.

"What's going on?" Pastor Harold asked.

"Is that Eloise?" Barbara Miller asked.

"What happened?" Theodore stepped up.

"You tell me," I said to Theodore.

"I don't understand," he said "What is it that you think I did? Did you find your aunt?"

I grabbed Porsche. "Pull Everett out so that he can testify."

She unzipped her coat and exposed a sleepy Everett. He eyed the crowd nonchalantly. In fact, he didn't seem to care that Theodore stood right in front of him.

Porsche and I looked at each other. "So much for testifying," Porsche muttered.

"Who's testifying to what?" Joan asked.

"No one," I said and motioned for Porsche to zip back up.

"Wren, do you want to go with your aunt?"

"Yes," I said and climbed into the ambulance. I looked back at Porsche. "Please take care of Everett."

"I will," she said.

They closed the ambulance doors and we took off. I grabbed my aunt's hand and held it between my own as the EMT in the back monitored her vital signs.

"Is she going to be okay?"

"I can't say," he answered. "I think she may have hypothermia."

"Was she hurt?"

"There's swelling in her ankle and leg. We're going to have to take her for X-rays and tests."

"She's cold and isn't awake."

"We know," he said and flashed a light in both of her eyes. "Could be a concussion. Right now there's no obvious bleeding. All we can do is monitor her vitals, keep her warm, and get her to the ER as fast as possible."

People are often surprised when they pick up a Havana Brown. These lithe cats are heavier than they look.

Chapter 23

They made me wait in a waiting room while they checked out my aunt. I paced. My wet hair stuck to my head and neck, causing me to shiver. Rubbing my arms didn't help.

"You need to get warm," Jim said when he entered the room. "Nurse, can you bring her some scrubs and a blanket?"

"Yes, sir," she said and walked off.

"I'm fine." But my teeth chattered to prove I wasn't fine at all.

"Here, let me help you get that wet jacket off," he said and unzipped my jacket. It was a very intimate act.

I gave him the stink eye. "I'm capable of dressing my-self." I tried to get the zipper open but my numb fingers refused to work. Finally, I blew out a long breath and gave up. "Fine. Please help." By this time, my entire body was shivering in waves.

The nurse came in with a blanket and a set of soft green scrubs. "There's a bathroom down the hall and to your right. Please go change. You look like you're in shock. Do you need my help?"

"I'll be fine." I grabbed the scrubs and hurried to the bathroom. Getting out of my clothes was almost heaven, as they had filled with sand and icy rain water. I splashed warm water on my face and washed the sand off my hands. Then, I reached into the jacket pocket and pulled out the key.

Aunt Eloise wasn't kidding when she said she had the key to the crime. I studied it. It wasn't a safe deposit key. It was bigger. More like a house key or a garage key. "What did you do to get this?" I asked my aunt. But she, of course, was unconscious and in an exam room some-where. So, it was a rhetorical question.

I stuck the key in the pocket of the scrubs and wrapped the blanket around me. The waiting room was empty. I sat down and huddled under the blanket. The Weather Channel was playing in the upper right corner of the room, but I wasn't interested. I pulled out the key and studied it. Aunt Eloise had gone to great lengths to get this key. It was up to me to figure out why.

"You look warmer," Jim said as he entered with a cof-fee cup in each hand. I slipped the key back into the pocket of the scrubs, wrapped a blanket around my shoul-ders, and took the coffee.

"Thanks for getting me something to change into. I'm sure Officer Jones and Porsche were just as cold."

"I haven't heard anything about your aunt," he said and sat down be me.

"They said in the ambulance she had hypothermia. She had a bump on her head and could have a concussion, plus she might have broken her leg or her ankle. Do you think the killer did this?"

"It was certainly more than a prank," he said and took a gulp of coffee and winced. "Hospital coffee gives the department coffee a run for its money."

"It's warm," I said and sipped.

"I saw you point Everett at Theodore," he said without looking at me. "The cat didn't respond."

"I know," I said. "I was so sure it was him."

"We'll keep looking."

"Someone set me up," I said. "They made sure I went into that shed and struggled to find something to get Everett out of the box."

"It was certainly clever, if they did."

I blew out a long breath. "I'm not a killer."

"I believe you."

"Then why all the suspicion about me and the shed?"

"It's what I do," he said and sipped more coffee. "I follow the breadcrumbs."

"You know we thought Agnes Snow was blackmailing people," I said. "We found her book with everyone listed and the amounts they paid her."

"Yes, we found your prints on her ledger. And was she blackmailing people?" he asked, still not looking at me.

"No, it turns out she was selling her craft work and the folks didn't want their recipients to find out."

"That's why I never suspected Woolright," he said. "I

knew Agnes was working on a special project for Mildred's seventieth-birthday celebration next month. Theodore was trying to keep it secret. It was a portrait of them done in grains of rice. He sat for Agnes several times. He had no reason to kill her."

"Well, that rules him out," I said. "Especially if Agnes died before she could finish the work."

"Miss Johnson?" A nurse poked her head into the waiting room. "Your aunt has been moved into a room. We are warming her and we want to keep her overnight to check for signs of a concussion."

I stood. "Can I see her?"

"For a little while," she said. "But then you should go home. We've got her. She's in good hands."

I looked at Jim. "What if the killer did this?"

"I've got a policeman stationed outside her door. She'll be safe."

"Thanks," I said and followed the nurse down the hall to my aunt's room. It was a double room, but the second bed was empty. Aunt Eloise was hooked up to an IV and a heart monitor. She looked pale and a huge bruise ran from her temple into her eye. "Hey," I said.

She fluttered her eyes open.

"What happened?" I asked.

She licked her lips. "So tired."

I took her hand. It was warmer than before and I squeezed it. "It's okay. It can wait. I'm glad you called me."

"I'm glad you came."

"That's enough for now," the nurse said.

I gave my aunt a kiss on the forehead and squeezed her hand. "They're going to take good care of you. Jim has someone stationed outside your door."

"Okay."

I hated to see how weak she was.

"It's okay," the nurse said. "By tomorrow she'll be right as rain."

"Come on," Jim said. "I'll take you home."

I draped the blanket over my aunt, and grabbed the bag of my wet clothes. He popped open an umbrella and escorted me to the squad car. I slid into the front seat. He went around and got into the driver seat. "I don't think you should be alone tonight," he said.

"Well, Porsche has her family and Aunt Eloise is in the hospital. What do you suggest I do? I'm not spending the night with my lawyer."

"I'm going to have Sanford stand watch at your back door."

"That's just miserable," I said. "In this rain. I'll be fine alone. Look at me, I'm not going anywhere."

His mouth was a thin line. "I'll have him watch from his squad car."

"Thanks," I said. "At least it will be warmer."

"I'll watch from the front," he said.

"You really don't trust me, do you?" I felt a pain of something in my heart. Maybe it was disappointment because I trusted him. Strangely, I wanted him to trust me back.

"It's not that I don't trust you," he said. "It's for your safety. Whoever did this to your aunt might want to do something to you next."

"Oh, right."

When we arrived at the shop, I jumped out and ran to the door and unlocked it. The door cackled at me and I reminded myself again to change the bells in the morning. Halloween was over. I turned on a light, locked the door, and waved to Jim. Then, I checked to make sure the back door was locked and went upstairs. A hot shower was in order.

A glance at my reflection in the mirror told me that I was a fright. Silly of me to think a guy like Jim would be interested in a murder suspect. Conrad had made it clear that a murder suspect wasn't datable. Especially one who looked like a drowned rat.

Thirty minutes later, I was showered and my hair dried. I had on my best flannel pajamas and a thick bathrobe and sat down at my desk and turned on my computer. I put the key on the desk and studied it. It looked like a house key.

I noticed some numbers across the top of the key. So, I searched keys and key numbers.

> *Keys* are typically printed with an alphanumeric code called a *key* identification *number*, a *key* code or a *key number* that allows locksmiths and compa- nies to replicate *keys* without the need to install a whole new lock system. *Key* codes fall into two categories: blind codes and biting codes.

Okay, what does that mean?

> The bit of a *key* is the part that actually engages the locking mechanism of a lock. (For example the tumblers in a pin tumbler lock.) The exact geome- try of modern *keys* is usually described by a code system. This is referred to as the *biting*. . . . A smaller number is typically a shallower cut on the *key,* but not always.

So, the numbers only told a locksmith how to cut the key. I tried again. This time I found the key manufacturer. It told me that this key belonged to a lock on a house door. So I called Porsche.

"Hello?" She sounded sleepy.

"Are you up?" I asked.

"I am now," she said. 'What's up? Are you at the hospital? Is Aunt Eloise okay?"

"They are keeping her for the night because of a concussion," I said. "I'm home and Officer Hampton has a patrol car at both my doors."

Porsche yawned. "So you called to check on Everett? He's curled up on my headboard." Porsche had a long headboard with three shelves on each side of the bed.

"Listen, Aunt Eloise gave me a key."

"What?"

"She gave me a key before they took her to the hospital. She said that the key was the answer to everything."

"Did you tell Officer Hampton?"

"No," I said. "But I went online. The best I can tell is it belongs to a house. It's a house key."

"Do you know whose house?"

"I suspect the Woolrights'," I said. "I know Everett didn't react to Mr. Woolright, but it doesn't mean he isn't involved. Can you do me a favor?"

"What?"

"In the morning can you buy a half-dozen bagels and take them to the Woolrights? Take Everett with you. See if he reacts to the house. Figure out the brand of door locks. If it matches the key, we might have something."

"Oh, you want me to spy?"

"I'd do it but I'm under house arrest."

"I'm all over it," she said. "I'll take the boys to school,

pick up the bagels, and see what gives. In the meantime, try to get some rest. Okay?"

"Okay." I turned off my phone and climbed into bed. In the morning, I'd know more. Aunt Eloise should be able to tell us what happened and with any luck, Porsche and Everett would find the killer.

I was up by 5 a.m. and made coffee. I took a cup to Officer Sanford and then went out front to take a cup to Jim. I climbed into his squad car. The inside was warm from his body heat and staying up all night. "I'm safe," I said. "You can go home now."

"As soon as it's light, we'll go," he said and sipped my coffee. "This is good."

"Thanks," I said. "It's French press, black like you like it."

"You're observant."

"Can you take me to the hospital?" I asked. "I want to be there when Aunt Eloise wakes up this morning."

"Sure," he said and put the coffee in the cup holder and started his squad car. We rolled out into the dark streets. This time of year the sun didn't come up until nearly 7 a.m. "Thanks for all your help," I said.

"Just doing my job," he said gruffly.

"I know you're going to want to question Aunt Eloise," I said.

"As soon as possible," he agreed. "I'd rather do it with you not there."

"I suppose I can respect that," I said and sipped my own cup of coffee. I played with the key in my pocket. "Do you think Mr. Woolright did this to my aunt?"

"Why would you ask that?"

"She said she was going to go see him."

"The beach is pretty far from his house," he said. "I sincerely doubt he had anything to do with this."

"Right." I went quiet and sipped my coffee.

"I'm sorry about your aunt," he said. "I don't like this rash of crimes."

"I guess it's the most excitement Oceanview has had since I've been here." We pulled up to the hospital and I got out. Inside the hospital was cool and dim and quiet. It smelled of disinfectant. The security guard at the desk must have been there all night, as she looked ready to go home and get some sleep. "I'm here for Eloise Johnson," I said. "She's in room 210."

"It's not visiting hours yet," the sleepy guard said.

"I'm her only family," I explained, letting the tears well up in my eyes. "I have to see her."

"Fine, sign in here." She handed me a clipboard. I signed my name and Aunt Eloise's room number, then hurried down the hall. My shoes squeaked against the waxed floor. I wondered how hospitals got away with waxed floors where everyone inside was a potential fall risk.

I knocked once and entered the room. "Aunt Eloise?"

I heard the sound of water running and she stepped out of the restroom. She clung to her IV pole. Her badly fitted hospital gown fell off her shoulders and her gray hair was a mass of wild curls. "Wren, am I so glad to see you. Can I go home?"

"We'll see what they say," I said and took a seat beside the bed. She climbed in slowly and tucked a blanket around her. "How's your leg?"

"They said badly bruised and my ankle is sprained but

luckily no broken bones. I'm still cold, though," she said. "Did you get the key?"

I glanced around looking for any sign of Jim, then leaned in. "What happened? What does the key mean? I looked it up. It's a house key."

"It's a house key," she parroted. Her eyes looked a little wild.

"Aunt Eloise, are you okay? Do you need some water?" I handed her a glass. I'd heard that as you got older you were in increased danger of dehydration. Aunt Eloise was hooked up to an IV but water seemed to be called for. "What happened? Why did you leave?"

"I told you I was going to get Theodore," she said and sipped the water dutifully. "I called but he didn't answer so I thought I'd grab my jacket and go see if he was home."

"I'm sorry that I left you alone."

"You weren't there," she said. "I called for you, but you and Everett were gone."

"I went to the bank. I told Josie I was going to be right back. Didn't she tell you?"

"No," she said. Aunt Eloise rubbed her forehead and winced when she found the knot that was still there. "I went to the Woolrights'. I remember it was dark. I wasn't sure anyone was home. I looked in the windows, but I didn't see anything. So I went around back. That's when I heard the arguing."

"Who?" I asked and leaned in closer. "Who was arguing?"

"Mildred and Theodore," she said. "I couldn't tell what was upsetting them. So, I went in closer and stepped on the back porch. They must have been in the living room because I couldn't see them when I looked in the kitchen window."

"Aunt Eloise, why did you look in the window?"

"I thought . . . it sounded like he was killing her."

"What? Who?"

"Yes, Eloise, who was killing whom?" We both turned to see Jim standing in the doorway.

* * *

Soothing Honey Face Mask

This simple mask helps smooth and soothe skin of
all skin types.

1 tablespoon raw honey
3 drops of your favorite essential oil* (I choose
   lavender)

*Be careful to choose an essential oil that is
gentle on the skin.

Mix the two in a small container. Then, dampen your clean face with warm water. Smooth on the face mask. Leave on for 15 minutes while you read your favorite cozy mystery. Set a timer so that you don't lose track of time. Rinse off with warm water and pat dry.

Chapter 24

Aunt Eloise struggled to sit up. "I didn't see anyone," she said quite clearly. "It was a man and a woman and they were fighting. I heard glass breaking." She glanced at me. "Then, I thought they were talking about the Snows' deaths. That's when he attacked her. I heard a scream and an awful thump. That's when he saw me."

"Who saw you?"

"Theodore," she said. "He had a baseball bat in his hand. When he saw me, he came storming out. I ran. But the stair was loose and I tripped and fell. He was standing over me with a murderous look in his eye." She grabbed her bedsheet and pulled it up to her neck. "I knew I was dead."

"But you're alive," Jim pointed out.

"Yes," she said. "It was a miracle. This orange tabby cat came out of nowhere and attacked him. I used the distraction to get up and run. He was chasing me. I had to get out of the street lights so I went to the beach. But I stumbled again and must have hit my head. The next thing I remember is waking up and hiding. I called Wren and she found me."

I scratched my head. The story didn't quite add up. Why the key? What did it mean? I wanted to ask, but I wasn't sure I should in front of Jim. "Well, you are safe now," I said and patted her hand. "I'm sure Officer Hampton will send someone to check on the Woolrights."

"Where did you get the phone?" he asked.

"The phone?" She looked confused.

I squeezed her hand. "You called me on a cell phone, but you left your phone at my apartment. Where did you get the phone you called me from? How did you remember my number?"

"I memorized your number, dear. Sometimes I call you from my home phone."

"Okay," I said. "That's great. I guess I should memorize your number."

"It wouldn't hurt." She smiled weakly.

"The phone," Jim asked. "Where did you get it?"

She blinked. "I don't know. It was in my hand so I dialed it."

"Well, it belongs to someone. It's in evidence now. I'll make a call," he said. "You ladies don't go anywhere." Then, he stepped right outside the door.

"Aunt Eloise, the key? What is the key about?"

"She threw it out the window," Aunt Eloise said. "During the fight. She threw it out the window and I heard her say it was to his den of sin. So, I picked it up and then went to the back window to get a better idea of what the fight was about."

"A key to his den of sin?" I tilted my head. "I don't understand."

"Don't you see?" she said. "I think Theodore was having an affair with Agnes."

"What?"

"The key is the key to the apartment where they met for their fling," Aunt Eloise whispered. "You need to go there. There will be proof of motive for the Woolrights to kill the Snows."

"I've got a patrol car going by the Woolrights' now," Jim said as he came back into the room. "My investigators are looking into the phone you had. We'll figure out where it came from."

The doctor came into the room. He took Aunt Eloise's vitals. "You two are going to have to leave. Eloise needs her rest."

"But I was hoping you were going to discharge her today," I said.

"Her heart rate isn't right," he said. "I want to run a few more tests. I'm sorry but she'll have to stay another night."

"But—"

"You'll have to leave now," he said and motioned to the nurse, who escorted us out.

"I'll be back in an hour to get her statement," Jim said.

"I'm staying here in the waiting room," I said and crossed my arms.

"Oh, no, you're not," Jim said and took my arm. "You're going back to the shop where I can have someone keep an eye on you."

"Why?"

"Until I find out who did this, I'm not taking any chances," he said.

I let him bundle me off into the squad car, but I refused to say a word to him. I kept my arms crossed and my eyes straight ahead.

"You would be wasting your time in the waiting room," he said gently. "Trust me, your aunt is in good hands."

"But she shouldn't be alone," I said. "You saw her. She's not making sense. She needs an advocate. Plus, what if the Woolrights come to finish her off?"

"I've got a police officer watching her room," he said.

I humphed and stared straight ahead. It all seemed like a ridiculous waste of taxpayer dollars. But I wasn't going to tell him that. He wasn't listening. Which meant it was going to be up to me to figure out the secret den of sin and why someone would kill Agnes Snow over it. All I had to do was figure out how to get around the Ocean-view Police.

I paced my apartment. From the second floor I had views of the front sidewalk and the back alley. Both were being patrolled by police officers. I closed the store for the day. I'd been up all night and Porsche deserved time off. I glanced out the kitchen window to the fire escape. If Everett could leave without climbing down the ladder, could I?

I opened the window and moved out onto the escape. I had a couple of folding chairs out there. Sometimes Porsche and I would have a glass of wine and watch the sunset over the ocean. I walked to the far end of the fire escape and studied the roof of the next door building. Technically it was within jumping distance if you were a cat. I'm not exactly the jumping kind. But I could try. I had a hunch I wanted to look into. If I went downstairs, I was pretty certain they wouldn't let me pursue it. But if I didn't, a killer might get away.

I climbed up on the railing and hung onto the gutter. "Don't look down," I muttered to myself. "Don't look down." I took a giant step and got my right foot on the Appletons' roof. Now, all I had to do was get my left foot over there.

Taking a deep breath, I went for it and vaulted myself to the roof. Not without making a ton of noise and scratching my hand on the gutter. A glance to the alleyway told me that no one was looking up. So, I pressed my hand into my sweatshirt to stem the bleeding and scurried across the pitched roof to the next flat roof to the end of the block and another fire escape. I winced as I jumped down onto the fire escape. I was certain I was going to be bruised and hurting in the evening, but for now freedom awaited. Scurrying down the ladder to the street below, I looked both ways and headed out. I had a hunch about the key and Theodore Woolright's den of shame.

Close to a mile later, I stood in front of a bungalow on the edge of the beach. It was built in the 1920s and stood quietly as if waiting to give up its secrets. I glanced left and right, but no one was on the street. No one to see me try the key. I hurried up the short walk and onto the blue painted front porch. A quick look in the windows told me no one was inside. Not that I expected anyone to be here, but it was better to be safe than sorry.

I slid the key in the door and it opened on silent hinges. Quickly closing the door behind me, I took down the hood of my sweatshirt and studied the area. The floor was solid wood. A room to the right had two walls of windows covered with sheers. Inside were shelves and boxes filled with every kind of craft material you could imagine. The supplies were colorful, but well organized. Everything was color coded and in rainbow order of red, orange, yellow, green, and blue. The entire room was filled wall to ceiling with color and sparkles.

This was Agnes Snow's craft palace. I remembered my aunt taking me here once a long time ago, when I first moved to Oceanview. They had been friendlier then and I hadn't forgotten the rainbow in the room.

I walked back into the combined living and dining room. In that area was a large quilt frame and a nearly completed quilt in Christmas red and green. There was a note pinned to it in Agnes's handwriting: "For Wilma Bitter. Xmas present. Don't let her see it." It made me smile. Mr. Bitter was one of the people on Agnes's client list.

I walked into the back kitchen and found a table with assorted containers of paints and glue. On the kitchen countertops were jars of seeds and shells and beads. Propped up on an easel near the back door was a large portrait of Mr. and Mrs. Woolright. On closer inspection it was created in seeds and tea leaves. Agnes had signed and dated it the day before she died. A sticky note on the frame read, "For Mildred's birthday surprise." A sadness washed over me.

Agnes Snow might have been my aunt's rival, but she was making people happy with her art.

The front door burst open and I whirled to see Mildred entering the house. She had a strange look in her eyes. "I thought I might find you here."

"Hello," I said. "I had a key." I raised the key.

"Maybe you did," she said and approached me. "Or maybe you just broke in."

"What are you talking about?"

"You came to hide the evidence that you and Agnes

had a fight the day before she died. And you came inside and replaced her lip balm with poison lip balm. You killed her."

"I didn't," I said and crossed my arms. "You did, didn't you?"

"No one will ever be able to prove it," she said, lifting her chin.

"You called this your husband's den of sin. You thought he and Agnes Snow were having an affair."

"They were. I caught him coming here on numerous occasions and staying for an hour. Then, when I saw he was bringing her money, well, I confronted him."

"But he denied it."

"Of course he would. I didn't expect anything more from a cheat like him." She started to breathe heavily. "It was my friend Agnes who broke my heart. I confronted her. But she laughed and said she wasn't having an affair. She told me I was delusional."

"She wasn't," I said and took a step back.

"Oh, and how are you so sure?" she asked as she strode toward me.

"Because she was creating an art piece for your birthday," I said. "If you don't believe me, look for yourself." I pointed to the portrait in the kitchen. "It's labeled. She labeled everything."

"No!" Mildred said. "No, that's not right. I saw them together. I saw him come here on a regular basis. I followed him." She sat down hard on the floor and covered her mouth. "I confronted him and he denied it." She looked at me. "I didn't believe him. I confronted Agnes but she just laughed at me. She laughed, but she didn't deny it."

"So you poisoned her," I said.

"She humiliated me and then laughed about it." There was horror in her eyes.

I reached into my pocket and pulled out my phone and carefully dialed 9-1-1, slipping my thumb on speaker so we both heard.

"Nine-one-one what is your emergency?"

"Hi, Josie, we're at 211 Pine," I said, not taking my eyes off the sobbing woman. "Mildred just admitted to killing Agnes Snow."

"Are you safe? Help is on the way."

"Am I safe, Mildred?" I asked and took a step back.

"I didn't know," she said over and over. "I thought they were sleeping with each other. She laughed at me."

"Stay on the phone," Josie said.

"Why did you frame me?" I asked her.

She looked up at me as tears rolled down her eyes. "I didn't."

"I don't understand. You used my lip balm to poison Mrs. Snow."

"Yes, but only because I knew it was the only kind Agnes used. She refused to use anything but your beeswax."

"What about Mr. Snow? Why did you kill him?"

"She didn't," Theodore said as he came in through the back door. He had a gun in his hand.

"Mr. Woolright," I said. "Put down the gun."

"I'm afraid I can't do that," he said. "You know too much."

"No, I don't," I said. "I don't know anything."

"I thought you were having an affair," Mildred said to him. "I saw you with her. I didn't know."

"I know you didn't know," Theodore said. "It's okay, baby, I'm taking care of everything."

I took a step toward Mildred. She was between me and the front door and she didn't have a gun.

"Don't take another step," he said and pointed the gun at me.

"The police are on the way," I said and raised my chin.

"Not soon enough," he said and studied me. "I thought you would be an easy target. I told Mildred to tell the police she saw you with Agnes. But you couldn't keep your nose out of things."

"Why kill Bernie Snow?" I asked.

"He figured it out really quick," Theodore said. "He came to the house to confront us. We told him to go home."

"He threatened to go to the police," I said.

"He didn't know anything," Theodore said. "He couldn't prove anything and neither can you."

Hearing sirens coming down the street, I took another step toward Mildred. "You should put the gun down now," I said.

His hands were shaking. "Mildred can't go to prison. She won't survive there."

"That's up to the courts," I said and took another step toward her.

"I won't go to prison, either." The gun shook in his hands.

"Oh, darling," Mildred said and stood. "Do it. We can go together hand in hand for all eternity."

"Don't!" I shouted. The doors burst open and officers ran into the house. They grabbed the gun and I fell to my knees.

The officers cuffed Theodore and Mildred and took them away.

Jim took my hands. "I'm going to put you in a squad

car," he said gently. "You are shaking and you need to be warm." He opened the car door and helped me in. Then, he went to the trunk and got out a blanket and wrapped it around me. "Stay here."

He closed the door and went in after the other officers.

I felt strange, like I was in a bad dream. My body wouldn't quit shaking. Soon an ambulance pulled up and the EMTs went inside. I watched as other police officers arrived. How could the tiny house hold so many people? I closed my eyes and thought of the rainbow craft room. All of this happened because Theodore asked Agnes to create a work of art. It was the saddest thing I'd ever heard.

Chapter 25

Later that night, Aunt Eloise and Porsche and I were huddled in my apartment living room with a bottle of wine and a tray of cheese and crackers. Everett was curled up in my lap.

"How did you know what the key went to?" Porsche asked.

"I remembered that Agnes had her own special craft house," I said. "Aunt Eloise took me there once for tea when we moved here."

"I knew you would figure out where the den of sin was," Aunt Eloise said.

"What happened the night you got the key?" I asked. "Where did you get the phone?"

"Frankly, I have no idea. I was a fool and ran onto the dark beach to get away from Theodore. I fell and hit my head. When I came to I was too cold to move, and the phone, well, it was in my hand."

"Someone must have put it there," Porsche said.

"If they saw you on the beach, why leave a phone? Why not call for help?"

"We may never know," my aunt said and sipped her wine. "Maybe it was Mildred. Maybe she felt sorry for me, but didn't want to call the police and stir up more suspicion."

"I'm glad you remembered my phone number and called me" I said.

"Me, too."

"I'm making a point of memorizing your phone number in case anything like this ever happens to me."

"Good girl," my aunt said. "We used to have to know everyone's numbers, you know. It wasn't automatic."

"The thing that bothers me is we'll never know who put Everett in the box in the shed," Porsche said.

"I suspect it was Theodore," I said.

"But Everett didn't react to him," Porsche pointed out.

"No, he didn't."

"Well, no matter," Aunt Eloise said. "At least now, the mystery is solved and our little town can go back to more important things like the Thanksgiving turkey trot and decorating downtown for the holiday season."

"There is one good thing that came out of this," Porsche said.

"Four people died," I pointed out. "What's good about that?"

"We have a scary Halloween story to go with next year's Halloweentown celebration," Porsche said. "Hey, you got to make lemonade out of lemons, right?"

Everett meowed his agreement.

Don't miss the next intriguing Oregon
Honeycomb Mystery

A MATTER OF HIVE AND DEATH

Coming soon from Kensington Publishing Corp.

Keep reading to enjoy a sample excerpt . . .

Chapter 1

"Oh, Wren, what do you think?" Aunt Eloise asked as she walked into my shop, Let It Bee. She held out her Havana Brown cat, Elton, dressed in a green alien costume.

"That costume really brings out the color of his eyes," I said. My cat, Everett, meowed his agreement. Elton was Everett's uncle. My aunt had bred Havana Brown cats for years until after Everett's mother died. Then she decided that encouraging people to adopt cats was a better way to go and started a Havana Brown rescue group.

"It's for the McMinnville UFO festival," Aunt Eloise said. "You're going, right?"

I winced. "I forgot about it. But in my defense, all my time has been taken up by the Let It Bee second-anniversary celebration this weekend."

"It's only Monday, and the festival doesn't start until next Wednesday. So you have plenty of time to get ready. I'm sure Everett is looking forward to it." My only living relative and near and dear to my heart, Aunt Eloise was a tall woman with the large bones of our pioneering ancestors. At least, that's how I liked to think of it. Anyone who's played Oregon Trail, the computer game, knows it took hardy stock to make it all the way out to the Oregon coast.

Eloise had grown up in Oceanview, Oregon, along with my mother. I, myself, had only spent three years in town before going away to college. But over two years ago, I returned and started Let It Bee, a shop featuring honey and bees in a 1920s building just off Main Street and a few blocks from the beach. "I'm bringing Emma and Evangeline. You know how Everett gets jealous when his sisters get to do fun things and he's left out."

Everett meowed his thoughts on the matter. I sighed. It had been years since I'd been to the UFO festival. Based on a UFO sighting in McMinnville in the 1950s, the festival was equal parts campy, with parades and vendors selling alien souvenirs, and serious, with speakers discussing the science behind sightings.

"Fine," I said. "We'll go for the parade and shopping, but I'm not dressing up."

"Oh, goody," Aunt Eloise pulled a silver costume out of the pocket of her long cardigan sweater. "I made him this! What do you think, Everett?" She held up the metallic spacesuit.

He jumped down from the cashier counter and walked to her. Aunt Eloise bent down, and Everett sniffed the suit delicately, then meowed and rubbed up against her leg.

"He likes it!" She straightened. The smile was wide in her strong face. Her gray hair was held in a bun on top of her head, and I caught a whiff of her orange-blossom perfume. "Now we can all watch the parade in style. Wait until you see my costume. I have a necklace that looks like a collar. The cats are the owner, and I'm the pet!"

"Well, that's certainly true of all cats," I teased. "But I'm not wearing a costume."

"You said that already," she pouted a moment, then broke into a wide smile. "Is it okay if I ask Sally Hendrickson to come with us? She would wear a costume. She's into cosplay."

"Yes, that's fine," I said.

The bells on the door to the shop jangled, and my sales manager, Porsche Allen, stepped inside the door. She shook off her umbrella, folded it, and walked into the shop. "Not busy today?" She looked around the currently customer-free store.

"We had a nice rush this morning, but between the rain and school getting out soon, there's a bit of a lull," I said.

"Typical Monday," Porsche said as she put her umbrella into the holder behind the cashier stand and pulled off her raincoat. Porsche was tall and thin, with gorgeous black hair from her Korean mother and sparkling blue eyes from her American father. Today she wore jeans, black booties, and a green sweater. "Hey, Eloise, what's up?"

"We're going to the UFO festival in McMinnville this weekend," Eloise said. "Isn't Elton cute in his little green costume?" She held up her kitty and placed the silver metallic costume on the counter. "I brought this one for Everett."

At the sound of his name, Everett jumped up on the counter and brushed by Porsche so that she could stroke his brown fur.

"Nice," Porsche said. "I took the kids to that festival last year. They had a blast."

I grabbed a zippered hoody sweatshirt off the coat tree near the counter, slid it on, and then grabbed my purse. "Please tell me you didn't dress up."

"We didn't," Porsche confirmed. "But the boys want to this year."

"Oh, good, we can all go together," Aunt Eloise said.

"Well, I'll let you two figure things out. I have an appointment. Thanks for coming in a bit early and covering for me, Porsche. Is someone picking the kids up from school?"

Porsche had two boys, River and Phoenix, who were ten and eight years old, respectively. "Jason worked from home today, so he can get them." Her husband, Jason, worked for a local tech company and was able to work from home whenever he wasn't traveling.

"Great, thanks. I've got to go see a bee wrangler about the fruit-tree honey," I headed toward the door.

"Tell Elias we said hi," Aunt Eloise said.

"I will." I waved my goodbye and pulled the hood up over my curly hair to keep it from frizzing too much in the soft rain. It rained a lot in spring on the Oregon coast. Unlike Porsche and her umbrella, most natives simply put on a hooded sweatshirt and stepped out, hood up. I guess we were used to being damp.

Elias Bentwood was a bee wrangler who lived in an old house on the edge of town. He'd trained me in the art of beekeeping and was my go-to guy for local honey. If Elias didn't have it, he could point me to where to get it.

I got into my car and drove the mile or so it took to get there. The house was a one-bedroom shotgun style, which meant you could open the front door and shoot a gun straight through the house and kill someone in the backyard. Aunt Eloise said that a bachelor lumberjack had built it in the 1920s, and it had been neglected until Elias bought it in the 1980s.

The tiny home was painted white and had sea-blue shutters. Elias maintained it well. I'd known him ever since I'd gotten out of college. Most of his hives were hired out at the moment to the farmers near Mount Hood. It was fruit-tree-blossom season, and bee wranglers would ensure there were hives close to the blossoms.

Bees typically foraged two miles from their hive, and even though some were thought to forage two to three times that distance, bee owners trucked hives in during blossom season to ensure the trees were properly pollinated.

Elias loved his bees and wintered some of his hives behind the house. It was Elias who had helped me design the glass-walled hive that took up a portion of my shop. Bees are important to the environment, and he'd been thrilled when I told him I wanted a safe way to give my customers a look inside a working hive.

He'd helped me build the hive on the exterior of my shop and introduced the queen bee and her court to the hive. It had become so successful that it was one of the biggest draws to my shop. The kids loved to come and watch the bees work, making honeycomb and depositing honey.

The rain stopped, and the sun came out as I walked up on the porch. I pulled my hood off, letting my curls spring out and knocked on the door. "Elias? It's Wren." There wasn't an answer, but I wasn't worried. Elias was probably out in the back with the one or two hives he hadn't hired out. I moved off the porch and followed the sidewalk around the side of the house to the back. The house didn't have a garage or even a driveway. Instead, there was a two-track alley in the back where Elias would pull his truck in and out to move the hives.

I heard someone moving through the back bushes. "Elias? It's Wren." Rounding the corner of the house, I came upon a horrifying scene. There were three hives tilted over, the roofs pushed off and the bees swarming, angry and confused. I caught the sound of car doors slamming and saw a blue car speed away down the alley.

"Elias! The bees!" Instinct had me stepping back to keep the side of the house between me and the angry bees. "Elias!" I called and peered around the house. Whoever did this must have taken off in the car. I didn't want to get stung, so I stayed on the side of the house and dialed Elias's cell phone.

I could hear ringing coming from the backyard. "Elias?" The only sound was the phone ringing, and it went quiet as I was dumped me into voice mail. If Elias was in the backyard, he might be hurt or, worse, attacked by the confused bees. The only safe vantage point to find out for sure would be from inside the house. I hurried around to the front of the house.

The door was unlocked, and I walked into the small living room. "Elias? It's Wren. Are you okay?" I made my way quickly through the tidy kitchen to the bedroom in the back. No one there. The bedroom was a mess of scattered papers and files on top of the made bed. I hurried to the back door that lead out to a tiny screened porch.

Elias lay on the ground, unmoving, while the bees swarmed around him. "Elias! Don't move. I'll get help." I knew better than to rush into a swarm of angry and confused bees. I dialed 9-1-1.

"Nine-one-one. What is your emergency?"

I recognized Josie Pickler's voice. "Josie, it's Wren Johnson. I'm at Elias Bentwood's house. He's lying on the ground in his backyard and not moving. I think he's hurt."

"Okay, Wren, I've got an ambulance and police on their way. Can you check for a pulse?"

"No," I said. "Someone has disturbed Elias's bees. They're swarming the entire backyard. We'll need bee wranglers with protective gear."

"I'll call animal control," Josie said. "Or should I call an exterminator?"

"Don't call an exterminator! I don't want the bees hurt."

"I'll advise the ambulance that bees are swarming," Josie said.

"Have them park out front," I said. "I know another beekeeper. I'll hang up and call him."

"Okay," Josie said. "Stay safe."

I hung up and scrolled through my contacts to find Klaus Vanderbuen's number. Klaus was a friend of Elias, and although he lived twenty miles from town, he was the only person I could think of to call.

"Hello?" Klaus's voice was deep and comforting.

"Oh, thank goodness you answered," I said. "It's Wren Johnson. I own the bee-themed shop near Main in Ocean-view. I'm a friend of Elias Bentwood."

"What's going on, Wren? You sound out of breath."

"I'm at Elias Bentwood's place. Elias is on the ground and not moving. I called emergency services, but some-one has vandalized his hives. Bees are swarming every-where. I don't think we can get to Elias to help him."

Klaus muttered something dark. "I'm on my way," he said. "Don't let anyone do anything stupid to the bees."

"I'll do my best," I said. "Please hurry. I don't know how badly Elias is hurt."

Klaus hung up the phone, and I walked back through the house to the front porch to wait for emergency ser-vices to arrive. I had some practice working with bee-hives, but they had always been docile. As angry as these bees were, there was no way I could reach Elias without help.

I heard sirens in the distance and ran off the porch to the street to wave them over. It was a police car. Officer Jim Hampton put the car in PARK. Riding with him was another officer I didn't know.

"What's going on?" Jim asked when he opened his car door.

"It's Elias," I said. "He's on the ground in the back, but someone has attacked the bees, and they are too angry for me to get to Elias."

The second officer got out of the car. "I can't help," he said, his dark gaze flat. "I'm allergic to bee stings. Got an EpiPen in the glove box."

"Show me where Elias is," Jim said. He was six feet tall, had blue eyes in a tan face, and looked a bit like the actor Paul Newman. "Ashton, check out the house."

"It's open," I said. "I found the door unlocked and went inside to get a better look at the backyard."

Jim frowned at me. "Elias is in the backyard, and you went into the house?"

"Yes," I said. "It was the only way to safely see the entire backyard. It's how I found Elias." We took off down the sidewalk as I continued to explain. "I called Klaus Vanderbuen. He's the closest bee wrangler. But he's about fifteen minutes out."

Jim followed behind me. I stopped at the corner and peered around the side of the house. Jim stepped around me and then ducked back beside me. "Those are some angry bees. Any thoughts on how to handle them? Should we smoke them?"

"Smoke them?" I asked.

"You know smoke tends to calm bees."

"I think that only works if you are gently moving parts of the hive," I said. "You need protective gear and maybe a bee box to capture them."

"I'll call it in," he grabbed his radio. As he spoke into it, I crouched down, wondering if I could somehow crawl slowly toward Elias. But the bees swarmed the entire backyard.

"Ashton," I heard Jim say into the radio when I moved back beside him.

"Yeah, boss," the radio crackled.

"Can you see anything from inside the house?" Jim asked.

"I'm looking out the bedroom window. Bees are swarming the back porch as well as the yard. Looks like we have one man down and three hives demolished. I don't see how whoever did this got away without being stung multiple times."

"I'll put a call into the ER to watch for bee attacks," Jim said. "Can you tell if Elias is moving?"

"I'm not seeing any motion," Officer Ashton said. "Looks like maybe blood pooling near his head. Also the back bedroom looks tossed."

"I can hear the ambulance," I said and hurried back to the front of the house. The ambulance arrived, and I rushed to the driver's side. EMT Sarah Ritter stepped out. She was five foot nine with short brown hair and serious eyes.

"What do we have?" she asked as she headed to the back of her rig to get out her equipment.

"Bees," I said. "Are you allergic?"

"Nope," she replied and opened the back door. I saw Jim go into the house as the second EMT came around and parked behind the ambulance.

It was Rick Fender. He was my height, and rail thin with bleached blond hair and a surfer look. He grinned at me. "Maybe you can lure them out with that honey candy you make."

"There are three hives of angry bees," I said. "I don't think my candy is going to soothe them. I hope you're not allergic."

"I'm not," he said and grabbed the end of a stretcher.

"Where's the victim?" Ritter asked.

"He's in the backyard, but the bees are there, too, and they're swarming. Listen, I called a bee wrangler." I glanced at my phone. "He should be here in about ten minutes."

"The victim could be dead by then," Ritter said and pulled the stretcher and her kit toward the side of the house.

"I don't think you understand," I said. "The bees are bad."

"I'm not afraid of a few stings," Ritter said and moved quickly down the side of the house.

"Fine," I said and threw up my hands. "Don't say I didn't warn you."

They rounded the back of the house, and I counted to myself. "Five, four, three—" Both EMTs came scrambling back to the side of the building without the stretcher.

Ritter waved a bee from in front of her face and stopped next to me. "That's more than a few angry bees. You run the honey shop. Do you have a bee suit?"

"No, I only wrangled for a season and used one of Elias's suits," I said.

"How far out is the bee wrangler?" Jim asked as he and Officer Ashton stepped off the porch.

I glanced at my phone, "Maybe ten minutes? Is there anything we can do in the meantime? Elias could be dying."

"I hate to break it to you," Jim said. "But until we get those bees under control, there's no getting to Elias."

"I can try a hazmat suit," Sarah said. "We have a couple back at the station. Don't know if they will be protective enough against that many bees. But it's worth a try."

"Go get it," Jim said. "Ashton and I will stay here and monitor the situation."

"Dispatch wanted to call animal control," I said. "But even if they have a bee suit, Klaus will get here before they can dig it out."

"What if Elias moves?" Jim asked. "Will the bees attack him?"

"There's a chance they will," I said.

"Then we'd better hope he keeps his head down," Jim said. "Fender, monitor the victim from a safe distance. Ritter, go get the hazmat suit."

"And me?" I asked.

"Stay out of the way."

Connect with

Visit us online at
KensingtonBooks.com
to read more from your favorite authors, see books
by series, view reading group guides, and more.

Join us on social media

for sneak peeks, chances to win books and prize packs,
and to share your thoughts with other readers.

facebook.com/kensingtonpublishing
twitter.com/kensingtonbooks

Tell us what you think!

To share your thoughts, submit a review,
or sign up for our eNewsletters, please visit:
KensingtonBooks.com/TellUs.